Tales From
FOSTER
HIGH

JOHN GOODE

Harmony Ink

Published by
Harmony Ink Press
5032 Capital Circle SW
Ste 2, PMB# 279
Tallahassee, FL 32305-7886
USA
http://www.harmonyinkpress.com/

Tales From Foster High

Cover Art by Paul Richmond   http://www.paulrichmondstudio.com

Print ISBN: 978-1-61372-718-8
Digital ISBN: 978-1-61372-719-5

Printed in the United States of America
Second Edition - Young Adult Novel
August 2012

First editions originally published in digital format by Dreamspinner Press:
Maybe with a Chance of Certainty – October 2011
The End of the Beginning – December 2011
Raise Your Glass – May 2012

This book is dedicated to Shayne, Dean, Chris, Eric and Jason.

Without them growing up gay wouldn't have been half as fun. Of course it would have been half as frustrating, but you have to take the good and bad. You take them both... damn. That's the theme of *Facts of Life*. Forget all that.

This book is dedicated to my grandfather. For a man who never graduated from the 4th grade, he was the smartest man I ever knew.

Author's Note:

I went to school at Shermer High School.

Even though it says different on my transcript and my permanent record would contradict that statement, I assure you I did all my growing up in those halls. I paid a buck to see Ted hold a pair of girl's panties in the boy's bathroom. I still think he stole them from someone. Me and some friends climbed up to the town's water tower and painted "Save Ferris" on the side one night. We spent the entire time pretty sure we were going to get caught, but it's still there to this day. I attended Saturday school the week after five kids got together and waged war against Principal Vernon. The week I was there the new principal, Mr. Rooney, was watching over us, and he was a complete dick. I remember the time the McCallister kid got left during Christmas and a couple of homeless guys tried to break into his house. Was a big fuss for a while since nothing really ever happened in the town, but after a while people forgot.

It was a nice place to grow up. It was small town, yet filled with a wide variety of people who never stopped showing me that no matter how different we were, at heart we were all the same person. Like take for instance Andie ended up going out with this preppie douche bag and everyone was up in arms. Most people thought she should go out with Duckie because they were similar but in the end let me tell you, the two of them made it work. Or the story about Keith who thought he had the hots for Amanda, who was one of the prettiest girls in school. Everyone thought they would end up together but it was his best friend, Watts, he fell in love with. Proof that no matter who you think you should fall in love with, your heart will always go down its own path every time.

The main thing I learned in Shermer is that no matter how different we all are, no matter what labels people put on us, we are all alike where it counts. We all want to be loved, we all want to be liked, and no one likes being hurt. I took those lessons with me in life, and when I moved to Foster I tried to incorporate them the best I could. After all, the entire point of being brought up in a decent place is taking those lessons and applying them in the rest of your life. Brad and Kyle could have gone to Shermer, I like to think. If the high school was still open, I have no doubt that they would be welcome through their doors, and though they might not have been the most popular kids in the world, they would have been accepted. Sooner or later, people would have embraced them.

I guess what I am trying to say is that these stories don't exist without those. Everyone from a certain generation forward owes John Hughes a debt that can only repaid by taking those moments he created and paying them forward. Being gay was never really covered in his movies, but I like to think that if he was still here, he would have dealt with the subject in the same caring and entertaining way he dealt with everything that teenagers deal with.

If these stories can convey even ten percent of what Hughes got through in his movies, then I am eternally grateful. And if you find yourself in these stories, even a little, then you went to high school in Shermer also. We probably were there at the same time. I was the guy two lockers down who never talked. Drop a note in my locker—maybe we have more in common than we thought.

From somewhere in Foster, Texas

John Goode

KYLE
HISTORY WHORE

JOHN GOODE

I DON'T remember the moment I knew I was broken.

I was seventeen and on the edge of an eighteen that seemed terrifying to a young man not sure of his sexuality. I knew I liked guys but was still under the delusion that an attraction to guys didn't make you gay just like drowning didn't mean you couldn't breathe, it just meant you were breathing something other than air. It made me different, and as we all know, in high school, there is nothing worse than being different. Though every TV show or movie will tell you the wacky, zany, oddball character is not only cool but a necessary component in most social settings, no one ever closed their eyes and wished they ended up being Screech.

I never assumed I was broken, coming from a single-parent family that consisted of a mom who spent more time drinking and partying than being an actual parent—not that I had any idea what an actual parent looked like. Pop culture had taught me that a mom was either baking pies in pearls and heels, Xanax smile pasted on her face as if she were a post-modern zombie, or the spunky single lady who worked hard and never seemed to secure herself a real romantic entanglement. My mom was neither of those, and the concept of a dad was about as familiar to me as walking on the moon.

I was emotionally retarded in a way that made connecting with another human being so daunting a task that even considering it could cause my heart to race and my breath to stop altogether. Since junior high, boys had made me feel funny, and not in a laughing sort of way. That clumsy, all feet and no balance stutter that most teenage boys feel toward girls, I would get in the locker room. Let me assure you, no one sounds slick stuttering like they are having a seizure. All sound would drain away as my vision zeroed in on the boy next to me taking his jeans off for gym. More than once I had found myself forcing my eyes to look away so I could finish dressing out for PE.

By the time I started high school, I had constructed a virtual igloo of emotional distance between me and everyone else. I projected a coldness that bordered on snobbery, and I knew it. I was the guy everyone knew of but no one could recall speaking to personally. I imagined myself an urban legend of Foster High School, like the Sasquatch or a chupacabra. Everyone had a friend who had seen me talking to someone, but no one had ever talked to me directly. I was a ghost wandering the halls, head down, backpack over one shoulder, eyes focused on where my next step would take me and nothing more. In a social environment where being cool and liked were currency, I was a monk who had taken a vow of poverty, which then necessitated a vow of celibacy. I sidestepped conversations, ate lunch by myself, and practically ran home after school.

I didn't know it, but I was broken in a way that wasn't readily evident to those around me.

As anyone who has read comic books knows, when one sense is taken from you, the others become almost superhuman, allowing you the ability to get by in life the best you possibly can. Since I was completely and utterly devoid of any knowledge of how emotions worked for other people, my mind had taken the unused space and used it to amplify what book smarts I already possessed to a Rain Man level of intellect. I was the person who never needed to study, never needed to read anything more than once, and always finished his test first. It may sound like I am bragging, but I assure you, these are not good things to other kids my age. I am sure in some alternate universe there was a high school where being a nerd was cool. That possessing a vast array of useless knowledge would be a badge of notoriety, and it would have garnered me some kind of social worth. Alas, I was not born there. Instead, my brain made me a geek at worst, at best the quiet, smart guy who never seemed to look up when he walked.

That's why I never saw him coming.

I knew who he was, of course; everyone did. His name was Brad Greymark, and he was one of those lucky few who walked on rarefied air as he passed you by in the hall. He was on the baseball team, and every image I had of him before we met was of him wearing a letterman's jacket, green with white leather sleeves adorned with a huge F on his lapel, making him look like a superhero amidst the rest of us normal people. He wasn't perfect-looking, though he was closer to it than most. He was good-looking enough to get you to turn your head at least once, and with Brad, once was all he needed. With his dark-red hair and green eyes, he was the very model of a modern teenage athlete: nice body, strong features with just a hint of prettiness that made him irresistible.

He had to know how popular he was, but it never came across when he talked. There was earnestness in his attitude that made you want to like him despite all of the obvious benefits already bestowed on him by the universe in general. Brad had hit the genetics lottery, yet from the outside he seemed oblivious to his effect on people around him. I never knew anyone to dislike or take umbrage with his obvious gifts as was so common in the high school ecosystem. Normally people like him were coveted and loathed behind their backs, but this wasn't true when it came to Brad. It was as if instead of pushing those around him down by reminding them of his physical superiority, he shared it somehow, like when you were talking to him, somehow you were made more popular as well.

I had, of course, never talked to him, but I had eaten lunch near the group of people that gathered at his feet every noon to break bread. Being in his presence was almost akin to listening to royalty speak. The way people hung on his every word seemed surreal at times. No matter what the subject, there seemed to be a gravity about it that made even the most trivial of subjects seem important. His voice was strong and soothing, containing none of the odd tones and subliminal insecurities most high school boys possessed. It was easily recognizable above the noise of a crowd, and no matter where he was in a room, it commanded attention.

Which is why, when I heard it coming from right in front of me, I almost screamed.

I had been walking through the hall as I normally did, head down, concentrating only on getting out of the building. Navigating a high school hallway is no easy task, since the inborn pocket of comfortable space most people possess seems to have no value when you have fifteen minutes to run to your locker, grab the books for your next class, and catch up with gossip before you are tardy. If you weren't careful, you could get body checked more times than a forward at a hockey game without even the briefest of acknowledgments by the person who had committed the personal foul. I had perfected an almost radar-like ability to pass by a crowd of people without them ever knowing I was there. This was one thing that TV never seemed to get right when they showed people in high school moving from class to class. They seemed to have an infinite amount of time to get from one class to another with time left over to discuss whatever plot du jour was unfolding in today's episode. There was never that much time in real life, it was hard enough just to grab your books and run to the next class.

So when I saw a set of size twelve Converse sneakers directly in my path that day, I swerved sharply left to avoid the collision. The sneakers moved to intercept me. As I tried to pull right, I heard his voice say, "Hey," and mentally, I lost it.

There is nothing worse than your body reacting to someone before your brain can even recognize who it is. It is a Pavlovian response when you run into someone you are attracted to and aren't ready for it. There is something that runs up your spine, as if every particle of your being is being magnetically pulled to the other person. Whatever automatic system your body has for keeping itself upright and moving forward temporarily fails, and inevitably you are going to stumble like your sneakers have grown three sizes too big.

And because I was a teenage boy, I began to throw wood.

There are few materials known to man more unforgiving to an erection than denim. It is coarse, dense, and not even the least bit interested in giving you an inch or two of room as the swelling member gets bigger. I don't know any male who has not felt the gnawing maw of jeans clamping down on his member at least once in his life. Sitting down, standing up, running laps, eating lunch—there is never a penis that is as comfortable hard as it is soft in a pair of jeans. The only thing worse than becoming aroused in the middle of a hallway while standing in front of a straight guy is adjusting yourself in the middle of a hallway while standing in front of said straight guy without seeming like you are playing with yourself.

I forced myself to focus on a spot between his eyes and tried to replicate the heterosexual male head nod that all teenage boys except me seemed to know, and responded with a, "Hey" that was a few octaves higher than I initially intended. My right hand was still gripping the history book and folder I had just retrieved from my locker, so as he began to talk, I tried to move the book in front of my groin as unnoticeably as possible.

"So you're kind of smart, right?" His question was far more rhetorical than an actual inquiry, since he kept talking without waiting for an answer. "Because Gunn is a cool coach, but he is a dick about grades."

This only made sense if you knew how our high school worked.

Coach Gunn was a bulldog of a man who spent his day coaching baseball and teaching history. That would seem to be a godsend to our school's jocks, who had to maintain a grade point average of 2.75 to stay on the team. They thought that since he coached them, his history class would be a breeze. So every year, the new group of jocks would do everything they could to make sure they got into his class.

And every year, a fresh group of boys found out that Coach Gunn did not believe in a free ride.

Brad had paused to wait for some kind of response from me, which was his second mistake; his first was expecting me to be normal in the first place. I wasn't used to talking to actual people, much less people waiting for me to respond to them. My gaze had moved from the space between his eyes and drifted to the almost luminescent green of his irises and had stayed lost there for a few long seconds. His eyes led me to the ruddy blush of his cheeks, which, upon closer inspection, seemed to hide pale freckles that made his skin seem that much more perfect with its newfound imperfections. His freckles led down to what I could see of his muscled neck. It was hidden by the collar of his jacket on either side, and I saw the first Adam's apple I was ever transfixed by. His neck led my eyes down to a thin white T-shirt that seemed to accentuate the hard muscles that made up the twin curves of his pecs instead of covering them. The way the cotton seemed to dip between them almost invited a person to see how deep the space between them actually was. I could see the impression of a chain underneath, and when he shifted his weight and I spotted the glint of silver between the white T-shirt and the jacket, I felt like I had almost seen the band of his underwear.

"You okay?"

My head jerked up so fast it was a blur as I realized I was still standing in the middle of a high school hallway instead of running toward him in the middle of a field while music played around us. On second thought, that sounds more like a fabric softener commercial than actual love, so never mind. "Yeah," I said quickly, not sure exactly what question I was answering.

Obviously he didn't either, because he cocked his head like a dog and asked, "Um, to which one?"

"What?" I asked, as confused as he was, if that was possible. And then whatever buffer that had frozen in my head freed itself, and time started moving normally again. "Yes," I said again, now answering his question, followed by a sharp, "No." Which didn't sound good. "I mean, I don't… what do you mean by smart?" I could see in his eyes that whatever hopes he had that I possessed any superior intellect were dwindling quickly as it became apparent I couldn't even string together a sentence. "I mean, there is street-smart, and there is, like, math smart, which I'm not because numbers suck, so not really, but if you're talking about…." I began to ramble.

"History," he said, cutting me off. "Coach Gunn teaches history, and you seem good at it." He was talking slowly now, as if he were trying to communicate with an alien. "Are you?"

"Yes," I answered, trying to swallow.

We stood there staring at each other for about five seconds before he just shook his head. "You know what? Forget it." He began to walk away.

And only then did I realize that one of the best-looking guys in school had just been talking to me and was now walking away from me. I tried to calculate all of the different possibilities that would have made someone like him talk to someone like me. Was I getting cooler?

Did he know I liked guys? Did he like guys? Did he like me? Was this a vain attempt to reach out and get me to understand that there was someone else in this world as lonely as me? Maybe he was trying to get across in code or something that he.... This was when my brain screamed at me. He needs help with his history homework, you retard!

"Wait," I said, turning around after him. He paused and looked back at me, and I felt my mind begin to get lost in the lines of his chin, so I blurted out, "I can help you."

He raised an eyebrow as the people walking past us stared, no doubt wondering what exactly that meant. I realized I had broken another cardinal rule of surviving high school besides "never look up" and "always bring your own lunch": never talk to someone else in front of people.

I was talking to someone else in front of other people.

I took several steps toward him to minimize how loud I had to speak. "With your history," I amended. "I can help you with that."

"I need to pass the midterm," he said in the same conspiratorial tone I was using. "If I don't, I'm toast."

I nodded to both the spoken and unspoken sentiments. I could indeed help him study for the midterm, and I was aware he would be tossed off the team if he failed it. And in a culture that is completely popularity-driven, like high school, being stripped of his letterman jacket was akin to being cast out from the pantheon of high school gods and forced to wander the barren earth with us commoners.

The ironic part is not once did I consider not helping him simply out of spite.

He was one of those golden boys who somehow seemed to deserve the spotlight of attention they received. Resenting or even trying to deny him that kind of adoration just seemed to be a cruel and unusual form of punishment. Imagining him not being one of the most popular boys in school was like picturing a beautiful golden retriever caked with mud or a masterpiece of a painting covered with years of grime and dust. I think that was his secret, the reason he was so well liked even though he didn't seem to try. People naturally wanted to help him, and I'm sure the fact that he resembled most people's concept of an ideal teenage boy in his prime didn't hurt.

"It's before Christmas break. We'd need to study pretty hard," I said, wondering what exactly I was getting myself into. "We could meet after school at the library—"

He shook his head, cutting me off. "I have practice, has to be after that."

I paused. "But the library closes at five."

He shrugged. "Then come over to my house, and we'll study there."

I froze.

"Or we could go to yours," he started to say.

"We'll go to yours!" I blurted out, not letting my overactive imagination have even a second to envision the horror of my mother stumbling out of her room, hungover and wondering why there was someone else in the house.

"Cool," he said, nodding to himself. "You need a ride, or do you have a car?"

"I do not have a car," I said tonelessly, still in shock as I realized that by not wanting him to come to my house, I had agreed to go to his.

"Cool," he said with an easy smile. "Meet me by the locker room after five; I can drop you off at home afterward, okay?"

My head nodded all by itself.

"Awesome. Thanks, Kyle," he said, turning around and then pausing. "That's your name right?" He seemed contrite and embarrassed all at once, which made him about a thousand times more attractive in my eyes.

I paused for an impossibly long moment as I realized I didn't know my name either. "Yes!" I blurted out as the memory of my given name stumbled across the tip of my tongue. "My name is Kyle!" I tried again, reinforcing it by saying it out loud again.

His smile turned into a wide grin as he held out his hand. "I'm Brad."

"I know," I said before I could stop myself. His hand closed on mine, and his head tilted to the right a bit as his eyes locked onto mine, as if he were considering those words carefully. I felt my stomach fall out from under me as I realized what the hell I had just said. "I mean, everyone knows you," I amended, and I followed that up with a nervous little serial killer chuckle that would convince absolutely no one I wasn't crazy.

He held my hand for a second too long as he said nothing and then slowly nodded. "Okay, Kyle. Cool." He let go, but I could still feel the warmth of where his skin had touched mine. "So after five?" My head did the bobblehead nod as I agreed. He laughed a little to himself as he turned away. "Awesome, see you then."

I tried not to stare at the way his jeans hugged his ass as he walked away.

I tried but failed pretty badly.

I GENERALLY avoided the locker room like a West Hollywood twink avoids solid food.

PE and watching normal guys get undressed was bad enough; the thought of actual athletes getting naked, standing around snapping towels at each other, soaping up under hot showers….

This is the gay equivalent of how straight guys view girls having a slumber party.

Brad came out, letterman jacket in place, duffel bag over one shoulder, hair damp and spiky from lack of product, fresh white T-shirt clinging to his chest. It was the hottest thing I had ever seen in the flesh. "Waiting long?"

All my life.

"Nah, not at all," I said, trying to replicate his casual style.

He chuckled at some internal joke. "You could have come in," he said, heading toward his car.

"Oh, no," I said, trying not to sound too strident about my refusal. "I'm cool."

He looked at me over his shoulder and grinned. "Okay. This is mine." He had stopped in front of a new, bright yellow Mustang that just oozed money.

"Nice car," I said as I eased into the passenger seat, terrified of somehow ruining the car. He tossed his bag into the backseat as he jumped behind the wheel.

"Thanks. Got it for my last birthday," he said cheerfully. Then, in a tone that sounded almost apologetic, he added, "My dad owns a dealership, so it's a lease." He turned the key, and the car roared like an angry sabertooth cat. It hit me that it was the perfect car for him. It was masculine, tough, and pretty all at the same time. Looking at him behind the steering wheel, looking over at me and grinning… it was like looking into the eyes of sex. "You okay?" he asked as I realized I was staring.

I turned my head quickly as I nodded. "Yeah, just kinda tired, I guess," I said as I faked the worst yawn in the history of faux bodily functions.

"Hey, if you're too tired for this, we can do it another day," he said, his voice dropping in concern.

"No," I answered way too fast and saw him smile as I looked back at him. "I mean, nah. I'm cool."

He shrugged and shifted the car into drive. "If you say so."

I was realizing I was really bad at this whole social interaction thing.

He lived in a house that exemplified everything that made him who he was. It was blindly normal in the middle of a good neighborhood on the good side of town where nothing ever seemed to go wrong. The cars were all polished and gleaming, the lawns immaculately groomed, making me wonder if any of them were ever actually played on. The suburban neighborhood should have been littered with kids struggling to milk the last rays of sunshine out of the dying day, dads standing in the driveway, watering the grass and waving aimlessly, but there was no one. It looked like every place I had ever wanted to live, but as with most of the actual world, it was just a bit off from the image in my head. But then again, all of my images came from movies and TV shows, so what the hell did I know?

"Nice house," I said as he pulled up in the driveway. There was an identical Mustang parked there, this one black as night and twice as tricked out as Brad's.

He shrugged as he reached into the backseat and grabbed his bag. "It's okay, I guess."

I wasn't sure if I was seeing it correctly, but it seemed like his gait changed as he approached the front door. His steps became smaller, his shoulders slumped, and the bag on his shoulder seemed to have weight for the first time. It may have been my imagination, but there was a half-second pause between when he reached up to the doorknob and when he turned it.

It was just enough time, I noticed, to say a silent prayer.

As soon as he opened the door, a wave of noise hit us like a freight train. The sounds of a man and a woman screaming at each other echoed from the high ceilings and Spanish arches that made the house so much more resalable in this soft economy. The replica Greek marble tiles in the front foyer were scrubbed perfectly clean, as if they'd never been walked on. Two sets of shoes were set off to the right with a coat rack mounted above them.

"Take your shoes off," he said in a whisper, which was completely unnecessary, since we could have walked in with a twenty-piece brass band and failed to be heard over the din of what I assumed were his parents fighting. "My mom is psycho about the carpets," he explained with more than a small dose of contrition in his tone. I step-kicked my shoes off as I watched him slip off his Converses and push them to the side. I found it amusing that in my entire life I've never seen any teenage boy untie his sneakers before taking them off. We all evolved into creatures that somehow gained the ability to dance/shuffle our shoes off, taking the same if not more time and effort than stopping and untying them manually would. I tried not to watch as he slid his jacket off. The muscles that seemed to show through the sheer whiteness of his shirt were distracting, at the very least. I pushed my jacket over next to his and was struck by how instantly different he seemed with his shoes and jacket off.

He ceased being Brad Greymark, star jock, lord and savior of the local high school, and became another teenage boy in socks. A flawless-looking, well-built teenage boy who never failed to turn people's heads, but a teenage boy nonetheless.

"My room's upstairs," he said, sliding across the floor à la *Risky Business* to the large sprawling staircase that led to the stars. "Let's head up," he said, trying to keep his voice down.

The screaming stopped.

"Bradley?" a woman's voice called out. "Bradley, is that you?"

He visibly winced as his mother called out his full given name.

A muffled male voice claimed that he hadn't heard anything as his mother cried out again. "Bradley, are you home?"

"Dammit," he muttered under his breath. He yelled back, "Yeah, it's me!" He turned to the staircase and then decided to add, "I have a friend here, and we're doing homework."

The sound of someone coming out of the kitchen and heading toward us seemed deafening in the echoing interior of the house. A man who looked like Brad, only twenty years older, sixty pounds heavier, and a shit ton angrier came barging into the foyer, two buttons undone, tie hanging loose, drink in a death grip. "What kind of friend?" he demanded, stopping in his tracks as he finally saw me. "Oh" was all he said.

"This is…." There was a pause, and then Brad said, "My tutor. We're studying history."

"Kyle," I said under my breath, feeling myself shrink as we stood there.

"History?" his dad said, not weaving or slurring in the slightest, but I had the distinct impression he was well on his way to being smashed. I had lived through more than a few drinking episodes with my mom, and I knew a drunk when I saw one. This man was dangerously intoxicated. He stood there, silent, for a long pause; I wasn't sure if he was waiting for us to say something or had just lost his train of thought, but after a few seconds he said, "Well, God knows you need some help" before he turned around and made his way back to the kitchen. "Just keep it down," he added.

Seconds later, he screamed, "I can talk to my son if I want to, Susan!"

"Come on," Brad said, climbing the stairs to his room. I followed, trying to remember how normal the house had looked from outside.

There was a "Do Not Enter" street sign nailed to the front of the door. From the pockmarks and chipped paint, it looked like an actual sign pulled down from somewhere. Brad pushed the door open, stepped inside, and kept his hand on the door, making it obvious he wanted to slam it shut as soon as I crossed the threshold. His parents' fight echoed upstairs as well, the acoustics of the house carrying the sounds to his room perfectly. "Come in," he said impatiently.

I hadn't even realized I had paused until he said something. Every particle of my being was telling me I should leave and leave now. I hated conflict of any kind and drunken conflict doubly so. Like a non-sparkling vampire invited into his room, I crossed the threshold, feeling a slight chill when the door closed behind me.

Like everything else in his life, his room was everything mine wasn't.

Whereas the walls of mine were covered in a patchwork collection of images torn from magazines and a few tattered posters I had bought over the years, his looked like those of a poster gallery: two framed images of cars in motion; a movie poster with five teenagers leaning over each other, staring intently out; and a trio of sports athletes, each frozen in mid-victory. A wide dresser supported a parade of gold-colored people all mounted on sports trophies, enough to populate their own country, it seemed, each one another log on the fire of differences between us.

I walked around, marveling at the maleness of the entire space. A small bathroom was set off the bedroom. The vanity counter was full of hair products, cologne, and a smorgasbord of goods devised to ameliorate teenage male insecurity. The room was like an alien planet to me; there was nothing that was not jock, butch, or alpha-male guy in or around it. Even the baseball-shaped alarm clock on the end table next to his bed shouted "I'm a dude!"

"So what do you think?" he asked, sitting down on the weight bench on the other side of the bed. The clothes draped over the bar indicated how much it was used.

I knew what he was asking, of course. I don't know how it is with girls, but with boys, there is very little as sacred as their room. It is the only area in the home that they are allowed to make completely their own, within reason; therefore, it is often a direct reflection of their personality. There is nothing more telling than a boy's room for showing who they are as a person, but you had to know how to read it. The cars were not indications of wealth but rather of the desire to get out. Movement and speed—they were horses that could carry us out of town as soon as humanly possible. That, and most of the time they were metallic red, and metallic red was badass.

The sports figures were about his desire, his drive, to do better and the person he wanted to become someday. I noticed that the three of them were all white, good-looking, and built like brick houses, much like Brad. They were the same sports figures I would have picked if I had to pick three sports posters and put them up on my wall. I noticed that even though they were superstars, not one of them was a celebrity outside of sports. Unlike some people who used their professional athleticism as a springboard to be something more, these people were known for sports and sports only.

But it was the movie poster that had me puzzled.

I mean, sure, everyone had seen *that* movie. Didn't matter what year it came out—that movie defined what being in high school was about. Though a complete fairy tale, it spoke of different people forced to spend a day together and realizing they had more in common than they ever knew. Real life never worked like that, of course, and even if it had, the spell would have been broken by Monday, and no one would have ever admitted anything out loud. That movie represented what every single high schooler wanted life to be, but it meant even more for those of us who didn't have a voice.

Finding that movie's poster in the room of one of the school's most popular people and seeing it hanging above his bed, the prime real estate in any boy's room, told me there was more to him than what everyone else saw. He could have come to school naked tomorrow and would instantly become more popular before someone offered him a towel. He could proclaim water to be uncool, and there would be hundreds of people who went thirsty the next day. To think that he had watched the same movie and wanted the real him to be heard....

Well, it was puzzling.

"I love that movie," I said, pointing at the poster.

I had thought I had seen the full arsenal of his smiles since he had talked to me in the hallway, but as he nodded, he flashed me a new one that put all the other smiles to shame. It wasn't until later that I realized that was the first time I ever saw him really smile. "So which one are you?"

Another popular question in high school, and though it seemed simple, it was a complex formula to figure out. You say the jock, you are trying to say you're in better shape than everyone else. If you say the princess, you're a bitch. If you say the criminal, you think you're cooler than you really are. If you say the nerd, you think you're smarter than everyone else. And if you say the basket case, you are hiding something that everyone else will want to know. There was no right answer.

"None of them, I guess," I lied, putting my backpack down on his bed. "So you wanna get started?"

Long seconds of nothing passed as I pulled my history book out and began to flip through it. When I looked up at him, I could see his wry grin was back, that "I know more than you" smile. He shook his head and moved over to the bed. I moved over and knelt beside the bed, knowing that was as close as I dared get to him. "Whatever you say," he said, lying down, his head toward the foot of the bed. "Where do we start?"

We started at Lincoln winning the presidency, moved through the Civil War, and rounded out with a little Reconstruction, all in about ninety minutes. That was a lot of material to cover in half a semester, and in a cram session like this, it was almost impossible. At the end of the first hour, we both knew two things. One, there was way more he didn't know than he did, and two, neither one of us had the concentration to go for more than an hour at the rate we had. In the last thirty minutes, things began to unravel, until he began asking random questions as he flipped through the book.

Like my own personal sun, he was not only too radiant to look at directly, I also found myself more and more drawn into his orbit with each minute. He had decided to lie back on the bed, book in his hands, as he leaned up against the pillows propped up against his headboard. This by itself was staggering, but his T-shirt had ridden up as he shifted around. The tan skin that had been exposed was just devastating to my ability to continue talking. The band of his white underwear was barely visible, and it was quickly becoming my own personal Waterloo.

"You know a lot about this stuff, don't you?" he asked, the words barely penetrating the fog that had descended onto my brain as I saw the ridges of what had to be his abs move with each breath. I had a stomach, a flat, skinny-ass stomach, but I had never once had abs. I wondered what it was like.

And then I wondered what they felt like.

And then what they tasted like....

"Kyle?" he said, waving a hand in front of my face.

I jerked back as if burned, which was when I realized my legs had fallen asleep under me.

I had been kneeling at the side of his bed for over an hour, and blood had long ceased to flow where it was supposed to and now was flowing where I definitely didn't want it to be. I went over onto my side as I stifled a sound by sinking my teeth into my bottom lip. The pins and needles that exploded throughout my legs as I rocked on the floor were as excruciating as any torture I had imagined. Seconds later, Brad's head popped over the side of the bed, his bangs falling down into his face. "You okay?"

My eyes were clenched shut as I nodded. "Peachy," I said, half grunting.

"You know, you could have sat up here with me." He settled in, resting his hands on his arms as he watched me try not to cry. "It's a big bed."

"I'm good," I replied, which was the most I could say.

"Ooookay." I could just hear that damn grin in his voice. "So what's your deal, anyways?"

My heart stopped. "Deal?" I asked, suddenly faced with a far greater agony than anything my body could throw at me.

"Yeah, deal," he said casually, like we were long-lost friends just catching up instead of relative strangers on either side of the social strata that made up high school. "I mean, you're not ugly."

This might have been the nicest thing anyone had ever said about the way I looked.

He was right; I wasn't ugly, at least not in the traditional sense. All of my damage was carefully concealed by a thin veneer of normalcy that, at times, felt like it failed to cover my entire body. Like a blanket two sizes too small, it could only cover one flaw at a time, leaving something else exposed to the general populace. If I could get past my crippling fear of talking in public, then my inability to avoid staring at people better-looking than me was revealed. If I covered that flaw up by keeping my head down, then the glaring reality that I had absolutely no friends whatsoever flashed like a neon sign. I had learned that the best I could do was to adopt a "duck and weave" strategy. I never stayed in one place long enough for someone to figure out my secret identity as the Hunchback of Foster High School, the discovery of which I just knew would be followed by torches and pitchforks.

I knew how this movie ended, and it wasn't with me walking across a football field, one hand raised in victory as Simple Minds played.

"Um, thanks," I said as I began to regain the ability to move my lower half.

"No, I mean, you aren't ugly, and no one has ever said anything bad about you, to my knowledge, at least." I could see his legs crossed over his head, white socks just hovering there, somehow making him even more attractive. "So then why the Harpo Marx routine?" His green eyes bore down on me, and I felt my stomach plummet.

And then my brain caught up with my ears.

"People talk about me?" I asked, completely ignoring the auburn eyebrow that arched in surprise. "Who?" This was news to me. I mean, as a recipient of the Claude Rains scholarship for the Recognition Impaired, I assumed no one knew who I was. I had imagined myself invisible, wandering the halls unnoticed, a not-so-short-nor-fat Bilbo Baggins without the foot hair, darting from class to class without engaging as much as a sideways glance. Who are these people who not only know who I am but actually discuss me?

He shrugged and rolled over onto his back. "Lots of people, I guess. I asked around about you," he added, reaching over to grab the baseball-shaped alarm clock with one hand. "It was all good, I assure you." He tossed it skyward with a casualness that I know would merit me a busted lip as gravity took hold of it and my own stunted reflexes tried to react. I have no idea why something so minor as tossing a ball could be so erotic, but it was.

"You asked around about me?" My shock was so great that I found myself quickly descending into a bad Jerry Lewis impression as I simply stammered Brad's own words back to him.

Another toss. "Of course I did. You think I just invite anyone over to my house?" Toss.

If blood had begun to flow back into my legs, it must have been draining from my face, because he glanced over at me, and whatever he saw shocked him enough that he forgot the falling piece of plastic that was hurtling toward his face. The sound of something striking flesh was like a crack of thunder. A loud "Fuck!" followed as his hands covered his face.

If my legs were still weak, I was unaware of it as I rushed toward him, real fear in my chest. Logically I understood the baseball-shaped alarm clock couldn't do any real harm to him, but for the overwhelming burst of panic I felt, it might as well have been a gunshot wound. I hovered over him, sitting on the bed next to his shoulders. "Are you okay?" I asked like an idiot. Of course he wasn't all right; he had just taken a line drive by a piece of plastic to his face. That was pretty far away from okay.

"Hit my damned nose," he said, the two huge paws that passed for his hands cupping his nose and mouth protectively.

"Let me see," I asked, not quite daring to move his hands aside myself.

"I'm okay," he said, his hands not moving one iota.

"Well then let me see," I reasoned.

Pause. "No, I'm fine," he insisted.

"Brad." I sighed. "Move your hands."

A weaker and muted "No," followed by an almost whispered, "It hurts."

"Move your hands," I said, taking hold of his hands and trying to pry them off.

"Stop it!" he exclaimed, his eyes wide.

"Let me see," I said, bearing down on his fingers, which he would not open.

"Let go!" he tried to demand, but it came out more whine than anything else.

"Let me see your nose, you big baby." I could see blood between the cracks of his hands and knew his nose must be swelling. Finally I stopped and looked down at him. "Seriously, Brad, let me see."

His hands refused to cooperate at first but then slowly moved aside. I hadn't noticed at first when he grabbed my wrists. "How's it look?" he asked as if inquiring about a missing limb.

It looked bad.

"It's okay," I lied, trying not to react to the sheer amount of blood that was gushing out of his nose and down his face. "Just put your head back here," I said, pushing his head over the side of the bed so it was upside down.

"Why?" he said, trying to sit up.

"Lay back!" I said, pushing him back down with a hard shove to his chest. I'm not sure if it was the shove or the tone, but he seemed shocked into compliance and lay back down slowly. "Just stay there," I said, as if addressing a willful dog or stubborn child. I got up with the intention of finding a wet cloth in his bathroom when I noticed his hand still grasping my own. I looked down my arm to his and followed it back to his face as if I couldn't quite grasp where this extra appendage had come from.

"Is it okay?" he asked, this time with real emotion in his voice.

"It will be," I said, smiling. "Let me get a washcloth," I asked, not willing to let go first.

With great deliberateness, he released my hand and brought his own back to his side. I didn't trust myself, so I turned quickly to his bathroom and began to search it for clean towels. Normally being this close to a place where I knew he showered would have made me curious at the very least, but we had wandered out of the places that made me clumsy and awkward and maneuvered into a place where I was very sure of myself.

I had seen blood before, more than I cared to admit.

The key to a swollen nose or lip was applying ice to it within the first few minutes, or it would swell at an alarming rate. If your nose and or mouth swelled past a certain point, then certain people would notice. If those certain people were teachers, then they tended to contact school officials. If school officials found out, they asked a lot of questions. If they asked a lot of questions, other people could end up angry.

And then you would get hit again.

I didn't see any ice, but a cold, wet cloth was a good start. I brought a wet and dry towel back over to him. He had been watching me upside down as he lay there. "You've done this before," he said as a fact and not a question.

"Hold still," I said, sitting down and wiping the blood away. Without the gore, it looked better than I had originally thought, no bruise and no cut skin. Most likely he'd hit his nose just the right way. I cleaned his face completely with the wet washcloth and then put the dry one under his nose. "Hold it tight, it's still bleeding."

His hand grabbed mine, and held the towel there by holding my hand still. His eyes seemed to sparkle as he looked up at me. "You saved me," he said, the wry grin evident even muffled by a towel.

"It's a bloody nose," I said, enjoying the way his hand felt grasping mine. "Hardly think I saved you from anything."

"Hey, this is my moneymaker," he said, his free hand making a circular motion around his face. "You know how much trouble I'd be in if this got hurt?"

Chuckling, I shook my head. "And how much money have you actually made with your moneymaker?"

"It's a work in progress," he said, his fingers moving down the length of my hand with a stroke.

I pulled my hand back rapidly, rubbing where he had touched me as if I could dispel the effect his touch had that easily. "Well, you're okay now," I said, beginning to stand up.

He sat up in a burst, scooting over until his face was level with mine. "I asked about you," he said, moving his hand away from his nose.

"Why?" I asked in a whisper. He had mesmerized me like a cobra mesmerized its prey.

"'Cause," he said in the same whisper, leaning forward. "I wanted to know you."

"You're bleeding again," my mouth said abruptly, completely against my will, I assure you.

A trail of blood seeped down his nose and over his lips as he pushed his mouth onto mine.

My eyes closed, and I tasted lust and blood as my tongue moved between his lips. I was shocked to find his moving back into my mouth. My arm slid around his back, and I could feel the hard muscle just beneath the thin cotton shirt that slid up as he leaned in. "Been wanting to do that all night," he said, resting his forehead against mine.

"Why?" my mouth asked, my eyes still closed.

I heard the chuckle move through his whole body as he pressed his mouth closer and whispered in my ear. "Because maybe I like you?" he said, his breath warm against my skin.

"Maybe?" I asked, not even aware I was holding my breath.

"Maybe, with a chance of certainty," he said, kissing the nape of my neck. "You like me?" he asked stupidly.

"What do you think?" I asked, smiling like an idiot.

"I think you need to get a bigger history book if you're gonna sport wood in the hallway from now on," he said, his tongue moving against the side of my neck for a moment, making me shiver from head to toe.

I could feel myself turning red as I took the compliment. "You noticed that," I said rather than asked.

"Oh yeah," he growled more than said as he began to move back up toward my mouth. "You're not ugly," he repeated, this time as a solid fact instead of an opinion. We kissed again, the copper taste of his blood reminding me of licking the tip of a battery.

I wanted to say thank you, but my mouth was already full.

I THANKED God for automatic transmissions, because he held my hand all the way home.

We had stopped kissing after hearing his parents' fighting begin to scale up the stairway with greater and greater intensity. He had scrambled off the bed and fled into the bathroom as I tried to collect my books before his parents made their way to his door like a pair of fairy tale trolls. The voices passed by after a few seconds, but my chest was tight with the same familiar fear I had lived with each night my mother and her boyfriend of the week had fought.

"You ready to go?" he asked, suddenly kneeling next to me. I was shocked to find him so close to me, his physical presence made my entire body jerk in reaction. His smile was like a force of nature, so all I could do was nod and pack my stuff up.

He took my hand out of my lap as soon as we cleared his driveway; his palms were callused from baseball and weights. My fingers traced the rough pads absently as he drove in silence. My hands were soft, disgustingly so compared to his, in my mind. I almost pulled my hand back, but his moved around and began to stroke the same pattern on mine.

"Your hands are so smooth," he said. I needed a second to realize it was a compliment. His touch felt incredible after what seemed like a lifetime of neglect and solitude. I squeezed his hand back, and his smile widened. He opened his mouth to say something and then closed it again as we continued to drive through the night.

The silence felt like it was forming a wedge between us as he turned the corner to my house. I was so stuck in my own private wave of misery that the need to be ashamed of where I lived didn't even register for once. We lived in a set of rundown apartments next to the local welfare tenement in a bad neighborhood on the shady side of town—a place where you had a better chance of getting shot than borrowing milk. I wasn't even aware we were in front of my building until he said, "I never knew anyone who lived over here before."

Fuck.

"Yeah, sorry about that," I said, grabbing my backpack off the floorboard. "I can't imagine your car is safe around here."

I tried to pull my hand back, but he refused to let it go, stopping me from leaving the car. I looked back and he said, "I'm not worried about my car."

And I understood where this was going, had known from the moment we walked out of his house, in fact. "Look, Brad, I don't expect you to talk to me tomorrow." He looked over at me, confused, and I amended my words with, "I know this isn't for real." I looked down at my feet, knowing there was no way I could get through this if I was looking at him. "I mean, you're you, and I'm me, and there is no way this is anything but… well, what it is. I don't want you to think I am going to go nuts on you or bug you at school or whatever. I mean I get it, it's cool."

He said nothing, which I took as silent acceptance, so I continued, "I know how this movie ends. We don't become fast friends on Monday morning and just forget everything that comes before. I'm not going to be a spaz and come up and try to talk to you in the hallway in front of your friends or anything. I'm not that guy." I took a deep breath as I forced myself over the emotions that threatened to get caught in my throat. "So don't worry, you're safe."

He stared at me, unblinking. "Okay."

"I mean it." And I did.

In my mind I had already thought about liking him, fallen head over heels, been blown off, and then hounded him relentlessly before he finally confronted me, telling me angrily that it had never happened, and he didn't like me that way. This would be followed by long weeks of me listening to emo music and crying my eyes out while thinking about killing myself. All in the matter of a seven-minute drive back to my house. "I'm not that type of guy." Even though I was completely that type of guy.

More not blinking followed by, "Okay."

"I'm not stupid, you know," I said, fighting back tears. "I know you can't go out with me." And it was true; even if I woke up tomorrow possessing a vagina and breasts, there was no way we could date in any high school known to man. Besides the fact that I would make a hideous-looking girl, there was no way a guy like him dated a person like me.

"Okay," he said again, confirming everything I already knew.

"So don't worry, I'm not going to be standing there wishing you'd walk over to my locker and say hi to me tomorrow." I slipped my hand out from under his. "But I'll help you study for the midterm."

A good ten seconds now, and then he sighed. The car was too dark for me to see his face completely, but from what I saw, he didn't look happy. "Thanks."

I grabbed the door handle. "And you don't have to kiss me for me to do it." Not waiting for a response, I opened and slammed the door and sprinted for my house like I was a blonde cheerleader being chased by the monster of the week. My key felt like it was purposely dodging the keyhole as the door began to blur from the stinging tears in my eyes.

The flimsy piece of wood flew open, and my mom stood there, her words slurring as she asked, "Where the hell have you...." And then she saw Brad's car pull off and into the night. "Who do you know that owns a car like that?"

I pushed past her, knowing that in the middle of her date with Jack Daniels, she would never notice how upset I was. The sound of my door slamming shut was as familiar as an alarm clock was in other houses. I tried not to throw myself on the bed and bury my head in a pillow like a twelve-year-old girl.

I tried, but I know I failed pretty badly.

WHEN I arrived at school, I prayed I wouldn't see him while looking everywhere trying to see him.

I moved quickly to my locker in hopes that I could get to first period without being seen, simultaneously hoping he could find me before first period.

This schism continued as I crept further and further down the hall. Part of me wanted so badly never to see him again because it would remind of me the fifteen-minute relationship I seemed to have imagined. The other part of me wanted to see him so much it was all I could think about. Somehow I had discovered a whole new level of hell to be miserable in. If you had asked me the day before whether high school could get any worse, I would have bet you everything I had that I had sunk to the lowest I could get. Yet here I was, at a whole new depth I had never imagined.

No one talked to me, no one glanced at me, it was the same as yesterday, same as every day I had gone to school, in fact. Yet today, being ignored hurt on a frequency so high that my self-imposed walls were starting to crack.

I wished that my locker were some kind of Narnian-type structure so I could just climb inside and never be seen again. It wasn't fair to go so long unnoticed, then to get noticed by what in my mind was the center of the universe, and then to metaphorically gnaw my own arm off to avoid being caught in a no-win situation, all within twenty-four hours.

If I had been a baby, concerned parents would have said I had had a long day and needed a nap.

That wasn't wholly true. What I needed I would never get. I slammed my locker door, wishing I could channel all of my pent-up sorrow and frustration into one physical blow, causing the metal door to fly off and ricochet down the hall, cutting nameless people in half, leaving them begging on the floor for a quick death. Crying out to an end of this misery called life.

Because I wanted them to feel just like I did right now.

But because I had not been irradiated with gamma rays or bitten by a radioactive spider, all the locker did was slam shut without the least bit of fanfare. That just pissed me off even more, and I turned to head toward first period—and I froze in place.

He was standing there, that small grin on his face. He had his backpack on one shoulder, his letterman jacket open to the waist, and his arms were crossed across his chest. He was leaning against the wall waiting for me to notice him. There was laughter in his eyes, which seemed to look straight through me, bathing me in warmth that, until that moment, I hadn't realized I missed. I felt my mouth go dry as my heart literally skipped a beat.

We stood there for what seemed like an eternity as my mind locked up. I had no idea what to say. I wanted to turn and run. I wanted to throw my arms around him and kiss him. I wanted to melt into the floor and just fade away. I wanted to do all of that and not say anything to shatter the moment.

And then he opened his mouth and, with a huge grin, said, "Hi."

I don't remember the moment I knew I was broken... but I do recall when I started to understand that it might be okay. It was the moment I fell in love with the boy with the green eyes.

No one starts a trip thinking that they might crash. Even though there is always a possibility, no one in their right mind ever begins a journey thinking that it's going to end in failure. There are only two types of people in the world who are aware and plan on crashing before they ever start: test pilots and teenage boys.

I must have stood there in the hallway in front of my locker for years as my mind struggled to decipher what my eyes were seeing. It had to be a mirage, an illusion of some sort created by my mind to show me what my heart truly desired. Maybe I was having a heart attack, and my life was flashing before my eyes. No, this never happened in my life. So maybe I was having a heart attack, and someone else's life was flashing in front of my eyes, which would have sucked because it seemed they got to go out with the hottest guy in the world while I was dying, and my last seconds were being spent being a creepy voyeur.

There was no way Brad was leaning up against the wall, grin on his face, just daring me to say something. I was frozen between wanting to pass my hand through him to prove he wasn't actually there and not making a move on the off chance he might vanish. Absolutely nothing came out of my mouth. Part of me was sure that this was the very moment my mind had snapped under the pressure of trying to be normal. That what little sanity I had squirreled away for a rainy day had finally gone bad, leaving me empty-handed and quietly going insane. Another part of my brain wondered what in the hell he was doing standing there after what I had said the night before.

"You keep staring, and people will think you have a crush on me," he said in a low enough tone that only I could hear.

That was enough to break me out of my stupor and finally react. I grabbed his arm and pulled him into the first empty classroom I could find, slamming the door behind us. Sounding angrier than I actually was, I demanded more than asked, "What are you doing?"

His grin didn't diminish, but the sparkle in his eyes seemed to dim slightly as he answered. "I was saying good morning—spaz much?"

My backpack slid off my shoulder as I collapsed back into a desk, sitting down. "I told you I was okay with this last night," I said, sighing, wondering how exactly something that seemed so incredible in my mind could be so sucky in actuality.

"Yeah, you said a lot last night." His grin vanished. "Now it's my turn," he said, moving toward me and leaning forward, fists on the desk. "Look, Kyle, I have no idea what this is, and I am not going to pretend I do, but I can tell you this. I didn't kiss you as some kind of payment for tutoring me." His voice was obviously angry, but I wasn't feeling nervous or apprehensive at all. "I'm not sure where that came from, but let me clear it up: you aren't some kind of history whore to me."

The phrase "history whore," by the way, is forever ingrained in my memory.

"You think you know me. Trust me when I say no one knows who the hell I am. Everyone thinks I'm…." He paused as he realized no matter what words came next, he was going to sound like a douche bag. He knew he was what passed for a celebrity at our school, most likely our entire town. Mind you, not "celebrity" as defined by Paris Hilton or anyone on Jersey Shore, but celebrity nonetheless. So if he said anything less than that, he was lying through his insanely white and perfectly straight teeth.

No one in high school ever admitted how popular they were unless they were extremely drunk or just a total bitch. Everyone labored under the impression that they were in some way a few notches below the top of the totem pole no matter who they were. It was only through other people's eyes that someone became the most popular kid in the world or the prettiest girl that ever walked these halls, so him saying anything that sounded like "I'm popular" now would violate every single social law of the high school jungle.

Instead he just shook his head and said, "Everyone thinks I am this person—everyone but me." He looked up at me, and it was the first time I had an inkling that no matter where somewhere is on that totem pole, there was always something pushing down from higher above. "I'm broken, Kyle, I'm broken inside…." His voice dropped to almost a whisper. "And I don't know what to do about it."

I think he might have said something after that, and I might have said something back, but whatever it was, it wasn't that important, because I had finally found something I didn't think existed. I must have been silent for a while, because he looked at me with concerned eyes and asked, "Kyle?"

I looked up at him and smiled, because I had just figured out something seriously important.

I had found another person to be with.

I wasn't sure where Brad and I were, but I knew it was Somewhere New. The bell interrupted and reminded us once more that we did indeed live in the real world, where things like linear time and consequences lived. Linear time existed because first period started at the same time every morning, and no matter how important this talk was, time was not going to change itself around us. Consequences existed in that if we missed class, we were both going to be in a crapload more trouble than either one of us wanted to court at that point in our young lives. So with great reluctance we parted ways, vowing we would talk about everything later.

"Later" being a time that didn't have a really precise definition.

Later, it turned out, wasn't lunch. Luckily we didn't have a lot of money, which meant I brought my own lunch every day because it saved me a lot of drama that other kids went through. Things like standing in line with other people, risking the chance of actually interacting with someone, or finding someplace to sit down. This saved me from the horrific experience of having people look me in the face and tell me to fuck off. Instead of suffering through that, I wandered the quad. I usually opted to retreat to the safety of the band hall steps, where I could rummage through my paper bag and retrieve the least distracting thing I'd thrown in that morning to consume.

The steps were also close to what was described by people as the Round Table. The name was ironic, since it was neither round nor a table but a long wooden bench with seats on either side of it. The name came from the fact that only the most popular of people ever sat there, the prom kings and queens, the elite of the elite of Foster High. And though everyone at the Table was usually called royalty in the most sarcastic of tones, it wasn't a table that just anyone walked up to, much less sat down at.

In retrospect, I have to plead temporary insanity.

Normally there was a better chance I would strip naked, roll around in broken glass, and then cover the wounds with Tabasco sauce than I would approach the Round Table. However, whatever I possessed in my brain that passed for common sense had left for the day and hadn't taped a "will return by this time" sign hanging on the door. I had my brown bag clenched tightly as I walked toward the Table. There wasn't even an average-looking person lounging around it. The least attractive person was a guy named Kelly Aimes, a short and stocky guy who was known more for his ability on the football field than his looks. Even he was still better-looking than most. The only thing that made Kelly less attractive than everyone else was that he was a total dick.

If you close your eyes and imagine every single movie bully you've ever seen pushing nerds, throwing people in garbage cans, and shoving geeks into lockers, then you have a good impression of what Kelly was like to be around. I hadn't noticed him, though, because all I saw was Brad. I'm pretty sure he wasn't standing there, one leg on the bench, as wind blew through his hair and an '80s rock anthem played softly in the background, but that was how I saw him. He was saying something that must have been engaging, since the circle of people who surrounded him seemed spellbound by what was coming out of his mouth.

I understood that sentiment all too well.

I got within nine steps of the Table before I heard a voice call out, "Hey, queerbait, where the hell you think you're going?"

There wasn't even a tiny little doubt in my mind as to whom those words were directed at.

As is the case in any high school or prison on earth, there is nothing more desirable to the general populace than free drama. There is a pack mentality that exists in those places that can only be rivaled by a group of people watching Christians being fed to lions. They want blood and lots of it. My head snapped up to see Kelly standing in front of me, blocking my way to the Table like a rude and abusive bouncer stopping me from entering a nightclub.

I looked past him and saw the Table had frozen in midsentence to look at me as well. Brad's eyes grew wide as we made eye contact, and he realized what I must have been attempting. I had to give him credit; he didn't shake his head or try to wave me off, since that would have given him away as well. Instead, his face was carved out of marble as Kelly knocked the lunch bag out of my hands.

"I asked where do you think you're going?" he said, his body drawing in close to mine. I winced as anyone with a badger in his face would. Not a good move, as anyone knows. In the dog-eat-dog world of high school, the paramount rule is "never show fear." "Oh! What's wrong, bitch?" he taunted, his chest bumping mine now, pushing me back a few stumbling steps, since he had at least forty pounds on me. "Not used to having a real man up in your face?"

To this day I don't know if it was fear, anger, or just straight-up loathing that made me respond with, "Why? Have you seen a real man around here?" If it had been a movie, you would have heard the record scratching sound effect as the assembled crowd processed what I had said.

And then came the laughter.

Part of me felt horrible for Kelly, because there is no worse fate than being surrounded by people laughing maliciously at you. Seeing someone, no matter who they may be, eaten alive in public is just plain disgusting. From the look on Kelly's face, this was the first time it had happened to him; the abject shock he displayed made staring at him akin to staring down a corpse. He looked to his left and right, verifying that everyone was, indeed, laughing at him. It was not a localized catastrophe involving just those people closest to us. I suppose I should have felt the flush of victory at that moment as the bully was hoisted by his own petard, but to be honest, all I felt was sick to my stomach at the thought of the very same thing happening to me.

And then he hit me.

One second I felt the blood race to my face as I realized I was inadvertently the center of attention, and the next I was on the ground. My right hand felt as if it had been dragged across broken glass as it hit the pavement hard; my left was clutching my chest where he had punched me. The look on my face must have trumped Kelly's by a country mile, as the laughter got louder, and I realized its focus had shifted to me.

I only knew two things.

One, this was the worst moment of my life.

And two, this was actually just the worst moment of my life so far.

"How's that for a real man, you fucking fag—" he had begun to taunt as he stood over me when his head snapped suddenly to the left, the sound of flesh hitting flesh echoing like a gunshot off the grassy knoll. The laughter had stopped as Kelly stumbled sideways and finally crashed like some great douche bag tree. I looked up and saw Brad standing over him, fists clenched, face etched with fury. He looked like an angry god fuming, deciding his vengeance. I looked around and saw people with their hands over their mouths trying to cover their delight at the new violence lest they be pulled into it. Everyone loved seeing someone get their ass kicked. No one wanted it to be them.

Kelly started to rise to his knees. Brad growled. "Stay down there." It wasn't a request. It wasn't even a suggestion. It was obviously a command, and he expected it to be followed. Kelly paused, his head still down as drops of blood pooled beneath his face. "You think it's funny going around picking on people smaller than you, Kelly?" Again, not a question. "Well, I'm smaller than you." Brad knelt down and locked eyes with him. "Pick on me."

It was true that Brad was a few inches shorter than Kelly, but only in physical height. Even though the two of them were both high school celebrities, it was only by the gift of sport that Kelly was able to share the same space with him.

Kelly's eyes watered as Brad thrust his face closer to him, just as Kelly had done to me. His abject fear was tangible as no one in the quad dared to breathe.

"Come on, big guy," Brad said casually, as if they were just discussing a sports score or the weather. "Pick. On. Me."

Kelly shook his head, blood from his nose and lip spraying out as he babbled. "I didn't mean anything by it, Brad!" His voice cracked, and it must have been obvious even to his own ears that he sounded like a little bitch. He swallowed and tried to control his tone. "I mean, I was just having a little fun.... " And he could instantly tell that was the wrong thing to say.

"Fun?" Brad asked as his eyes flashed with rage. I had never seen anyone that angry this close up before unless their anger was directed at me. He grabbed the front of Kelly's shirt and hauled him to his feet as if he weighed nothing. No one Kelly's size could be used to being manhandled like that, and from the way his feet refused to steady themselves under him, he wasn't. Brad pushed him toward where I still sat on the ground, no doubt in the same level of stupor as the rest of the crowd. "Let's have some fun, then," Brad hissed harshly in Kelly's ear from behind. "Look at him and apologize."

I felt my throat go dry as Kelly looked down at me, and I became the totality of his universe for the next few minutes. I knew people were staring, I knew I should get up and run, but I couldn't. Instead, I just sat there like a lump, speechless.

In a voice barely above a mumble, he said, "I'm sorry."

Brad's knee came up against the small of Kelly's back, making him bark out in what was probably more shock than actual pain. "I said apologize," he ordered through gritted teeth. "Not just say sorry like a fucking girl. Try it like a man." Small pause. "For once."

I saw Kelly's face redden in both anger and embarrassment as a few people in the back laughed. As he looked at me again, I saw the coldness in his eyes, and my chest tightened. I could tell this was not the end. This was not even the middle. As he said in a monotone voice, "I apologize for knocking you down and being a dick," I knew beyond a shadow of a doubt.

This was just the beginning.

"It's okay," I said in what had to be just louder than a squeak.

"And I'm a fucking tool," Brad said softly as he shook him.

"And I'm a tool!" Kelly said, almost shouting.

"And I have a little dick, and it makes me do crazy things!"

Kelly's head sagged down, and in the most defeated voice I have ever heard another human being use, he echoed, "And I have a little dick, and it makes me do crazy things."

The crowd exploded in howls of amusement as Brad pushed Kelly to the side. He fell hard, his hands scuffing on the pavement as mine had. I was horrified, not just by the attention, but by the knowledge that Brad had just made the whole mess a million times worse than before. He took a step toward me and held out his hand. "Come on," he said to me in a low, kind voice. "Let me help you up."

I looked up at him in shock for several seconds before I pushed myself to my feet, trying not to wince as my hand screamed in protest. I stopped there for a moment, inches away from Brad's face. His eyes belonged to a stranger, and I realized I didn't know him at all.

I turned and pushed my way through the crowd, praying that if I was going to start bawling, no one would notice until I was past them. I know he wanted to follow me, but there was no earthly reason why someone like him would run after someone like me.

And for once, I was happy for that.

There was nothing left to do but flee after a scene like that. I had just received more attention in the last five minutes than I had in the entirety of my time in school. Though everyone has Ferris Bueller-like dreams where they jump up and sing "Twist and Shout" in front of thousands, the reality of having all those people looking at you is a completely different situation. I was mortified beyond belief, and the thought of going back to school ever again was daunting.

I ran home.

The joy of having an alcoholic party mom was that if you came barging through the door hours before school was out, you didn't receive so much as a raised eyebrow in response. I pushed the door to my bedroom open and froze in place when I saw Brad sitting on my bed, thumbing through a well-worn copy of *The Outsiders*. He looked over with a concerned look on his face. "Hey."

"You have a friend here!" my mom called from the living room.

Sighing, I closed the door as I dropped my backpack to the floor. There was nowhere in the small room to sit other than the bed, and there was no way in gay hell I was going to sit next to him near a bed again. Instead I leaned up against the far wall and tried to look as intimidating as I could. "How did you get here before me?" I asked, my confusion interrupting my anger.

He tossed the book back to the ground. "I have a car, what did you expect?"

Dammit.

"So what do you want?" I asked, knowing whatever anger I had hoped to express in my voice was lost after such an idiotic question.

"How's your hand?" he asked, looking at the way I was clutching it.

"Fine," I said with a clipped annoyance. "What do you want?"

He paused, his eyes boring into me with an intensity that, frankly, I wasn't prepared for. "Are you pissed at me?"

"What do you think?" I shot back.

"I think that if you are pissed, I'm not sure why." In fact, he sounded angrier than I ever was, for some reason.

"You're pissed at me?" I blurted out as my mind struggled to connect the dots.

He dropped his head, breaking eye contact for a moment as he muttered to the ground, "Well, I'm not filled with love at the moment."

The sarcasm was like a blade to me for some reason. My indignation and frustration evaporated under the sudden and overwhelming urge to apologize to him. I had no idea what I should apologize for, but the desire remained nonetheless. Finally I was able to ask, "What did I do?"

He looked back up at me, and our eyes met. "What in the world made you walk towards the Table?"

Normally I would have been disgusted by the way his voice emphasized its importance, somehow changing it from a table to the Table, but I was literally shocked by his question. "What?" I sputtered as my mental gears ground themselves to a standstill while I tried to process his words.

"Oh, come on," he said, standing up suddenly, reminding me again of our physical differences. It was daunting to have him here in such a familiar and enclosed space. My bedroom was barely large enough for me and my issues, but with an angered Brad standing not three feet away from me, it was positively microscopic. "You were making a beeline straight towards it, and you know it. What possessed you to do something that stupid?"

[38]

And my mind finally found a gear. "Excuse me?" I said, more of a demand than a question. If he had been any more shocked by the change in my demeanor, his jaw would have literally hit the floor as I continued to berate him, uncaring whether I upset him or not. "Who do you guys think you are, anyways?" I took a step toward him and felt far too much enjoyment at seeing him stumble a half step back. "Do you honestly think people need permission to get near your precious table?" I saw his face blanch as my voice conveyed seventeen years of disdain when I snarled. "I get you guys are popular, but I know you did not come all the way to my house to tell me I'm not good enough to walk towards a fucking table." Another step, and he fell back onto my bed with a half yelp. "Because I thought at the very least you and I might be two people that could at least talk without me asking for diplomatic immunity first!"

The look on his face gave me a clue as to how I must have looked when he confronted Kelly: he just gaped at me, wide-eyed.

"I'm a human being, Brad, and I can walk up to any place I want to." I stood over him, my breath coming quickly as my heart pounded from the adrenaline. Even with him flat on my bed I held no illusions that he wasn't more physically imposing than I was. But a crack had snapped open in that bravado he wore as a set of armor. And what I saw underneath was as alluring as it was intoxicating.

I want to say it was the thrill of the moment. I want to blame the moment on his vulnerability. I'd love to blame it on a half-dozen different things, but the honest to God truth was I did what I did because I knew we were starting to crash, and I didn't want to go out like that.

I fell on top of him, his hands moving to my waist automatically as our hips met. My mouth moved over his like an animal staking its claim. I bit his bottom lip as I pulled away. I felt his hands grip me and pull me closer as I kissed my way to the side of his face and down his neck. I could hear the whispered "Oh God!" as I felt the tendons clench between my teeth, the unmistakable rush of domination filling my senses. Feeling his chest move against mine as I nibbled the muscles where his neck met his shoulder, and the pressure of his crotch grinding upward as I licked my way back up to his ear was like the first hit of a drug.

My head was swimming as I pulled his head to the side, savagely plunging my tongue into his ear. His gasp twisted tighter, into a near squeal, as his entire body reacted as if touched by a live wire. I tried not to focus on the fact that I had one of the most popular jocks in the school writhing under me and just enjoy the physicality of it, but I had to admit that who he was made it as enjoyable as what we were doing. I bit lightly at his lobe as I felt him take a halting breath. In the lowest of voices, I whispered, "You like that?"

He nodded quickly, and I could tell he didn't trust his voice right then. I felt him moving his hips so that he rubbed against me again and again. I may have been skinny, but I wasn't lacking in every department that made up a man. His eyes got bigger for a moment in surprise, and then the smile spread across his mouth. "Not such a mouse after all?" he asked as he squeezed the head softly.

I closed my eyes in ecstasy as I pressed my forehead to his chest..

His voice purred in my ear as he echoed my own question. "You like that?"

I nodded, trying not to groan as he began to move his hand up and down.

"God, you feel good."

I looked up at him, confused, not sure he was talking to me. When I saw he was, a smile came over my face.

"You're hot," I said, pressing my hand over him, beginning to rub. I felt him buck up into my touch as his eyes clenched in the moment. I was entranced by the way he bit his lower lip, his tongue snaking out for a brief moment as I began to rub harder and faster. I went back to his ear, probing around the sensitive skin. "You want that?" I whispered between licks, the feeling of him moaning under me, his body unable to resist me, like nothing I had ever felt before.

"Oh God, Kyle," he murmured, his voice trailing off into incoherent sounds.

I said nothing as I moved harder.

"Oh Jesus!" he cried as his hips stopped moving.

I kissed him, his tongue thanking me in ways language would never have been able to replicate. His arms had pressed against my waist, pulling me against him as his hips literally bucked off the bed in response. He was panting like a dog as he held me close to him, his body shaking with each little earthquake his member produced. His hands slid up my back, pulling me down into an embrace as he settled back onto the bed.

After a few seconds he asked in an amused tone, "So do you do that a lot?"

I didn't look up as I traced a circle around one of his nipples through his T-shirt. "Never."

He moved my face up as he kissed me again. "Seriously?"

I nodded, embarrassed.

He didn't move for a few seconds and then whispered, "Thank you," before he kissed me.

His hand moved down to my jeans slowly, and I laughed in nervousness.

This was the exact moment my mom chose to pound on the door. "Leaving!" she bellowed. "Back later tonight."

I'm not sure if I kicked him away or if Brad threw himself away from me, but I do know that if there was a world record for buttoning a pair of 501s and jumping up while smoothing out your hair, I broke it at that very moment. I could literally feel my heart pounding as if threatening to detonate my rib cage from within like an action movie explosion. I glared at my lap angrily, blaming it for what was obviously going to be death by embarrassment once my mother saw me with a hard-on.

Neither one of us even drew a breath until we heard the front door slam shut.

I collapsed back onto the bed with an audible sigh while Brad slumped back against the far wall. "Oh my God," he half moaned.

"I think I just had a stroke," I said, pulling a pillow over my face.

There was a pause before the bed shifted, and I felt a weight over me. The pillow moved aside, and his face filled my vision. "Well, I can tell there is some swelling." His grin made the innocent phrase so dirty that I felt my body react despite my state of terror.

"You're crazy," I said, not pushing him off me.

"I might be a little impaired," he said, drawing closer, his lips barely ghosting over mine.

"What if she comes back?" I asked, not able to draw a full breath from anticipation.

"I jump again," he said as his lips touched mine.

And the sound of the front door opening was like a gunshot going off next to us. This time I did push him off of me. The sound of him hitting the far wall was a pretty solid thud. After a second, my door opened, and my mom poked her head in. "You might want to move your car," she said, looking at Brad. "There are a couple of guys across the parking lot eyeing it pretty hard."

He looked like a puppet being jerked up by his strings he went from sitting to standing so fast. One hand was digging in his pocket as he looked over at me. "We okay?"

I nodded.

"Call me tonight," he said, rushing past my mom and out the door.

She watched him leave and looked back at me. I felt myself internally cringe as she focused on me. "Nice boy."

I nodded again.

Her gaze felt like a slow-moving drill boring into my skull as we stared at each other for a moment. I could see questions like "So what's he doing with you?" and "So what's wrong with him?" brewing in her mind, but she had nothing to complain about yet, so she didn't have a toehold to use as a starting point.

Yet.

Her gaze told me I was on report with her. She knew something was up, and she was going to find out what it was. "Be back later," she said, finally closing my door and leaving.

Five minutes later, I let out the mental breath I had been holding since I had first walked in and seen him sitting on my bed.

"I am so dead," I said to no one.

I COULD still feel him under me even though he was gone. I could still taste him in my mouth even though hours had passed since he had left. Like an afterimage from looking at the sun, everywhere I looked, all I saw was him. I wandered around the house, dazed. The fact that Mom was not there, coupled with the fact I had just made out with a real boy on my bed, made me feel the closest to drunk I'd been in all my seventeen years.

I tried to throw a leash on my mind as it began to wander over the details of what had just happened and began to imagine what might happen. I knew it was dangerous territory, and in my experience, nothing good ever came from straying down that path. Every time I had dared to hope for something in my life, it seemed that fate, like a small, angry child, went out of its way to make sure I not only didn't get it but was instead rewarded with the exact opposite. In my mind, hope was as illusory as unicorns and leprechauns, so when I felt my thoughts move from what was to what could be, I tried to stop them.

But it was too late.

I could see us, secret lovers behind everyone's back, every day pretending to be nothing but acquaintances, every night, so much more. I envisioned us holding hands in the darkness of a movie theater, his leg pressing up against mine, our bodies silently passing messages to each other. In the distant future I could see us sitting together, both of us stuffed into the oversized chair we owned, watching a movie and sharing a bowl of popcorn. I could feel the warmth of him as I leaned into him, completely ignoring the movie.

I wondered if we could keep it hidden for long. I mean, eyes wander, smiles linger. Only a fool would not be able see what was going on between us. His being one of the most popular guys at school might make it less shocking than I was thinking it would be. He could come by and pick me up for school, I'd see him between classes, and we could have lunch….

"Sonofabitch!" I said, jumping up from my bed.

It had taken me almost three hours to remember that we never actually finished the conversation we had started. The shock and humiliation of the afternoon came rushing back in an instant, and my previously dispelled anger suddenly reappeared. I had no idea where my cell was, so I was forced to grab our old house phone and jab Brad's number into the receiver, as if it had been complicit in Kelly's attack.

Brad picked up on the third ring. "Hey, I was wondering if you were going to call," he said, the smile evident in his voice.

"You never answered me," I said, trying my best to keep his grin from infecting my own face.

"About?" he asked, backpedaling a bit.

"About me being a human being," I said, the anger seeping into my voice slowly.

"I agree that you're a human being," he said, obviously thinking this was some part of a joke.

"I'm serious."

"So am I," he said, his voice becoming more serious. "You are a human being." After a beat, he added, "Unless you're a vampire or a werewolf. That'd be weird. You're not a vampire or a werewolf, right?"

"I'm serious," I said, my patience fading.

"So am I!" he said, obviously having fun with this. "On one hand it means I'm into necrophilia, and on the other, I'm into bestiality. Either way I'd be a sick puppy."

"Brad," I said, interrupting his monologue.

"Seriously, what is wrong with those movies?" he rambled on.

"Brad," I tried again.

"I mean, they are good-looking dudes, but at the end of the day, you're dating a dead guy or a dog, and who wants that?"

"Answer the fucking question!" I roared into the phone.

There was silence for agonizing seconds, and then I could hear his voice, filled with as much emotion as any computer. "What was the question?"

Fair point. I hadn't actually asked anything since that afternoon. "Do you think I need to ask permission to approach your table?"

The shock in his voice was so genuine that I felt like a complete ass. "Is that what you're upset about?"

"You think I shouldn't be?" I shot back, feeling more upset than angry.

He was quiet for so long I thought for a moment he had hung up. I wanted to ask if he was there, but we were two teenage boys in a standoff, which meant we were not going to just talk about what was wrong but play some stupid game of emotional chicken with each other instead.

Finally I heard his voice say, with a coldness that startled me, "I'm coming over." And he hung up.

"Brad?" I asked, hoping that maybe I had gained the ability to jump back in time five seconds and stop him from hanging up and somehow avert this whole train wreck.

But it didn't happen.

It took him less than fifteen minutes to knock on my door. I considered just turning off the lights and pretending I wasn't home, but since I wasn't in the middle of a bad sitcom, the odds of it working were pretty slim. Instead, I took a deep breath and forced myself not to shrink away as I normally did when confronted with conflict.

The door was barely open when he barged in, sounding like he was continuing a conversation we were having just on the other side of the door. Obviously furious, he snapped, "Is that what you think of me?" while coming to a stop in the middle of the living room.

I closed the door and locked it on the off chance my mom was going to make another impromptu appearance. The lock would at least give us a few seconds warning this time. "Like what?" I asked back.

"Oh, come on. I already tried to pretend I didn't know what we were talking about. Now you're gonna take a stab at it?"

I paused for a moment, not sure how to proceed. This was all too familiar to me, and that was throwing off what I was sure was righteous indignation. "I don't—" I blurted. "I mean I didn't—"

"You think I am seriously someone who would think other people are beneath me?" He was demanding answers now, and his tone and manner were entering dangerous territory as far as my mind was concerned.

He was starting to sound like my mom.

"That isn't what I said." I choked, trying to bite back the bitter, metallic taste that filled my mouth.

"Then what did you say?" he said, taking a step forward. "Come on, Kyle, what do you really think of me?"

I held my ground the best I could, but the sheer power of his anger coupled with his frame made it an intimidating task.

"Come on, Kyle! What kind of jock douche bag am I?"

"Brad, I—" I started to say under my breath.

"What?" He took the final step toward me. "I can't hear you," he said as he reached out toward me.

I am sure it was an innocent gesture. I'm sure he probably meant to just make me look up at him so at the very least he could see my lips move. Maybe he was trying to reassure me by placing a hand on my shoulder. I'm sure there were half a million reasons he could have made a move like that, but my mind only knew one.

I drew back and flinched. Not the flinch of someone who was scared or concerned. Not the flinch of someone who was nervous and caught by surprise. And certainly not the flinch of someone who was supposed to be having a heated discussion with the guy he had been making out with mere hours before.

It was the flinch of someone who was used to being hit.

He froze instantly. His entire body looked carved out of wax as his expression morphed from anger to horrified shock, while mine dropped into a panicked cringe of abject terror. The second I did it, I regretted it. I cursed as I took a few stumbling steps away from him as I tried to compose myself internally.

"Kyle," he said in a voice barely above a whisper. "I wasn't going to—"

"I know," I said abruptly, his concern stinging worse than the panic. "I know," I repeated more softly as I felt my eyes begin to sting. I was embarrassed, angry at myself, but most of all, I was tired. I was so tired of feeling like this. I was tired of being afraid of everything. My legs gave out under me as I wilted to the floor, more a move of surrender than an actual fall.

He raced toward me like a fairy-tale prince. His arms encircled me as I tried to draw away weakly. Brad's sympathy was worse than his anger, and I cursed myself for being so fucking weak. He pulled me close as the dam holding my emotions broke, and they came flooding out in a sorrow-filled sob. I laid my head closer to his heart and began to explode with seventeen years of pain and wrath rushing out in a meltdown of nuclear proportions.

He ran his fingers through my hair as he tried to soothe me. We rocked there for several minutes, my mind incapable of thought. I heard him say, his voice devoid of all emotion again, "I know, I know." Then, after a few seconds, sorrow began to saturate his words. "My dad hits me too."

And then we began to cry together.

IT must have been more than twenty minutes before we regained
enough composure to make it off the living room floor and to my bed.
Though he was physically larger than I was, he clutched me like a
drowning man clutches an overturned lifeboat. There was something
about him hurting that made me forget about my own pain instantly.
Maybe it was because, in my mind, he was some kind of high school
superhero, and the thought of a lion that cute with a thorn in his paw
was just too much for me to handle. Maybe it was because deep down I
thought he was just a better person than I was, which meant his agony
was far more valid than mine. Maybe it was because it was easier to
focus on someone else's pain than my own.

Maybe it was because when he hurt, I felt an ache in my own
chest.

"I sounded like him," he said in a voice so withdrawn that it was
like nails on a chalkboard. "I sounded just like my dad when he yells at
my mom." A silent, half-swallowed sob racked his whole body, and I
felt it reverberate through my own, a sympathetic pain that resonated
from having been treated the same all my life. It was as if, for that
moment, we were one person in pain, each of us sharing the other's
pain somehow. I squeezed him tight in commiseration, reassuring my
imagination he was a real person and not a madness-induced
hallucination.

"It's okay," I said, sounding as lame as another human being ever
has.

He looked up at me, his eyes red, watery orbs of anguish. "No it's
not." His fists gripped at my shirt. "I don't want to be him, Kyle; I
never want to be him." His head sank onto my chest, and the rest of his
words trailed off as he began to cry again

I knew that feeling well.

If I had had a choice between being caught by a band of roving cannibals who were competing in a sadistic new reality show where I was the main course or growing up to be my mother, I would have started to marinate myself to help ease the cooking process along. I remember seeing the echoes of what Brad might become when I saw his dad drunk in the foyer, his bloodshot eyes scouring me up and down, judging me and my entire life in one intoxicated stare. I could see how Brad might end up like that man one day, bitter, angry, his best days behind him, a life of popularity and high school fame long dead, mired in a life he wouldn't wish on another soul. Silently screaming for a pardon from the purgatory of his own creation, if even for one, memory-blurred night.

"You're not like him at all," I lied, knowing what he needed to hear. I knew it because I had wanted someone to say it to me most of my life—a proclamation that I was more than the sum of my genetic heritage. That I was not condemned to a life sentence of looking into the mirror and seeing someone else staring out at me.

"Some days I hate him so much," he said, nuzzling me, our legs intertwining as if just holding each other was not close enough. "I hear him downstairs, and I just feel this rage inside of me... and I want to just—"

I felt his body tense next to mine, and again, I knew how he felt, and unlike him, I had words for it. "You just want to run out of your room and start swinging until they shut up," I said, envisioning the well-worn fantasy in my head. "You want to just start hitting them again and again. And you don't want them to pass out, because if they pass out, they can't feel it anymore. And if they can't feel just a little bit of the pain they've caused you, then what's the point?"

I felt tears roll down my face as I stared up at the ceiling, blinking the images away. I saw him move toward me, his eyes reflecting the abject shock he was feeling. "Is that how you feel?" he asked.

I felt my face grow warm as I nodded.

"Oh, Kyle," he said, and he pulled me into his embrace. "I never want to hurt you," he said as I felt the fresh wounds on my heart begin to bleed. "I promise you I will never hurt you."

And he meant it, I'm sure he meant it.

"I didn't mean what I said before," he said as his arms tried to protect me from the world around us. "I didn't mean 'What were you thinking approaching the Table 'cause you don't deserve to be there.' I mean, what were you thinking doing that when Kelly was there?"

I felt my mind pause as the idea I had been completely wrong about him tried to work itself out.

"He's a complete dick. He lives for doing shit like that. I thought everyone knew about him, and that's why no one ever tries to sit with us."

I mentally berated myself as all of the things I had thought in anger about him came echoing back in my mind. Every time I thought I had him figured out he threw me a curve ball, and I ended up scrambling for cover.

"I want you to come sit with us tomorrow," he said, pulling me back so we could see each other.

"No," I said, shaking my head quickly. "I was just going to ask you something," I said, physically trying to pull away from him.

His hands kept me pinned as he said in a calm voice, "I'm serious, I want you to sit with us and see we aren't the stuck-up fuckers everyone thinks we are."

I still hadn't stopped shaking my head no.

"Kyle, I'm serious." His voice dropped an octave, sending a chill down my spine. "Please sit with me tomorrow at lunch."

My head stopped moving.

"Seriously?" I asked.

Instead of answering, he kissed me. It was so much better than any yes could have been.

THE next morning I was a wreck.

I had a very specific pattern to the way I dressed. I called it social camouflage. Since we didn't have a lot of money, I couldn't afford a bunch of name-brand stuff anyway, so I did most of my shopping at places most kids my age wouldn't admit to knowing existed. Nothing had bright colors, nothing other than a T-shirt and jeans, nothing that could ever be picked out of a lineup with a dozen other invisible kids standing next to me. So far it had worked, even though there were days I hated being that person. I wanted to be more than just invisible, more than just playing it safe. I wanted to be the snappy dresser or the stylish guy who always wore clothes that looked like they were made just for him. People like Brad made things like a letterman jacket and a white T-shirt look like they were part of a movie wardrobe, and they drove me crazy.

My first instinct was to dress down even more than normal. I mean, I was testing the limits of my ability to be ignored sitting at that table, and I had no idea how to proceed. Should I try to increase my blandness when everyone was going to stare at me anyway, or should I use the moment to break out of my role and show that maybe I was more than the high school ninja I had been up to that point?

Or maybe I would just throw up all over myself and call in sick.

I got to school and didn't see Brad anywhere. I was hoping maybe we could go over our lines for lunch, since we really didn't get past me asking "Seriously?" before making out for the rest of the night. During my first few periods I went over some topics I could bring up in case conversation seemed to be lagging. After all, I at least wanted to seem interesting to these people. The period before lunch, the desire to puke returned, and I spent half the time in the bathroom, splashing cold water on my face and trying not to pass out.

When I went to my locker to ditch my books for lunch, I saw the small note that had been slid through the grille lying on the bottom. I unfolded it and saw Brad's writing. "Meet you at the Table," it said. I had never been happier in my entire life.

I walked out of the hallway and into the quad. The sun seemed brighter, and the air smelled sweeter. I am pretty sure there were no cartoon birds circling my head as I made my way across the quad, but I saw them all the same.

I saw him across the way sitting on the Table. There was a pocket of space around him and his friends, as if there were an invisible velvet rope warding the common people away. I could see Kelly standing there, looking more like a guard dog than a bouncer, and I wondered why I had never noticed him before. Brad looked up and saw me; he smiled and waved me over. It was like finding a golden ticket in your candy bar.

I tensed as I walked past Kelly; he seemed to ignore me, but I could see him give me a sideways glance. It was part "Hulk smash!" and part "They really will let anyone eat here nowadays." I ignored him as I heard Brad call out, "Kyle, over here, man."

"Hey," I said, moving closer to him.

"You know everyone?" he asked, knowing I didn't.

"This is Tony, Adrian, and that's Cody," he said, gesturing to the three insanely good-looking guys sitting at the Table and staring at me like I was an alien life form.

"That's Susie, Deanna...," he said, gesturing to the two cheerleaders sitting to the side.

"And this is Jennifer," he said, smiling at the beautiful blonde girl sitting next to him.

"My girlfriend," he finished as the blood drained from my face.

"Pleased to meet you," I said automatically, my face a mask of congeniality.

I ALWAYS hated fairy tales.

I mean, one, the name is completely demeaning as well as misleading. Precious few of them have actual fairies in them, so I never understood why they were called that in the first place. Two, most of them feature incorrectly named happy endings for all involved. That sucks, because from the very beginning, the reader is encouraged to believe that things will work out for the better in the end. Anyone who knows anything knows that almost nothing ever ends, and when it does, it rarely ever does so well. And the third and most important reason was that I hated watching useless people waiting around to be saved.

I mean, honestly, who just sits around in a house with a bunch of short guys waiting for their prince to come? So your mom is a bitch and wants to kill you because her mirror told her to. Cry me a river, why don't you? Your big plan is sitting around, cleaning house, waiting for the other shoe to drop?

And speaking of shoes, everyone has been picked on by mean girls. You do not wait for some old lady to pop in and transmogrify some innocent rodents just so you can sneak into a dance under false pretenses. And let's say you do sneak in. For the love of all that is holy, take your mask off and look the guy in the face and say, "Hi, I'm Cindy from down the street. I have this thing at midnight; can we do coffee later?" This nonsense about a shoe and searching the entire village for one girl—it's crap.

And if it wasn't crap, I didn't want to know, because I knew if I left a glass sneaker behind after some dance, no one would have spent five seconds looking for me afterward. I didn't want to be a victim, some princess locked away in a tower, waiting to be saved. I wanted to be the hero of my story; I didn't need to be saved. At least I didn't want to be.

After a while, there is a trick you learn when dealing with unpredictable drunks. When someone is drunk, everything about that person becomes amplified in one way or another. Angry people get furious, sad people become miserable, and my mom becomes downright paranoid. I see TV programs that portray drunken people as incoherent, stumbling fools who slur their speech and have no idea what's going on around them. It makes me angry, because my mother is never like that when she's wasted. She becomes hyperaware of the people around her and reads more into their facial expressions than should have been humanly possible. I learned quickly to suppress any and all emotions just in case one might pass through my brain and show as an expression on my face at the wrong moment.

[53]

When Jennifer reached out to shake my hand, my face held all the expression of a wax figure.

"So you're Brad's tutor?" she asked in a voice that was bubblier than that of any girl I had met before.

"History whore," I said with a completely straight face. I heard Brad choke on something as he tried to intervene.

"Excuse me?" she asked, her head cocking exactly like a curious cocker spaniel's.

"Okay, you're excused," I said, still not missing a beat.

"Can I talk to you for a second?" Brad asked, his face red with emotion.

"It was great meeting you," I said in a tone that would have held up in a court of law as genuine and pleasant.

"Same," she said slowly, obviously not sure of what just happened.

Brad grabbed me by my elbow and dragged me away from the quad and out of earshot. "What the fuck are you doing?"

My face would have been more expressive if it had been crafted from diamond. I refused to break down in front of Brad over what had just happened. I was not going to pick up my dress hem and flee into the night. "You have to be kidding me," I said in a tone barely capable of reaching his ears.

"You had to know about Jennifer," he said, making it sound like I was trying to argue that the world was flat despite the globe standing between us. "Everyone knows we're going out."

Truth was, he was right. Everyone did know that Brad and Jennifer were a couple. They were the high school equivalent of Brad Pitt and Angelina Jolie. Everyone knew but me. You see, high school reputation and gossip were dependent on word of mouth. And word of mouth involved people talking to other people. No one talked to me. The fact that Brad had already found his princess and I might just be the comedic sidekick—or possibly the talking animal—was starting to dawn on me.

"I didn't. If I did, I wouldn't have done anything with you," I almost hissed through gritted teeth.

And now he cocked his head to the side like a baffled golden retriever.

"Why would you think I would fool around with you?" I demanded, realizing that we might have been existing in completely different stories the entire time.

"Because we like each other," he answered automatically like it was the most obvious answer to a question on some odd test.

I refused to cover my face with a kerchief and flee across the quad. "Enjoy your lunch," I said in a tone that, on its best day, would have been referred to as "frosty." I turned deliberately and smiled at Jennifer and the rest of the people whose names I had already forgotten. "Was awesome meeting you," I called to her with a half wave.

As soon as I rounded the corner of the music building, I threw my lunch in the trash and took off like a bullet.

This was what I meant when I said things that ended rarely ended well.

I'm not sure how high school kids survived before campuses became open at lunch, but I imagine it must have been a lot like living on the wrong side of the Berlin Wall. The freedom to just leave campus, even if only for a few minutes, was invaluable.

The area around Foster High was considered remote at best. It was built on the outskirts of the town proper, and our student population was an odd mix of the town's wealthiest and poorest kids. The school district straddled the old projects where we lived and a strip of new housing developments where Brad's house was. In a way, the school was considered to be a no man's land.

Behind the baseball diamonds and soccer field stood a fence that marked the end of school property and the beginning of the woods.

Now, calling the sparse collection of trees that lined the property "the woods" was ironic at best and sarcastic at worst. No one who had ever been in actual woods would have referred to the motley grouping as anything else but what it was: the back of the school grounds. But for us, it was our place.

Or, more correctly, since I was a student here in name only, it was better called Their Place.

It was a place where the stoners went to light up between classes, where the older kids sneaked a cigarette at lunch, and where couples went to make out whenever they wanted. The dense overhang effectively cut the light to almost nothing, making it virtually impossible to see what was happening inside without actually going in. I had never been out there before, but unlike Brad's relationship with Jennifer, I knew it existed.

How did I miss them going out? I spent more lunches stalking that table than anyone else did, but somehow I missed he had a girlfriend? Maybe I didn't miss it; maybe I just ignored it because I wanted it not to be true. I could feel the same heated shame creep up my face again at the thought of what a fucking fool I must have looked like, thinking that Brad could ever have been mine. He was one of the most popular people in my world; how could I have ever thought he would pick me?

Motherfucking fairy tales.

Again, my common sense had been hijacked and corrupted by tales of down and out girls who barely registered in their worlds as ordinary. They were bookworms and shut-ins who ended up being picked out of a crowd as a beauty, a diamond in the rough, or even a princess. Though I didn't want to be that kind of person, I had to admit that the thought of one person in the world choosing me over everyone else sounded incredibly desirable, even if it was total bullshit. I would never be the princess, and the sad part was that I had never wanted to be before I met him. It was hard to stare into those bright green eyes and not fall in love at least a little, but to have him over you, kissing you? It was just unfair.

Before him I had been happy, well no not happy.

Before him I had been content, no, not that either.

Before him, I had settled into being quietly miserable for the next four years, and Brad had come and fucked all that up. And now? What was I now? A weak and shattered stereotype in the middle of the dark woods, pining over the love he never truly had. All I needed to do was fall asleep, wake up, find it was dark, and stumble into a house made of candy or some crap. Because no matter how much my mind was trying to tell me Brad and I were something real, I knew the truth.

I had fallen for the happy ending.

I spent the next hour or so packing my emotions back into the containers from which they had escaped. Previously mint-condition desire and love, still in the box, were now forever ruined as I taped up the plastic covers and tried to stack everything back where it belonged. This was not my story, and I had been a fool to think it ever could be. That is the true crime that fairy tales commit—making people like me think that we counted in this world. I was neither hot nor in shape. I was just a normal boy in an extraordinary world, and stories like that, no matter how misleading and destructive, would always appeal to people like me. The Brads and Jennifers of the world didn't need a storybook to tell them about happily ever after; they were consigned to that fate the moment they opened their perfect eyes and gazed out across the world. They didn't need a trio of Alzheimer's-impaired witches to warn them away from cursed spinning wheels, because even if they did succumb to such a cruel deception, someone would come along and make it all better.

As I looked back at the school, I realized I hated *The Wizard of Oz* even more than I had before. I readied myself to accept my return to my black-and-white world, but unlike that retarded Kansas girl, I was not going to sing a song about it. Returning to a world devoid of joy and light where I simply woke up, went to school, and waited until the day was over so I could go home and go back to sleep was not, in any definition of the word, a good thing. Lather, rinse, repeat. I had no idea how long I would be forced to endure it or what happened next, but I knew wishing for more than that was just foolish.

I packed up my regret, using far more mental packing tape than necessary to make sure it didn't open up on me by mistake, and placed it in with the rest. A thousand little feelings all locked away, each one of them screaming at me to reconsider. I sighed softly as I closed the box and made my mind up.

Once upon a time there was a boy who didn't get to fall in love.

The End.

EVEN after all of that, I expected him to be there waiting for me again.

I shouldn't have, of course. After all, why would he be? My mom was gone, which meant another night of foraging for dinner, but I had absolutely no appetite. I fell back onto my bed in what I was sure anyone else watching would have seen as an over-the-top dramatic flourish. At the moment, I was feeling pretty emo, so I didn't care.

I tried to push thoughts of him out of my mind, to put him back in whatever box his memory had come from, but it was a waste of time. Every time I pushed mentally, he pushed right back. I closed my eyes, and I could imagine him over me again, the feel of his weight on top of me, reminding me that he was a real person and not some cartoon prince.

But was he?

My eyes opened as I stared at my ceiling for a long time. Was I really someone to him or was I just someone to fool around with on the side? Part of me thought I understood what had been going on, but after today, I only knew one thing for certain.

Brad and I were on completely different paths, and this moment in time was where they had happened to meet.

What we had done was simply satisfying a curiosity for him—a dalliance in a place he would never settle down in. He was just passing through the neighborhood. I knew in my heart the neighborhood was where I was going to live my life. The whole liking guys thing was something he was going to work through, a stage. I was going to be the guy he brought up when he wanted to seem more worldly than he was. "Oh yeah, I messed around with a guy in high school." And he would be the guy I brought up once I'd had two drinks too many. "Yeah, he was my first love, and he was straight."

I couldn't blame him. After all, he was who he was, and I would always be me. I had always known deep down I was different, but now I had a name for it.

Gay.

The very thought of being gay gave me chills. Not because of what I thought of it but because of what others would. Kelly's words came echoing back in my memory. Queerbait, bitch. All words that I was going to become very familiar with as time went on, I was sure. I didn't have the same choices Brad had. I couldn't just stop and walk away, end up dating some girl, settling down, and raising two and a half kids, average job, mortgage, bills, pretty much what the rest of the world considered normal. I wasn't normal, and no matter how hard I tried, I was never going to be.

And though I didn't hear it at the time, a small part of me exclaimed, "Good!"

At some point, the darkness of my room gave way to the inside of my eyelids, because when the phone rang, I nearly jumped out of my bed. I looked around in confusion, not quite aware I had fallen asleep. The house was pitch black, and I hit every single sharp corner in the apartment on my way to the phone.

"Hello?" I asked, still not sure how awake I was.

"Hi," he said, his voice sounding small and miserable.

"Hi," I said back, feeling exactly how he sounded.

"I tried calling your cell. Can you talk?" he asked, which confused me for a moment until I saw the time. It was after ten at night, a time that any normal kid would get whaled on for getting phone calls.

"Sure," I said, taking the phone back to my room.

He was silent as I fell back onto my bed, the darkness feeling almost welcoming to me in my misery. I could hear him breathing on the other end of the connection, but it was obvious he had no idea what came next. Finally he said, "I'm sorry."

And he was; I could hear it in his voice. He was truly sorry, and the very sorrow that his tone conveyed over the phone tore me apart. All I could think of was his pain and his suffering. Even though I was in fourteen types of pain, the only thing that was real was his hurting.

"I know" was all I could say back. What was there to say? I'm sorry too? For what? For kissing him back? For feeling too much? For not knowing he had a girlfriend? My eyes stung as I realized that everything was climbing out of the boxes I had just sealed. Little creatures of discomfort in my mind, pinching and tearing at anything they could find as I struggled not to make a noise.

"I wasn't just…," he began and then stopped. I'm not sure if he was close to crying or just choosing his words carefully, taking cues from some invisible attorney who was there to make sure his client walked free from any and all guilt. He finally let out a huge sigh and said, "I don't know, Kyle. I didn't want to hurt you."

"I know," I said in the quietest voice I could muster.

"But I did," he said, not even bothering to frame it as a question.

"I know," I said again, trying to keep everything held in but failing miserably and beginning to cry.

I could hear him on the other end, the choking sounds of his own sobbing mixing with mine, making the saddest duet of ruefulness I had ever heard. Finally he sniffled and said with more conviction than I could have mustered at that point, "I'll make this right, I promise."

He was making a vow, a vow right there to right what was wrong. Just like a prince.

And damned if it didn't feel good.

I heard the muffled voice of his mom talking on the other end for a second, and then he came back. "I need to go. Can I drive you to school tomorrow?" I didn't even know I was just nodding like an idiot until he asked hesitantly, "Kyle? You there?"

"Yes," I answered quickly. "And yes, you can drive me to school."

"Sweet," he said, something other than grief entering his voice. "Night."

He hung up, but I continued to hold the phone to my ear for a long time after.

He was going to save me. I just knew it.

I BARELY slept that night.

I tried to banish from my mind the image of a prince showing up with a horse-drawn carriage, tried to tell myself my life wasn't like that. But no matter how I tried to ignore that fantasy, I had to admit Brad would look incredible as a Disney prince, his dark red hair carefully swept back as his bangs danced playfully above those soulful green eyes. In our school, he was practically royalty already. It wasn't a huge leap to imagine him in the line of succession to an actual throne.

"But you're still not a princess," I heard my own voice comment as my alarm clock went off. I felt completely miserable for a moment as the images in my dream drifted out of reach until they flickered out, fireflies heading off to bed in the dawn.

I shook my head and got out of bed. Whatever had bothered me was only a dream. The reality was he was coming to pick me up, and that meant things had a chance to be right again.

Not a huge chance, but any chance was better than what my life had been so far.

I threw on whatever I pulled out of my closet first. I was so excited that I didn't care what other people thought. Brad Greymark was on his way to drive me to school, and the rest of the world could burn. I ran myself through a shower so quickly that I am sure there were whole parts of my body still dry when I got out. I squirted some hair product in my hand and spent the next twenty minutes trying to make my hair anything better than it was.

Twenty-three minutes later, I jumped back in the shower and washed it out of my hair.

I grabbed my backpack and flew out the door, half expecting to see my prince astride his bright yellow mount, sunlight gleaming off his teeth as the wind moved through his hair. When I saw he wasn't there, I sat on my front step and waited, knowing it wasn't going to be long.

Ten minutes into waiting, I put my backpack down. He was going to be there; he was just running late.

Twenty minutes and I started to pick at my shoes. Morning traffic could be horrible, I had heard once.

At thirty, I knew he wasn't showing up, but I waited anyway.

At forty minutes, I was going to be late for first period.

I snatched my bag up and sprinted down the street toward Foster. I cursed myself silently because I knew I had fallen for the fairy tale again. Instead of sticking to my guns and letting it go, I had to be the one romantic idiot holding up a lighter and asking for more. Life had promised me that this time I would be able to kick the football, and as always, I was lying on my back, staring at the sky and wondering what exactly had just happened.

I knew what had happened. This was the kind of happy endings people like me got.

I could hear the tardy bell ring half a block away, and I stopped running. Ten seconds or ten minutes, late was late. Unless I developed super powers in the next half second, there was nothing I could do about it. When I got to school, I could see his car in the parking lot, and the one last, small shred of hope I had been counting on faded away. Instead of calculus, I plodded to the office, knowing I was going to need a late slip.

As I stood in line behind the other losers who couldn't get to class on time, I wondered why we couldn't get late slips for life. "Please excuse Kyle from heartbreak, as he has lived a sheltered life and has no idea how to handle something as simple as a crush."

With my luck, I'd get the note and my mom would refuse to sign it.

I groaned under my breath as I realized that they were going to call my mom and tell her I had been late, which meant having to come up with an explanation that didn't end up pissing her off even more. Once again, I had to label this the worst day of my life.

"I thought nerds like you were never late for school," Kelly's voice said from behind me.

Correction, the worst day so *far*.

I forced myself not to tense up or turn around to confront him. I simply picked a point in front of me and concentrated on it as if it were the center of the universe. It was an oldie but goodie when it came to dealing with stress in my life. The thousand-yard stare, zombie brain, Franken-stare, all nicknames I had cultivated over the years for basically the same thing: shutting down every part of my brain that reacted to outside stimuli.

"Don't pretend you can't hear me, you little faggot," he said, whispering harshly as the various people who worked in the office milled about us. "I know you can."

The "don't pretend you can't hear me" gambit had been a classic in my mother's repertoire of tactics to Generate a Reaction from me, though Kelly's "faggot" variation was new. Regardless of what style was used, my defense remained the same: continue to stare straight ahead as though the person had not spoken.

His elbow impacted the small of my back, something between a nudge and a punch. "So what happened?" he taunted. I could see his sneer even though my back was to him. "End up taking too much time to put on your makeup? I know how you girls are, getting ready in the morning." He thought he was funny, as he half chuckled at his own words. He could have been doing his homophobic stand-up in front of a mannequin for all the response he got from me. I was surprised at how little his words stung. And I continued to dissect the far wall in front of me. I had thought that having verbal grenades hurled at me would hurt, yet all I felt when Kelly continued to taunt me was exhaustion. I was seventeen, and I was already weary of the world.

Kelly's give and my not-take limped along for a few more minutes as person after person in line ahead of me stood in front of the assistant principal and gave them their sob story of why they were late for first period. I'm not sure why we worried so much about what we were going to say. No matter how creative the excuse might be, we were still going to have a tardy slip pushed into our fingers, and they were going to inform our parents. I tried to focus on the stories instead of Kelly in hopes that, at the very least, it would dissuade him from continuing.

The girl in front of me walked in, and despite all of my intentions, my mind began to prepare an excuse.

I'm sorry, but the guy whom I had imagined into my boyfriend promised he'd pick me up, and like the pathetic little boy I am, I waited for him until there was no way for me to make it on time without using a rocket pack. Can I get a "I'm a new homosexual and fell for my first straight guy" pass and move on, please?

At precisely the same moment, Kelly finally succeeded in getting me to react to something.

"Don't think I won't kick your ass," he warned darkly. "Your boyfriend Brad isn't here to save you."

I spun around, dropped my backpack, and shoved him as hard as I could with both hands. "He isn't my boyfriend, asshole, and I don't need anyone to save me!"

Kelly fell back on his ass with a loud thud as the people behind him backed away in startled panic. However, if anyone was going to take home the award for Most Shocked, the race was a tie between Kelly and me. He gaped up at me, eyes wide not from fear or pain but from complete and utter outrage. My eyes were wide, not from anger or frustration but from complete and utter terror.

"What the fuck did I just do?" I muttered under my breath.

"What the fuck did you just do?" Kelly roared, jumping up to his feet. He looked like a bull charging, his face red, nostrils flared. I suppose a quicker man than I would have moved out of the way, but frankly I was still too stunned. I had actually put my hands on someone else in anger.

If I had ever held any illusions about my ability to play football, they were quickly shattered as his head, fist, arms, and shoulders made contact with my abs, and I felt what air I had left in my lungs relocate to someplace less violent than my body.

I went down like a straw man, Kelly's momentum throwing us into the assistant principal's office. The girl who was in the middle of her well-rehearsed excuse let out a screech as she stared down at the nightmare sight of two teenage boys struggling for dominance at her feet. I couldn't draw a breath to save my life, but the fact that I wasn't fighting back wasn't slowing Kelly down in the least. He connected two solid hits to my face before Mr. Adler pulled him off me.

My body curled automatically into a fetal position as I struggled to haul any oxygen in the vicinity into my lungs. I could already feel the side of my face pulsing from his punch. Part of my brain judged it to be a solid six out of ten, good impact, decent follow-through, bruising for the next two weeks, and tenderness for at least a month. I'd been hit better by girls—well, by my mother specifically—but for a first-timer, Kelly had made a decent attempt.

It was the second time that week I had to be saved from that troll, and it was getting old fast. As I hesitantly began to draw breath again, I forced myself up off the ground, pushing past the pain that made up my face. Someone as old and out of shape as Mr. Adler could hold someone as built as Kelly only because Mr. Adler was an authority figure. Kelly was the same age as I was, but from that point on, we couldn't have been more different. Kelly had had respect for adults and their word ingrained into his head since he could walk.

I had never once in my life ever respected any adult. My mother was my daily reminder that behind all of their talk and bluster, adults were just taller assholes who could drive.

Kelly saw me turn toward him and, the second before I swung my fist into his balls, tried to get free of Adler's grip. I had never thrown a real punch before, but I had been on the receiving end of more than enough blows to know how to hurt someone. Operating on pure instinct, he jumped back, trying to avoid as much of my hand's impact as he could. Kelly's legs propelled him back into the assistant principal, who hadn't even been aware that I had taken a swing. The two of them fell back in a tangle of screams and cursing.

It took everything I had not to jump on Kelly when he was prone and keep whaling on him. My mind refused to recognize what we were doing as a scuffle or even a fight. Kelly wasn't just another guy who was picking on me; he wasn't just a homophobic douche who would not let up on me. Kelly had become more than just one person; he was the symbol of everything that was menacing in my life. He was a dragon, and I was done waiting for someone to slay him to protect me.

I'd do it myself.

"Touch me again and I swear to you I'll kill you," I snarled as Kelly rocked back and forth on the floor, his hands cupping his aching testicles. I'm not sure if he heard what I was saying, but it didn't matter. I wasn't saying it for his benefit. "I don't care who you are; leave me the fuck alone!"

I looked up in time to see someone hold their cell up and snap a picture. The flash made me blink a few times as I tried to clear my eyes. The faces of the people in the office were burnt into my mind in that split second. The look of abject horror and shock on every single one of them stopped me cold in my tracks. I knew that look; I knew it well. I'd seen it too many times in my life, but never once had it been directed at me.

They were looking at me like I was the monster.

Me? I wasn't the monster, he was. I was the hero; I was the knight who had put this ogre in his place and….

I looked down and saw Kelly still gripping his crotch, his eyes closed in obvious agony. And here I was, standing over him, screaming at him. The same way he had been in the quad.

"But I'm the hero," I muttered as one of the many adults who had come rushing at the sound of a fight clamped a hand down on my shoulder and led me away. This wasn't the way the story was supposed to go. I thought the hero was rewarded after he slew the dragon.

I was tossed into an empty office. I think it might have belonged to a guidance counselor. A dilapidated poster of a pissed-off cat hanging onto a rope telling me to Hang In There looked like it might be older than I was.

I always felt sorry for the people who actually trained to do guidance counseling. Trying to inspire a generation of, at best, apathetic teenagers who weren't able to conceive of life past the end of the current week, much less college, had to be a lot like running full-tilt at a wall and hoping you would somehow pass through it instead of slamming into it. No one cared less about the future than a high school student. The future had no bearing at all on the all-important now. Nothing was more important to us than now, and right now, I was screwed.

The only silver lining of this very, very dark cloud was that between being told I had been late for school and that I had teed off on a guy's junk while he was being held by the assistant principal, the tardy thing would be a distant second in my mother's mind. I had no idea what had gone wrong in my life. Exactly one week ago, I had been a faceless nobody wandering the hall; now I was going to be the guy who punched Kelly Aires in the balls.

Shortly after that, I'd be known as the guy who got killed by his mom.

Twenty minutes later, one of the principals walked in. His face showed that this was far too early in the day to be dealing with something as serious as two students fighting. He had a file in his hand, and before addressing me, he had to look down and check my name. "Kyle, can you tell me what happened?"

I said nothing. I was pretty sure of my rights, and though it was highly dubious that I was going to get read my Miranda rights for a high school scuffle, I held my ground nonetheless.

If he had been expecting an answer, he didn't give any indication as he kept flipping pages. "Kelly is the same boy you had a problem in the quad earlier this week, isn't he?" Again, the Geneva Convention stated... okay, I had no idea what was in the actual Geneva Convention. For all I knew, Geneva had been the site of a gathering of foreign chocolate tycoons and had nothing to do with actual prisoner rights, but at least I knew that it was a thing. I would have given my name, rank, and serial number if I had possessed them. I was fairly certain that saying "Kyle, complete loser" followed by my school ID would have confused the man. So I sat and said nothing.

"Look, Kyle," he said, sighing as he closed the file. "You seem like a good kid. Great grades, no tardies or absents; before this week, I don't think I've ever seen you in here. When something like this happens, it can be the start of a pattern. Things like fights and arguments out of nowhere are usually cries for help. Is that what is happening here?"

I looked up at him, acknowledging him for the first time since he had entered the room. He paused when he saw my reaction. "Why?" I asked with absolutely no emotion in my voice whatsoever.

"Why what?" he asked, confused by the query.

"Why would you care if it was a cry for help?" I clarified.

His voice gave off a pleasing, concerned tone, and he said, "Because we want to help."

"Okay," I said, frankly not caring anymore about anything. "My mother is a drunk, she is rarely home, and when she is, I'm terrified of what I might say or do to set her off. I think I'm gay and may have fallen in love with a guy who can in no possible way love me back. And I'm pretty sure that Kelly and I are on a collision course that is going to end with one of us killing the other. And we both know who is going to win that fight. So please, help me."

His face had gone pale as the exact toll of everything I had just rattled off sank in.

"Can you get me a new mom? Can you sober her up? Can you make me straight? Can you make him gay? Can you stop Kelly before he kills me?"

He shook his head no slowly; I'm sure he didn't even know he was doing it consciously.

"See, this is the problem with cries for help. Even if people hear them, they can't do a damn thing about them."

We sat there, him stunned into silence as he came to the realization that teenage problems might not be as easy to face and resolve as he had once believed and me lamenting that even with the confession, my life was still in the same, completely shitty place it had been before. "Can I go back to class, or am I suspended?"

He didn't say anything for several seconds, and then he realized I had asked a question he could answer. "We can't get ahold of your mother. Do you feel up to finishing the day?"

I grabbed my backpack and leveled him with a look. "No. But when has that changed anything?"

He didn't stop me as I walked out.

I'm not sure if the word had traveled by some form of telepathy or just insanely rapid texting, but by the time I walked into third period, everyone knew what had gone down. They all stared at me, whispering as if I was Edward Cullen, except not as tall and nowhere near as handsome. Also, I didn't have diamond skin or weird yellow eyes. I realized quickly I didn't like my newfound celebrity at all. I didn't want to be stared at, and I certainly didn't like being talked about. The worst part was that their buzzing was just below my threshold of hearing. I caught my name, Kelly's, once even Brad's, but anything else drowned itself out into the repetitious droning that made me think of grown-ups talking in the *Peanuts* cartoons.

By the time lunch rolled around, I was in an even worse mood than I had been when I had arrived to school. I dreaded stepping foot into the quad. I wasn't sure who I wanted to see less, Kelly or Brad. I opted to just stay away from people altogether and eat my lunch by the backstops of the baseball field. There was never anyone there outside of gym and practice, and that suited me just fine. Once in a while, I saw a lone straggler make the trek past me to the woods, but no one saw me. That worked for me.

I took a bite of my tasteless sandwich and tried to count how many days I had left before I was out of high school.

"You sure don't make it easy for a guy to find you," Brad said, poking his head around the corner of my backstop.

I felt my throat constrict in panic, and I began coughing violently as I tried to swallow. He rushed over to me and began patting me on the back, which never seemed to do anything for anyone but which was the physical action of choice when one was choking. "Hey, come on," he said, pulling a can of Pepsi out of his jacket pocket. "Here, take a drink," he said, popping the top open before handing it over.

I took a greedy gulp and felt the lump of food go down and air return to my lungs.

I coughed a few times as I handed the can back to him. "Thanks."

He shook his head and pulled another out of the opposite pocket. "That one is yours, keep it."

I tried not to marvel at the fact he had bought an extra one for me and concentrated on the fact that he had left me high and dry this morning. I took another drink as we sat there, staring out across the field in silence. "So you had a day," he said casually.

I glanced over at him for a second to see if he was making a lame attempt at a joke or if he was actually asking me a question. The way the afternoon light hit his skin and shone on his face was distracting, so I looked away quickly. "One way of putting it."

"Was the fight about me?" he asked, still not looking over at me.

I sighed, knowing it had been and yet knowing it had nothing to do with him at the same time. "No. Kelly just pissed me off," I said, taking another bite.

"You pissed at me?"

I looked over at him. "Why shouldn't I be?" I said so bitterly that he finally stared directly at me. "Do you know how long I waited for you to show up?" I forced the stinging in my eyes away. I wasn't going to be a whiny little bitch. I refused to collapse into myself under the crushing weight of self-pity. "Do you know how that made me feel?"

He looked down as he saw the raw pain in my eyes. He must have known that most of it had been caused by him. "I know, I'm sorry," he said, sounding more like a sad child than a teenage jock.

"Where were you?" I implored, wishing I could keep the pain out of my voice.

"Jennifer called and needed a ride and I—and I just—" He put his head between his hands as his words disintegrated into murmuring.

"Look, Brad, I didn't ask you to pick me up; that was your idea. I didn't ask you to kiss me; that was you. And I didn't ask to be put into a situation where you were going to push me to the ground out of sight every time someone walked by. I am not going to sit here and be treated like an embarrassment by you. It was nice knowing you. I hope you find what you're looking for," I said as I tossed my bag into the trash and got up to leave.

"And if what I was looking for was you?" he asked.

I paused as I saw the naked emotion on his face and knew it was reflected on my own. But I was done running at that football only to have it pulled away at the last second. "Well, congratulations. You found me," I said miserably.

He said nothing as I walked away.

I had almost made it to the door nearest my locker when Kelly spotted me from across the quad. He was obviously sick of having to explain his side of the story to every person who walked up and asked him. Punching Kelly was an act of either incredible bravery or plain stupidity. Either way, I had no proper response for people's questions. From the viewpoint of Kelly's friends and teammates, him being hit by me was a different story. For that news, there was only one reaction that seemed proper: laughing out loud combined with a huge amount of pointing.

So when he saw me trying to skulk away, he knew he was being given one chance to change the story once and for all. "Hey!" he screamed as he made a beeline toward me. "Where you running to, fag?" he added.

I stopped and turned to him.

He had brought a crowd, of course. There was no way anyone was going to miss what people sensed was coming next. Normally people paid good money to see a fight like this on pay-per-view. To find it free in your own backyard, well, that was just too tempting.

I should have been scared; I should have been terrified by the attention. Half the school was staring at me, every person waiting for me to get my ass kicked. But I wasn't—not scared, not terrified. I'd had enough, and to be honest, I wasn't talking about Kelly or Brad. I'd had enough of running away from my life, of holding my breath waiting for things to get better by themselves.

We are told in fairy tales that evil always loses and good eventually will triumph. That is what makes those stories so desirable to the general population. They want to believe that karma works and the bad guys are always defeated in the end. But in a world where no one thinks they are the bad guy and everyone plays the victim, it is harder and harder to find the black and the white of a situation. We are all the hero, and we are all the monster.

It just depends on which way you look at it.

Kelly started off by pushing me, which, as first moves go, has been a steadfast classic for boys since the second grade. I didn't go flying back; I didn't cry out from the impact. I braced myself and pushed him back as hard as I could. His eyes widened as he realized I wasn't going to beg for mercy in front of everyone.

What Kelly didn't see was that I was no longer just standing up to him and his actions of the past few days. In my mind, this wasn't about him and me and what we had done to each other. This was about a life spent in fear. A fear of people finding out who and what I really was. A fear that if I ever exposed who I really was, I would be shunned and hated for it. A fear that my mom would beat me up because she suspected who I was.

But honestly, how was that any different from the way I was already living my life?

I was alone, friendless, and generally considered odd by the few people who even realized I existed, so what did it matter if they found out? I was done running—from being gay, from my mom, from myself.

I was the hero of this story, and it was damn time I started acting like I was.

"So you think you're a tough guy now?" Kelly sneered, jabbing another finger against my chest to make his point.

I slapped his finger away and took a half step toward him. "I didn't start this, Kelly," I said in a calm voice. "But if you think I'm afraid of you, you're nuts."

He jumped at me suddenly, and I jerked back, realizing too late he was only trying to get a reaction out of me. He laughed, and everyone echoed him. "You seem pretty scared to me there, fairy."

"What the fuck is your problem?" I roared back, the words clawing up from deep inside me.

Kelly flinched and brought his fists up to defend his face automatically.

"What did I do to you, Kelly? What have I ever done to you?"

"Queers like you make me sick," he said, almost spitting.

"Why is that? Why do you care about what I am, Kelly?" I countered.

His eyes narrowed. "You saying you're queer?" He looked around him. "Did you hear that? He admitted it!"

"So what if I am?" I said, not caring anymore. "How does that affect you?"

His expression froze as he realized I wasn't going to argue with him about my sexuality. And I understood suddenly that mocking my sexuality was the only club in his bag.

"I mean, seriously, Kelly? Why would you care about what I do or don't do? Are you so messed up that just having someone different around you is a threat? Are you that scared about catching the gay that your only answer is to start hitting people?"

There were a few chuckles from the crowd as it started to turn on Kelly.

"I don't give a damn what you do," he shot back.

"Then why are you always in my face about it? I mean, come on, Kelly, what have I ever done to you?"

He sputtered as he tried to rattle off something, but I didn't give him a chance.

"People are different, you douche bag. Every single one of us likes what we like, and no one ever asked you for permission." There were a couple of shouted "Yeah!"s from the back of the crowd, and I felt emboldened. "I don't care if you like me or not, Kelly. And I don't care if you like the way I live my life or not. But I am not going to run scared every time you feel threatened by my sexuality. Real men aren't scared of things like that."

"You saying I'm not a real man?" Kelly growled, and I realized I was about to get punched.

"I'm saying you aren't a real man," Brad said from the side, grabbing everyone's attention instantly.

"You don't have to do this," I said to him quietly, trying to give him a way out.

"Yes, I do," he said to me solemnly.

"What is your problem anyways, dude?" Brad asked as he strode toward Kelly. "You think anyone who likes guys is a girly guy? Some kind of fag that you can just beat down whenever you want?"

Kelly laughed. "You calling that a real man?" he said, pointing at me.

Brad looked back at me and smiled. "I think he's the only real man here right now." And then he turned back to Kelly. "He is standing here, unafraid, backing up who he is and what he believes in. If that don't make him a man, I'm not sure what does."

"Slobbering on some guy's knob sure doesn't," Kelly answered.

"Why, Kelly?" Brad asked, pausing for effect. "When we were in junior high, you slobbered on my knob at football camp pretty well, if I recall."

There was an explosion of stunned gasps and laughter as Kelly's face turned dark red. "Bullshit! You can't prove that!"

Brad shrugged. "Don't have to. Why would I lie about that?" he said, more to the crowd than to Kelly. "Who cares anyways?" he said. "No one here is who they say they are. And we all know it." He began looking around the crowd. "Some of us throw up to stay skinny, some of us have sex to stay popular, some of us beat up people to hide what's inside." And he paused and looked at me. "And some of us hurt the ones we care for just to stay hidden."

I shook my head no, but he ignored me.

"I like guys too, Kelly," he said, still staring at me. You could have heard a pin drop in the shocked silence. "And if you have a problem with Kyle, you have a problem with me."

"I don't need you to save me," I said softly.

"I'm not," he said, taking another step closer. "I'm saving myself."

And he kissed me.

Some people looked away, some people stared gawking, and others cheered as I felt myself kiss him back. Time seemed to stop in that moment, and it was just the two of us, caught forever in that kiss.

He pulled back and said out loud, "So anyone else wanna call me or Kyle here a fag?" No one said a word. "Because the next time I hear it, I'm not going to let it slide."

Kelly gaped at Brad and then at me, and damned if he didn't look a little jealous. "Fucking queerbait," he said before pushing his way out of the circle of people.

The crowd began to disperse as the first bell rang for fifth period, leaving just him and me standing there. "Why did you do that?" I finally asked.

"Because I wanted to," he said, moving closer, putting his hands on my shoulders. "Because I'm tired of thinking I'm broken or fucked up. And you made me realize back there that I wasn't those things at all."

"I did?" I asked, still feeling very much broken and fucked up.

He nodded and leaned in for another kiss. "Maybe we're not broken," he said, pressing in closer. "What if we were just two parts looking for the other piece?"

"So what do we do now?" I asked.

He shrugged again. "I don't know," he answered honestly. "But I know one thing."

"What?"

"We do it together." And he kissed me again.

I don't remember the moment I knew I was broken… but I do know the moment I began to feel fixed.

It was the day the green-eyed boy fell in love with me.

BRAD
81 CENTS

MY name is Bradley Greymark, and I used to be the most popular guy in Foster, Texas.

I know that doesn't mean much to you, and to be honest, before yesterday, I didn't think it meant much to me either. I mean no one sets out thinking "I am going to be the most popular guy in school," and then it happens. Those people are always just too weird and eager to ever be actually popular. The key to being popular is acting like it means absolutely nothing to you. It's like life goes out of its way to give you what it thinks you don't want, which would make life kind of mean if you think about it.

I know I'm not supposed to say things like this, or I end up sounding like a colossal douche bag, but I am okay with that too. Over the last day I've realized what I used to have and how much I had really liked having it. In twenty-four hours I've gone from Top Dog to persona non whatever that word is, and I can say with great certainty that it sucks. I didn't know how much I had enjoyed being popular until I had a large Coke thrown in my face.

There is a TV show that I really don't watch where unpopular kids get cold drinks thrown in their faces just walking down the hall. They kind of gasp and then wipe their faces as the colored liquid drips down the front of them while people around them laugh. I suppose it makes for a good bit of comedy, but let me tell you, the reality sucks balls.

My problems started when I was sitting in the backstop during lunch a few days ago while the guy I had a huge crush on told me I had hurt him. The really bad part was that I knew I had hurt him and didn't have a good answer for why I had. Well that's not true I guess, I was afraid, so I did what I always do; exactly what I needed to do at the time and then hoping my smile would get me out of trouble. In this case it didn't so much as get me out of trouble as it just hurt him even more. So I had to make a decision to stay the guy I had always been and hated or find the guts for once to be someone else. Someone better than I was.

Someone more like Kyle.

So that meant standing in the middle of a crowd declaring that I liked guys too. Which wasn't a thing I had ever told anyone else before now, but Kyle was standing there by himself being so brave that I couldn't just stand there and let him hang by himself. So I had stood up with him and said I liked guys also and that if anyone had a problem with that, they could take it up with me. I'm not sure what I thought would come after that, but I knew it wasn't going to be something good.

That morning I just sat there and panicked.

Normally, I got up early, showered, dressed, and made my way to pick up my girlfriend Jennifer. Girlfriend is a term I'm hesitant to use in retrospect, but I'll get into that later. I'd hang out in the student union before first period and shoot the shit with the other guys and talk about who was having what party this weekend and if it was worth going to or not. Then I'd doze off in class, counting the seconds until lunch came around. Come noon we'd all sit at what everyone else called the Round Table, which was where everyone who was anyone ate and pretended to like each other. That would then lead to a countdown until practice after school where my day truly started.

Nowhere in the world am I happier than on the baseball field. The sun, the wind, the smell of the cut grass, all of it is just perfect to me in a way that is hard to describe to others. Some guys like it because it wasn't being cooped up in a classroom. Others seem to like it because it's physical; smacking the ball around is a great way to get out all the pent-up frustration that could accumulate during a day of school. Most of the guys like it because being on the baseball team makes you cool.

Not me. I love baseball because being out there is the only place in the universe where I can be myself.

Out there I wasn't Nathan and Susan's only boy. I wasn't a high school student who was unable to maintain a 2.75 without help. And I wasn't one of the nameless kids who were born, bred, and died of boredom in Foster every year. Out there on the diamond, I wasn't a disappointment; I wasn't too dumb, and for a couple of hours a day I wasn't stuck in Foster. From the moment I walked onto the field to the second I stumbled back into the locker room, I was in a place that, if anyone asked me, I would have said was the closest to heaven that I am ever going to see. It was the entirety of my life standing on that grass chasing after fly balls. I know it sounds corny, but it really was the only bright point of an otherwise shitty life.

Normally, my entire day would be a prelude to that moment. Nothing else mattered to me as much as standing at home plate, holding a bat, waiting for a ball to try to get by me.

But today wasn't going to be normal. Today was the very opposite of normal, and there was no way I was going to avoid that fact. I sat on the edge of my bed, not sure what I should do with my time. I couldn't go pick up Jennifer; she had taken off from school after my announcement and so far hadn't called me. Of course, I didn't have the balls to call her either, so I wasn't too surprised. I was pretty sure my little announcement had destroyed her world along with mine, so calling her wasn't my first choice. In all honestly it wasn't my second, third, or even my tenth.

I wasn't sure if I could go sit with everyone in the student union. I mean, what could I say? "Hi, guys. So anyone else come out yesterday?" I'm sure that'd go over like a fart in church. I mean, I wasn't even sure if I was gay or not. Sure I liked Kyle; that I knew. I didn't know about the rest of it. Did telling the whole school I liked guys count as coming out? Could I take it back? Did I even want to?

So I sat there and thought about faking a heart attack so I could skip school for a few months. I mean, they wouldn't let a kid with a weak heart deal with something as harsh as high school, would they? It wouldn't fly—they would take one look at me and see I was fine. But then I knew my mom, though; she would overreact to the point we'd end up in the emergency room, where she'd throw a fit, all the while proclaiming that no one would see her son. The doctors would find out in two minutes that I was faking and my mom was nuts, no guarantee in that order, either. We'd end up with no ride home because the two Xanax she would swallow in the middle of her panic attack would kick in, and she'd be useless. They'd call my dad to tell him what had happened, and then the shit would hit the fan.

The thought of my dad finding out I liked guys almost made me throw up.

I could hear my parents' shower running, which meant I needed to be gone now. I threw on clothes and went over to pick up Kyle as quick as I could. It took every iota of control I had not to squeal my tires as I pulled out of the driveway and took off toward his house. Kyle had given me the impression that his mom wasn't a morning person, so I didn't call to let him know I was coming over. I knew what it was like to have a friend fuck you over by waking up your parents, since I had caught shit more than once after one of my drinking friends called at three a.m.

Kyle didn't live on the nicest side of town, but then I wasn't sure what that meant any more. Our family was supposed to reside in one of the priciest areas in Foster yet the people I knew there were more fucked up than any family in town. Sure the people over on this side of town didn't have as much money as everyone else, but in my own personal experience, money only makes people meaner and nastier. I couldn't imagine Kyle was proud about living in a place like this, but honestly, he had nothing to be ashamed of.

Kyle was a great guy, but I didn't have the same amount of faith in the rest of the people who lived around him. I knew more than a few guys in my own neighborhood who would get off on screwing up a car like mine for kicks, and those guys had a lot more money than the people around here. If anything happened to this car, my dad would beat me to death and leave my body hanging in the front yard as a warning to anyone that passed by. Everyone thinks he bought me this car for my birthday, but it was just a lease from his dealership. Sometimes I thought this car was the epitome of our family. A costly present that on the surface looks like it is a show of compassion but in the end is just a symbol to show the neighbors we have money to burn.

Even if we didn't.

It wasn't even eight in the morning, so honking for Kyle was out of the question, which meant I needed to get out of my car to knock on the door. Luckily I could park right in front of his apartment and could keep one eye on the car as my knuckles rapped quickly on his door.

After a few seconds the door opened, and Kyle stood there in his boxers. His hair was sticking up from sleep, and there was a toothbrush in his mouth. He looked so cute that I forgot all about my concern and worry about the previous day's proclamation. I had to smile. "Morning."

He yelped something unrecognizable as speech and slammed the door shut.

I knocked again. "Come on, Kyle. I already saw you."

"What do you want?" I heard him ask from the other side of the door.

"Well I was here to pick you up for school, but now I want to take about a thousand pictures of you looking like that," I said, knowing he was so wound up he wouldn't take my cheery words as a joke.

"Wait out there," he said after a few seconds.

"Kyle, let me in," I replied, leaning up against the door. "We both know you ain't got nothing I haven't seen personal—"

He swung open the door, and I fell backward into his apartment. "Shut up!" he exclaimed, looking down at me. From down there I could see him blushing, and it made him even cuter.

I grinned and craned my head back. "Nice boxers, you know I can see up your—"

"Fuck you," he said. He turned away and sprinted into his room.

I laughed as I got up and closed the door quietly.

The apartment wasn't as clean as I expected it to look based on how clean my other friends' parents kept their houses. Last time I was here, his mom had let me wait for him in his room; there hadn't been time to really look around the place. It wasn't a wreck, but it was obviously not as clean as my mom liked to keep ours. There were a few beer bottles on the table and an ashtray full of cigarette butts in the living room. I looked through the ashes for a second and could see not all of them were tobacco. His door opened, and he poked his head out. "Get in here!" he whispered frantically, gesturing me in.

I walked over calmly and slowly, knowing the pace would drive him even crazier.

"Will you hurry up!" he hissed. He was really cute when he was upset.

"Thought you said to wait out here," I said casually.

Kyle grabbed my arm and pulled me in his room. He had thrown on a hoodie, but he was still in the boxers. They were pale white and about the cutest thing I had ever seen on a guy. "I meant outside, not in the living room," he said, exasperated.

I shrugged, knowing well what he had meant but playing dumb. "How was I supposed to know?" He rolled his eyes, which finally made me laugh out loud. I grabbed the front of the baggy hoodie and pulled him close. "Come here before you have a stroke or something." I kissed him hard, needing to hide in his embrace, if even for a few seconds. I felt him stiffen in my arms for a second, and then he kissed me back, his arms slipping under my letterman jacket and pulling me close.

"You're going to be the death of me," he said, smiling up at me.

Looking into those deep blue eyes, I swore I didn't care what anyone thought anymore.

"Death by kissing," I said, cupping his ass through the thin material of his boxers. "I can think of worse fates." I squeezed, and I felt him jump.

"We need to get to school," he said, swatting one of my hands away.

"Let's cut," I said, the almost forgotten dread coming back to me.

"What?" he said, pulling back. You'd have sworn I'd just asked him to head off to Dallas and kill the president from the way he looked at me. "You can't just cut school!" he explained as if the thought of ditching classes was a federal crime.

"Sure you can," I assured him, sitting on the edge of his bed. "We do it all the time," I added, leaning back with my hands behind my head. I paused for a moment because I realized the *we* I was referring to was gone. There was no longer me and a bunch of friends,. That was gone. There was just Kyle and me now. That was my *we*. It was a sobering moment.

He turned around, grabbed a pair of jeans, and yanked them on. "It's wrong, and we'll get in trouble," he chastised me.

His remark brought me back to the here and now, I forced a grin to cover the fact that part of me was screaming inside. "So's hitting people in the balls while the assistant principal holds them back. But that didn't stop you," I teased.

"I'm going to be in enough trouble over that," Kyle said, pulling the hoodie off with one hand and pawing through his drawers for a T-shirt at the same time. "I don't need to give my mom any more ammunition."

I sighed as I plopped my head down on the bed. "School's gonna suck," I said, staring up at his ceiling.

He climbed on top of me, straddling my waist as he looked down at me. "Are you sorry you said anything?"

I wanted to tell him the truth: I was terrified about what I'd done and had no idea what it was going to mean. I wanted to just spill my guts and have it done with. When I looked into Kyle's eyes, I knew I couldn't do that. He had spent his entire high school life trying to be as invisible as possible, when Kelly had taken it upon himself to choose Kyle to be the guy he was going to torture for a day. What Kelly hadn't known was how much I liked Kyle. Maybe he did, though. Kelly and I had fooled around more than once, so he had to know I liked guys a little. He never said anything because he knew between his word and mine which one would win. But this couldn't be jealousy, could it?

"You do know long pauses just make me think you're trying to find a way to say yes and not break my heart?"

He looked just as scared as I felt, and the only thing that he could count on was that I was with him. He needed me.

I smiled and shook my head. "No, I'm not sorry at all," I answered with as much conviction as I could muster. I pulled him down on top of me; he moved up next to me, his head on my chest. "We're together, and I don't care who knows," I said, praying the words didn't sound as hollow as they felt.

He squeezed me tight. "Thank you, Brad."

I looked down. "For what?"

"For just being you," he said, the two of us falling into a comfortable silence as we lay there.

It was a nice statement. Now if I only knew who I was supposed to be.

"You better run a comb through your hair," I said after a while. "You look like a hamster nested up in that joint."

He punched my stomach as he got up. "I wasn't expecting company."

I laughed as I followed him. "Looking like that, it didn't look like you were expecting to leave the house."

"I wanna see what you look like first thing in the morning," he threatened.

"Play your cards right and you might," I said, wagging my eyebrows and shooting him an evil grin. He blushed right on cue as I pulled out my phone and snapped a picture. The flash made him blink as I looked at the screen. His face was so perfect, so adorable that I felt something move in my chest. I wasn't sure if I liked the way it made my heart skip a beat slightly or not.

"You dick!" he screeched as he tried to grab the phone away from me.

I held him back as I slipped the phone back into my pocket. "No dice. That one is a keeper." I leaned in and kissed him quickly. "I'll wait for you outside."

He was shocked just enough by the kiss to give me time to retreat out the front door. I breathed a sigh of relief when I saw my car was still there and untouched. I leaned on the Mustang's hood and waited. I couldn't help pulling my phone out. I looked at the picture again. It made me smile. He was everything I wasn't, and for once in my life, that wasn't a bad thing. His picture was like a totem, a pocket of calmness in the absolute chaos my life had become. Minutes later, he came bounding out, hair slicked back. He toted his ever-present backpack over one shoulder. I was honestly surprised he didn't lean to one side when not lugging it around.

Seeing Kyle ride in my car was like watching a kid opening a present at Christmas.

My other friends all have cars and are all pretty blasé about them. They pretend like it's no big deal having a shiny, new car, but inside, we all know that those four wheels are one of the most important things in our world.

Clothes, cars, reputations: these were the only currency that was accepted at Foster High by those who mattered. To be honest, I had gotten bored with my car. It was more a chain around my neck than an actual object I took pride in because of the way my dad had forced it on me. He had gotten me the car from his dealership, making a huge deal that his son was driving a top-of-the-line model, and never took a break from reminding me about it every chance he could. What had started out as an awesome gift had degenerated into just another weapon of mass misery my parents used to try to one-up the other in the disaster they called a marriage.

I had forgotten what it was like not to have a car, and though it's a crappy thing to say, there's no way a guy like Kyle could afford a car like mine. Hell, the truth was I couldn't afford a car like mine, either. I would have been happy with some old muscle-car junker, something I could spend the summer fixing up. However, my dad, as always, took things to the nth degree and insisted that no son of his was going to drive anything less than a new Mustang around town. God forbid anyone know we weren't rich.

To my family, clothes, cars, and reputation were the only things that counted as well.

The Mustang was something I used to get out of the house and go to school. But looking at the car through Kyle's eyes made it so much more all of a sudden.

"This is awesome," he said over the music—and wind, since I had put the top down.

I had to smile back as I reached over and took his hand. "Yeah, it is," I agreed, not talking about the car at all.

I slowed as we neared the student parking lot, and I turned the music down. "Last chance. Everyone loves a cut day."

I saw him bite his bottom lip, and I knew I was wearing him down.

"It's a Friday. They aren't going to do anything anyways," I said, not that I actually knew what the fuck happened in class on any day. At least I sounded good. "We could head out to the lake, grab some sun, eat lunch—just the two of us."

"What about when they call my mom?" he asked, sounding like he was talking about what if Darth Vader came and asked if they had found the Death Star plans.

"Who cares? Tell her it was a mistake… that you were there." Kyle looked like he was leaning back toward school. "Come on!" I pleaded. "I just wanna spend time with you today. I'm not ready for everyone else."

I saw him sigh and knew he wasn't ready for everyone else, either. "Okay, cut day it is."

I felt bad that I hadn't told him the real reason I wanted to skip, but I had told him enough to make me not feel like a complete piece of shit. His hand snaked under mine as we drove off, and I put my worried thoughts behind me. I had a whole weekend to figure out how to deal. Monday was a million years away.

Lake Foster was about twenty minutes outside of town. It was about the only thing we had as a place to go on the weekend.

Sorry, was the only thing the group of people previously known as *we* had as a place to go on the weekend.

A night of entertainment was pretty much heading out and drinking all night, but when you grew up in Foster, it was the only something we knew. Our town was hours away from any city worth a damn, so if you wanted to go somewhere on the weekend, you didn't have a lot of choices. We could go to the Vine, which was our crappy theater that played two ancient movies back to back. People only went so they could make out in the back row or sneak a couple of bottles of schnapps in and get wasted while everyone laughed at the screen. Or we could head over to the bowling alley, which was akin to hanging out in a doctor's office, it held so much joy. Only thing that was even close to fun was midnight bowling, when they turned on these black lights, and you bowled with glowing balls. Honestly it was only fun when you were drunk, which seemed to be the only way Foster was manageable. Or you could go to the lake and get wasted in peace without any adults around waiting to narc on you.

I have spent more time at the lake than I would choose to admit, but never at the bright and sunny beginning of a November morning. I had left it at that time, but showing up this early was a first. The lake was deserted when it wasn't summer or the weekend. I saw a few boats out there with retired men who spent their afternoon fishing, but besides them we were alone. I parked next to the campsite we usually hung out at on weekends. There was a bench under a tree, a grill, and a nice little stretch of land that connected to the lake. It was prime real estate for Foster Lake, and we had it all to ourselves.

I had no idea what to do at the lake at eight thirty in the morning.

We sat and watched the lake in silence. I cursed myself for thinking that there would be anything to do out here so early on a week day. I should have checked to see if my mom had left for her yoga class and taken Kyle to my place. Hell, I could have taken him to Nancy's, the diner across from the Vine. We could at least have had breakfast. I was running away from my problems again, which was pretty much how I lived my entire life, and now I was dragging someone along with me.

I can say, with no joy or ego whatsoever, that I've never once stood up to a problem. I've smiled my way out of them, lied my way past them, and once or twice, bullied my way over them, but never once looked one directly in its eye. I hated that about myself. I never solved anything; I just pushed it aside until either it blew up in my face or didn't matter anymore. I'd never broken up with a girl. I just stopped calling them until they got the hint. I never told someone I didn't like them anymore. I just spent time with someone else until they went away. And then there was Kelly.

I couldn't do this to Kyle.

I opened my mouth to tell him this was a mistake and we should go back to school, but before I could say anything, he turned to me and said, "This is so awesome! I've never been out here before."

I saw the awe and the wonder in his eyes and was struck dumb by the intensity of his emotions. I assumed he meant in the day, but I realized mutely that he'd never been out here before, at all. He just wasn't popular enough to have been invited out here, so this was a whole new thing to him. I remembered the first time I came out with a few of the older players and how much I had been blown away I was actually at the lake with them.

"Thank you," he said, trying to move over closer. The center console stood between us.

"You wanna sit in the back seat?" I asked and saw his head nod so rapidly I was afraid he'd pass out. I shook my head and laughed as he put the top up and climbed into the back seat. Where the bucket seats are prohibitive to snuggling, the back seat seems made for it. I had spent a night or two back there with Jennifer, but for some reason, it seemed a lot more comfortable with Kyle.

I slipped my jacket off and bundled it up behind me to lean on. I liked the feel of him pressing up against me; he wasn't as frail or as small as the girls I had been with. There a weight to him, a solidness that I had to admit was turning me on. He smelled like a guy—his shampoo, his cologne, even his deodorant all mixed together and reminded me beyond a shadow of a doubt that I was in the back seat with another male.

And I found that erotic in a big, bad way.

I kicked my sneakers off and pulled him into my arms. "Hey there," I said, grinning.

"Hey," he answered, a little breathless.

I leaned down to kiss him. I liked the way he kissed me back instead of just taking it. Most of the girls I had dated were a little on the passive side. They knew my reputation: I was the kind of guy that went after what he wanted. Not many tried to stop me, since they wanted the same thing.

Kyle was different. He wasn't just there because he wanted to date the star second baseman or wanted to wear my class ring. He was here because he liked the real me, and he wanted to be with that guy. I wasn't sure who that guy was, but Kyle seemed to like him a lot. I have no idea how someone this special had been ignored for so long, but the more time I spent with him, I liked him more and more.

Safe on the edge of Lake Foster, I didn't have to worry about everyone else.

I buried those thoughts as I cupped the back of his head and kissed him harder. I wasn't here to think about what I was running from. I was here to enjoy what I thought I was running toward.

I felt him react. I wasn't sure he had a lot of experience being intimate with anyone, but I can tell you, the boy had skills. What he may have lacked in experience, he more than compensated for with passion. It was different being with someone so expressive, who didn't have a poker face when it came to what they liked and how much they liked it. Jennifer had known I was cocky and never let me once believe she had liked me as much as I liked her, which was a point I had debated with myself a thousand times. It was always a game with her that made me keep my own cards close to my chest so I wasn't the one with my eyeballs hanging out of my skull while my tongue unrolled like a carpet. At first it was a challenge to score with the hottest girl in town, but what started as dating became more like combat the way she dangled affection in front of me like the cheese at the end of a maze. I had no choice but to fight back, and what started as a hot romance became a cold war.

Or in other words, we were just like my parents.

Kyle liked me and didn't care who knew.

He was half kneeling against me, pinned in the corner as he kissed me passionately, and it was hotter than anything else I'd experienced. My hands went under his T-shirt, and I couldn't believe how small he was. He looked like a beanpole, but there wasn't an ounce of fat on him. He was all coiled muscle and leanness that drove me nuts. I have always been a big guy, and though I lift and run every day, I had always secretly wanted to be built like Kyle. Every time I looked in the mirror, I saw myself a few bad years from becoming my dad, and that image made me work out even harder. Kyle, though, with just a couple of weeks in the gym, would be cut as hell and clueless about how cute he was.

His blond bangs hid his eyes, which was a shame because the inner sparkle of their blueness was alluring. He looked like a skater, all elbows and knees, and there wasn't a way that he didn't turn me on. I felt him giggle under my touch, and he pulled back slightly. "Tickles," he whispered.

"Oh really?" I asked, smiling evilly.

"Brad, don't!" he begged as I began to tickle him in earnest. "Oh please stop!"

His laughter was like music, so pure, so real that it was infectious. No one I knew laughed like him. The people I hung out with would be caught dead before they made this much noise over anything. He spasmed in my grasp as, attacking him, I wrestled his shirt over his head. I threw it in the front seat at the same time I pulled him against me midlaugh. He gasped when I nibbled on his neck. His skin was salty as I kissed and tongued my way to his nape. I could feel him shiver as I continued to lightly bite him, moving to his right nipple. His hands grabbed the sides of my head as I licked the nipple, feeling it harden under my ministrations. They were small and pert. For some reason, knowing they were a live wire to his sex drive turned me on.

"Brad!" he exclaimed under his breath as his hands dug into my hair. I moved to his other nipple and brought it to the same state of excitement instantly. He seemed shocked by the sensations he was feeling. I knew, then, he was a virgin. I don't know how, but I just knew this was the farthest he'd ever gone.

"You like that?" I asked with a wide grin. His arousal only added to my own titillation as I got turned on turning him on. He nodded, unable to form words.

"Oh Jesus," he moaned as he pressed himself against my hand.

I moved my other hand around and unbuckled his belt. He wore jeans that were easily three sizes too big for him. I remembered when I had talked to him in the hall, and he had gotten hard. He had thought he was being slick covering it with his folder, but honestly, there was nothing short of hiding behind a brick wall that could conceal that.

I had fooled around with exactly two guys before Kyle, and neither time was it serious.

The first was Cody Peller, a guy on my football team when I was thirteen. We had won the last game of our season and had stuffed ourselves celebrating at Panky's Pizza before crashing at my house. My mom was already unconscious for the night, and my dad was locked in his den with orders for us to shut up or else. Cody and I had sat on my bed and watched *A Cinderella Story,* since both of us had claimed a huge crush on Hillary Duff. I had never told him that even though I thought Hillary was cute, my eyes had always been on Chad Michael Murray. Instead, we both acted like the little horn dogs we were, bragging about what little we'd done with girls and boasting about what we'd do if we actually got our hands on one. We both got excited while we watched the movie, and once the lights were out, we got a little handsy.

We never talked about it again, but I was terrified Cody would tell people what we'd done. I kind of ignored him whenever I saw him again, and he treated me the same way, which was fine with me. I tried to put it out of my mind, but there was no denying I had liked what we'd done.

That summer my dad sent me to football camp. He was determined that I was going play football when I got to high school—

just like him. The fact that I liked baseball more didn't mean a damn thing.

Kelly and I were already friends. I had gravitated toward him after Cody and I had our falling out. He seemed more than happy to be my friend, so much so that when we got to camp, I began wondering if he was like me or not.

By the second week, we were inseparable. He was really expressive, like a dog that just loved to jump up on you and lick your face repeatedly. Football camp was a lot like any other type of camp: a ton of useless activities during the day to keep us occupied, a couple of crappy meals, and then as the sun went down, we were told to fend for ourselves until lights out was called. Guys began to pull apart into packs, different cliques of people that seemed to hit it off in a quasi-sexual kind of way. You'd be surprised how much of professional sports is really just homosexual energy channeled into alternate means of activity. Guys I played ball with were very close. We had no problems putting our hands on each other and thought that roughhousing while naked was funny.

During that summer I realized, though, there was a line for me that others didn't seem to approach. I wasn't just wrestling with guys to prove I was top dog and to put them in their place. I knew there was a sexual edge to what I was doing. I danced around that fact for years to come.

No one ever guessed a thing. I was the type of guy other guys liked being around. I was easy on the eyes and cocky enough to pull it off. They seemed to like following me for some reason. I was usually made team leader or squad officer or whatever we were doing. Coaches loved to put me in charge, and no one else seemed to mind. The guys I kept around me were people that weren't bright enough to be able to see through my bullshit and catch me. I'd love to say that it was an instinctual thing, that I wasn't smart enough to do it on purpose, but even I'm not that dumb. People like Kelly were too enamored with just being friends with the Popular Guy that they would never once look twice at me or question a word I said.

My closest friends were like attack dogs, a pack of loyal guys who never once asked why I told them to do anything.

I was surrounded by people, but I was always alone as hell. I didn't know what was going through my mind, but I knew I wasn't like them. It felt like everyone around me was two-dimensional, and I was the only person who had that extra something that let me see through the bullshit around me. It wasn't that I was smarter or older than anyone else; it was more like I spent so much time worrying about real things—like if I liked guys or not—that smaller things like if I was good-looking or if girls would go out with me seemed lame in comparison. So that summer with Kelly, I was the closest I had ever gotten to being me than I'd ever been before or since.

That was, of course, until Kyle.

When we were alone, Kelly gushed on me—it was never overtly sexual because I don't think he had a name for it either. He just genuinely liked me and had no words to explain why. But I did. I could see the same confused hunger in his eyes that I had seen in my mirror more than once. I wish I could say I was really attracted to Kelly. I mean he was a good-looking guy with a decent body. Truth was, though, that we were both almost fourteen in the middle of that awkward phase. Our hormones were raging like magma moving under the surface. I would have dry humped a chair if I thought it would get me off. Kelly was just convenient and not completely gross, so I decided on him.

I still feel guilty as hell about that.

Though we had been handed out cabin assignments, the coaches had no idea who we were outside of pads and jerseys, so we had switched to be with our friends early on. All the coaches and counselors cared about was that they saw a body in a bed. The exact identity of the body was very much unimportant. At first Kelly and I shared a cabin with two other guys, but as the camp went on, one sprained his ankle and had to go home, and the other ended up moving out and bunking in one of the larger cabins with six beds. No one cared about the two of us in our cabin alone. If anything, as soon as dinner was over, our cabin became the cabin to be. Everyone would come over. We'd play music, arm wrestle, sometimes play cards, though none of us really knew the rules. We just goofed off until the counselors came pounding on the door saying everyone had to be back in their cabins in bed.

Kelly slept in the top bunk, and I had claimed the one on the bottom as mine.

Thirty minutes after lights out, the whole camp became no-man's land because no one was going to check on you unless someone raised holy hell or turned on a light. Kelly and I had no plans on doing either. We didn't want to draw attention to ourselves. He'd slip down and crawl into my bunk. Our excuse was that we could talk and not have to raise our voices, but the truth was that the bed was small, and we were almost lying in each other's arms. Both of us wore only boxers, and just moving around, skin on skin, was pretty much the most erotic thing either one of us had done up to that point. I mean, sure I'd been under the shirt, above the bra with Melissa Carver, and Britney whatshername had gotten me off the night of the Sadie Hawkins Dance, but skin on skin like we were during those nights was farther than any girl would have allowed at that age.

Kelly rubbed himself against me like a dog. We went like that for the first few nights we had the cabin alone. Him lying with me, us talking about the day and the plays we'd run, and then lapsing into silence as we ground against each other. I remember him laying his head on my pillow, his lips on my shoulder, his tongue barely touching my skin. I'd move his hand over me, using him like the object I considered him to be. This was good to get off for the first four days, shooting in silence and him climbing up to his bunk as I drifted off with a sigh.

The fifth day, I moved his face to my chest. He complied, nibbling on me as he thought he understood what I wanted. As he moved lower, I pushed him farther and farther down. I slipped my boxers off so he knew what I wanted. The rest of the summer went a lot like that. I never reciprocated, of course. The only way I could assert to myself that I was straight was because I never touched him back. That was stupid and petty, but it was nothing compared to what I did to him next.

Kelly was a nice enough guy, but he wasn't the most personable of types. I am sure a lot of the demons that plagued him have a place in my head as well, but at the time I didn't care. As the summer went on, most of the guys began questioning his closeness to me. Of course, I was golden, so I never got any looks. They all wondered what was wrong with Kelly and one day brought it up to me.

I remember my heart freezing in place as I stopped breathing altogether.

I don't recall much of what they said. All I knew was that Kelly was suspect and that meant I was by association. That same night, when he climbed down into my bunk, I pretended to freak out, asking him what he was doing. He had no answer, since it was the same thing we'd been doing the entire summer. The huge difference was that he had done things to me the entire time, and I had done nothing to him. It was stupid, but I can assure you that in thirteen-year-old-boy logic it made perfect sense. The next morning I shunned him pretty hard. That afternoon I moved out of the cabin and moved into the last bed in the huge cabin, where in the night I sat in the dark and told stories about him with the other guys.

Kelly never knew what he did wrong, and I never explained it to him. When I got back home, I went to my mom and told her that I didn't want to play football anymore, that I liked baseball, but I was afraid to tell Dad. Just as I had figured, my mom used the information as a weapon against my dad, blaming him for forcing his own ideals on me against my will. I felt lousy, but I didn't say anything to anyone. I moved into junior varsity and never played football again. Another two years passed before I saw Kelly in high school. My knowledge of what he had done allowed me to keep him under my thumb with just a look.

This was the little spiral of guilt and doubt that never allowed me to think I was as good a person as the people around me thought I was. I was living a lie, but the lie was so much better than the truth in my head. They had no idea who the fuck I was, and I never wanted them to know. I began dating girls aggressively after that summer with Kelly. I liked sex, and girls liked me, so it was never a stretch for me to date a girl for a while with relative ease. I made sure I was never really into any one girl; most believed I was another player, as most jocks were. I talked a good game, and again, most people wanted to like me, so it was easy to hide in the role. The first two years of high school, I got lost in the role a little. I'd hang with the older guys on the team, get smashed at the lake, and let some girl take advantage of me under the stars. I earned a reputation and used the reputation to my own needs. By the time Jennifer set her sights on dating me and stalked me, she knew that, at best, I was going to be indifferent toward her. I honestly didn't think she was dating me; she was dating my letterman jacket. That was fine since she was one of the hottest girls in school.

We traded popularity, and no one was the wiser.

"You okay?" Kyle asked after a few minutes.

I looked up, not realizing I had drifted off in the middle of what we were doing. The crushing weight of everything I'd done to hide who I was and the realization I might do worse to Kyle pounded into me, and I began to tear up. "No," was all I could say before I began to cry.

He hugged me tight, though he had no idea what was wrong. Him hugging me was the nicest thing anyone had ever done for me. My life was spinning out of control, and all I could think about was running away from it. I didn't want to hurt Kyle, but I knew what I had done before. If I followed suit, I would hurt him the same way I'd hurt Kelly and Cody. And I so didn't want to do that to Kyle.

"What's wrong?" he asked, moving me around until he was leaning back, and I was being pulled against him. No one had ever done that for me before. My parents were not the expressive kind of people; as an only child, I was left on my own more times than not. As I grew up, people assumed I was going to be that guy, the one that people listened to, the one that they followed. No leader shows their weakness to those around them, and the more people I seemed to collect, the farther and farther away I hid. I couldn't just break down in front of someone. Jennifer would have been mortified to see me cry like such a bitch. No one gains any popularity points for going out with a crybaby.

"I just—" I choked out, not even sure I was willing to say. After a second I shook my head and just gave up. "I don't know."

"It's okay," he said, holding me close. "It's gonna be okay."

I wasn't sure he knew what was upsetting me, but it sounded like he was talking about what I was freaking out about. Was it going to be okay? How was I supposed to go back to school and not be that guy? "How do you know?" I asked, hating myself for sounding so weak

He smiled at me, and I could see his eyes tearing up as well. "Because we have each other."

I looked away and hated myself even more.

"I'm sorry I ruined the mood," I said, sniffling.

"Hey, that was the first time I've ever gotten close to that mood," he said with a toothy grin. "So that's cool."

I laughed and lay my head against his chest. His heart was pounding, and it was reassuring because I knew it was beating partly for me. We lay like that for a few minutes, and then his stomach grumbled loudly under my ear.

"Sorry," he said as I burst out laughing.

"You hungry?" I asked, sitting up.

He looked at me sheepishly. "I was going to have breakfast before I got dressed."

I rolled my eyes as I got up and grabbed his shirt from the front seat. "Then let's go get some food."

"What if someone sees us?" he asked, like we had just robbed a bank.

I climbed into the front seat. "Trust me, Kyle. You're with me." I turned around and gave him my thousand-watt smile. "You're untouchable."

YOU have to understand that I was never a person but instead a well-groomed bargaining chip.

My parents were high school sweethearts, which is a term that means "too stupid to use a condom." When my dad went to college, my mom was already pregnant with me. That translated to "no matter how far my dad thought he was going, it wasn't going to be far enough." He had earned a scholarship playing football. Unfortunately, he also had operated under the delusion that since someone was paying his tuition because he could hit people hard, it was okay if he continued to hit people hard off the field.

It turned out when he hit people at a local bar and sent someone to the hospital, no one paid for his bail. It turned out when he was arraigned for assault and battery, no one paid for his lawyer, either. And it turned out when he was put on probation and missed three practices in a row, people stopped paying for his tuition. My dad had escaped Foster for exactly five and a half months. I know, because he screamed that at my mother every time they argued about nearly anything.

He married my mom and went to community college, managed to come out with an associate's in business. From what I gathered, there wasn't an actual shotgun involved, but my grandfather on my mom's side had never been shy about sharing the fact I had a father because of what he had said when my dad started backpedaling before the wedding.

Growing up in a fucked-up family was a lot like living with a pack of tigers.

I did my best not to get anyone's attention, and if they were calm, I made sure they stayed that way. Early on I understood that conversation in our house was what other people considered yelling in theirs. My mother took candy that made her happy and made her sad. The candies made her fall asleep, and they made her wake up. My dad, on the other hand, drank grown-up stuff that made him even angrier some nights. When I was younger, I didn't get quite why they took what they did, but I also understood that if they stopped, things got worse.

It was assumed by both of them that I was going to grow up being the all-American boy.

I was going to play sports, be well-mannered and expected to be the kid from the happy family no matter how much bullshit the whole "happy family" thing was. Everything was about outside impressions; the fact that we were miserable human beings didn't matter. If we had a nice car, then everything was all right. My dad loathed my mom's ever-breathing guts, but that didn't count. If she had real pearls and people knew they were real, then she was happily married to a great man. And the fact that my father had no patience for a young child and never missed an opportunity to tell me that while berating me as a burden didn't matter as long as he sponsored whatever sports team I was on at the time. I had a great dad who was engaged in his son's life, and I should be grateful for that.

I hated everything about my life.

As I grew up, I learned that complaining resulted in nothing but misery. Mom and Dad both knew that we were all caught in some kind of domestic purgatory until I graduated high school. Bitching about it was only going to exacerbate the situation. Instead of love and compassion, we substituted (or traded in) emotion for money. My dad ended up using what little local celebrity he had in Foster to sell cars and sell a lot of them. He ended up being made a partner in the dealership, which meant even more money, which meant even more status to maintain.

We moved to a bigger house, which meant better furnishings and better cars. The result: the more money became not enough money, and that meant more fights. I heard some weird saying once: "Keeping up with the Joneses." Now I have no idea who the fuck the Joneses were, but we were in a race to keep up with the Greymarks, with the fictional versions of ourselves. Let me tell you, the fictional us were kicking the real us's ass.

I always had the newest bike, the best clothes, and the most elaborate backyard setups in the neighborhood. We had a pool, a huge tree house structure that my dad had made for me by three contractors, and equipment for half a dozen different sports back there. Every kid within six blocks came to my house to hang out during summer. When I was young, it was awesome, because I was stupid enough to think they were there to hang with me. As I got older I figured out I was just the kid whose parents were buying him popularity in spades.

After that it became pretty shitty to be me.

There is nothing worse than a ten-year-old kid who knew that no one liked him for who he was. Every laugh was hollow, every smile just my lips going through the motion. I started to be a dick. Knowing that they were there to use my shit, I made it cost them to do it. I was a little asshole, turning guys against each other so that they'd fight to come over and be my friend. People wanted things, and if you had the things, then people wanted you.

The bad part was that everyone I knew was just like me.

All of my friends were rich kids, and they had come to the same realization I had around the same time. We became the stuck-up little bastards of the town, living up to every crappy stereotype about privileged kids ever dreamed up. We drank in junior high; we stole stuff we knew we had money for; we trashed shit because we hated the town.

I think it was when I realized that I stared at the other guys longer than was necessary while we dressed in the locker room and that I was doing more than just comparing when we showered that I was nothing like the other guys. After Cody, I knew I was nothing like these people, and once I realized that, I was disgusted—in myself, in them, in the entire lifestyle we were living. I would begin to get nervous changing out, shaking before games as I feared that any little thing would give me away. I was so scared of it that I just walled it off, built a facade around me of the guy everyone already thought I was. There was a small part of me that wanted to scream out the truth, but much like my parents, I literally had no idea how to live any other way. I had always had a ton of friends, even though they didn't really know me. I had never been disliked by a majority of the people, even though they didn't like me but the image I projected. I had never been considered anything but attractive, although, if those people were to look inside me they'd know I how ugly I was inside. I was stuck with no choice but to conform and hating myself for conforming.

I had been miserable for so long I'd grown numb inside.

Kelly had been a mistake, and I knew it. There was something inside of me I didn't want to face. I discovered that staying completely still and drinking a lot didn't help the pain go away, but it made me less aware it was there. At the same time, I felt trapped in my own life. When I made varsity, I could feel the noose tightening around my neck. I was running out of options. Varsity meant the next year and a half would be spent playing my ass out for scouts. If I was very good, I'd get a pass out of Foster, either into college ball or onto a farm team playing for next to nothing but swinging at the chance for the pros. I also knew as much as I felt restricted playing ball in high school, in college or on a professional team, it would get much worse.

I didn't live with the illusion I was good enough for pro ball, but a free ride to college would be the only thing that could get me out of Foster. The only problem would be that I'd either have to become an incredible slut, fucking every girl who threw herself at me to prove I was a guy, or marry Jennifer. If the assumption in high school was that all jocks, including me, needed to have a girl, in college it would only multiply tenfold.

Every time my thoughts started to spiral toward the future, I could feel my heart begin to race and my stomach contract as if I was going to throw up. There wasn't a night I didn't fall asleep wishing I was just like everyone else, a mindless high school jock wandering the halls like a sheep grazing in the field. I promise you the only thing worse than being a rat trapped in a maze is being aware that you were that rat.

"And you, honey?"

My head snapped up, and I blinked, surprised. I wondered how long the waitress at Nancy's had been waiting for my order. "Four-egg-white omelet with cheddar, onions, and a side of hash browns." I saw Kyle's eyes widen at my order, and I shrugged as I handed her the menu. "I'm a growing boy."

He looked over the selections a few times and then opted for some pancakes.

The waitress smiled and took the menu as she asked me, "Who's your friend, Brad? He on the team?"

"A friend," I said way too quickly. "Just a friend." That was no better. "I mean a friend who...." I realized there was no way for me to get out of this with my dignity intact, so I just gave up and said. "No, he's not on the team."

She gave me a long look, the same look she'd shoot me if I was being held against my will and needed her to call 911 or something. I smiled and looked away, knowing I had fumbled that pass in just about every way possible.

A few seconds later, Kyle said quietly, "Well that wasn't awkward at all."

I tried to give him a big smile, but I knew my heart wasn't in it. "I'm sorry. First time I had to do that."

"You've never brought anyone to eat here?" he asked. We both knew he wasn't talking about that at all.

"First time I ever brought a guy I had just been making out with in my back seat." I saw him blush, and I knew my grin had won the day. "We'll get better at this," I said, knowing the second I opened my mouth I was committing myself further into something I was in no way comfortable with, since it meant the inevitable destruction of this carefully crafted snow globe I called a life.

"We kinda have to, right?" His voice was hopeful, and that hope was like a tiny stab in my chest.

I sighed and took a drink of my orange juice, looking across the street at the Vine. It was barely ten in the morning. I don't think anyone was even there yet. They had a noon matinee double feature that the guys and I had used more than once to skip the after-lunch classes. People didn't usually go to the matinee, so the Vine was a good place to take a girl and fool around or maybe catch a buzz before heading back for practice. Nothing was funnier than watching five half-wasted guys struggling to run laps around the backfield without throwing up everywhere.

The rest of them took their cues from me, and with me gone, no one would have the guts to actually speak something and suggest skipping and heading over after lunch. No one would be there since I wasn't at lunch to bring the idea up.

Kyle's fingers snapped in front of my face.

"You okay?" he asked when I looked back at him. I nodded, trying to focus my attention on him, but I couldn't dam off the rest of the voices in my head. "I was asking you what you wanted to do with the rest of the day." I'd seen that look before from other people. He was asking me what to do, and suddenly, I couldn't fake an answer.

"I don't know, Kyle," I snapped out of nowhere. "I don't have any fucking answers." His face paled in amazement, and I shook my head, trying to calm down. "I'm just not in a good mood. I'm sorry."

The waitress came back and put our plates on the table in front of us. There had never, in the history of awkward conversations, been a more fortuitous arrival of food, ever. "You boys need anything else?" she asked.

A time machine and a gun?

"We're good, thanks," I said, giving her another reassuring smile.

"Holler if y'all need anything," she said, walking away.

I began to scoop food into my mouth, hoping that the meal would stave off any more verbal missteps on my part. He paused for a long while before he began to eat as well. Skinny or not, he could put some food away, which meant I had bought myself some more time.

Time that was not going to do me any good because I was no closer to figuring out what to do than I had been back at home. My brain was telling me to just end what we'd started, nip it in the bud, crush his spirits in one fell swoop, and try to take back what I had said yesterday. Of course up to this point, the thinking that I'd done had snarled my life into a mess, so what did I know?

A part of me, albeit a small part, knew that standing up next to Kyle was the best thing I'd ever done. The feeling of finally shrugging off this disguise and talking with my own voice for once was refreshing. It was more than refreshing; it was liberating in such a way that it was almost like being drunk. That sounded better to me: I was drunk on emotion, and that was why I'd told the entire school my secret.

Even I didn't believe that one.

Jennifer had to have done the math as well about where we were heading because she had been talking about the future more and more. What colleges I was thinking about, what scouts might be coming to watch me play, and where their farm teams were located. She never flat out told me that she was already making plans to move when and where I did, but the implication was crystal clear. If baseball was my ticket out of this town, I was Jennifer's in a big, bad way. Other than complete academic excellence, which Jennifer was never going to pull off, there weren't many ways for a girl to get out of Foster save fucking a guy and holding on for dear life. Foster and Granada, our rival school, laughed at the concept of women's sports. I had a better chance of curing cancer than a girl had of getting a sport's scholarship.

If I fucked up, I wasn't just consigning myself to a lifetime of getting drunk in the back of a pickup every weekend and working a shitty job in a nowhere town, but I was fucking her future over too.

People thought Jennifer was a bitch, but that was because she was the best-looking girl in town. Once any guy reached the age that he knew what his dick was for, he wanted to get in her pants. Foster is a small town, and girls had it pretty bad because of the double standard as far as sleeping around went. We were good ol' Texas boys, and people assumed that we'd try to fuck anything that moved. No one ever called us a slut or a whore; they called us healthy boys. But a girl spreads her legs with anyone she hadn't been dating for a year or was engaged to and she was considered a complete waste of flesh.

I never understood, because who did they think we were supposed to fuck: the cows? For every all-American boy sowing his oats, there was an all-American girl who should have been doing the same; yet one walked away with a pat on the back and a beer and the other was shunned until someone took pity and married her. Jennifer was cold and standoffish, but I couldn't blame her. After all, in a town full of "delicate Texas roses," she was considered the best of the best. She had hunted me down as the guy to date when we were both sophomores. I'd like to think it was because I was so damn hot, but I always worried there was a deeper reason she would never guess.

I had almost no interest in trying to fuck her.

I flirted and fooled around because it was expected, but I never felt an overwhelming urge to throw a girl down and screw her to death. Only when I was drunk, and even then it wasn't the best of experiences, would I find myself horny enough to actually seal the deal. My lack of interest and subdued sex drive were a perfect fit for Jennifer's needs, and she was the exact thing I had been looking for.

Someone to hide behind.

No one blinked twice when we started to go out. I know it sounds arrogant, but we were the best-looking of our bunch; of course we ended up pairing up. Kelly never said a word, and it wouldn't have mattered if he had. Even if he'd admitted to sucking my dick, Kelly would have been called a fag and ostracized. Worse, he would have been accused of being a liar, since I was Brad and untouchable. I hated the whole crappy mess so much.

Jennifer and I had never once had to talk about the unspoken rule that said we covered for each other in public. I was always the aloof but faithful boyfriend jock, and she was the pretty and chaste cheerleader. We played our parts. I know at least for me, I hated every second of it. I didn't hate her, but if I had to choose the kind of person to spend time with, she wouldn't have been that person. I could never tell if she felt the same way toward me, and every time I thought too hard about it, I got flashes of my mom and dad.

We had finished the bulk of our breakfast and were picking over the carcass trying to extend the silence as long as possible when he sent a shot across my bow.

"We don't have to do this," he said softly.

"A little late since I already kissed you in front of everyone?" I asked, pushing my plate away.

From the look on his face, it was the exact wrong thing to say.

"I was talking about today," he said, all the indecision and doubt evaporating from his voice, revealing the steel underneath.

"Oh," I said, knowing I had shown my cards too soon.

"Oh?" he said as his voice got louder. "What's that supposed to mean?"

"It means oh," I fired back. "Sorry, it's all I got."

"Really, Brad? 'Oh' is all you got?" I shushed him and gestured for him to keep it down.

"I'm sorry, but this isn't easy for me," I explained, realizing how crappy that sounded even as I said it.

"Right, 'cause it's a cake walk for me," he countered, and I knew he was right and wrong at the same time.

"I just don't know how to handle this yet," I elaborated. "I have a lot of things to consider, and it's just fucking me up."

"Fine," he said, pulling out his wallet. "Because I am just a loser who has nothing to worry about, because who cares if I'm gay, right?"

It wasn't until that moment I realized he might have a lot on his mind too.

"I didn't mean that, Kyle." I paused. "What are you doing?"

"Paying for my breakfast," he said as he thumbed through the obviously empty wallet.

"I got it," I said.

He began digging through his pockets. "No, it's okay, Brad." His voice was like ice. "I don't want to end up owing you anything." He slammed his hand down. There was eighty-one cents. "I'll get the rest to you tomorrow." He turned to walk out, and I grabbed his arm.

"Come on, please don't do this," I pleaded.

He looked at my hand and then to me. "You better let go. You don't want anyone to think we're queer."

I took my hand away as if burned.

"Good-bye," he said, sounding more defeated than angry.

I didn't know what was worse, me making him that mad or the fact that I didn't chase after him. I chalked them both up as equally shitty and waited for the check in silence.

I left a wad of bills and walked out to First Street. Foster isn't known for its killer traffic, and before lunch, the street lay almost empty. I saw Mr. Parker out in front of his sporting goods store sweeping the sidewalk, and a couple of ladies walked out of the flower shop next to him. Kyle was nowhere to be seen. I wasn't really expecting to see him. I still wasn't sure if I'd gotten what I wanted when he'd taken off, or whether I had just lost what I needed. Either way, I was alone.

I saw the front doors open to the Vine and Ms. Garner turn on the marquee. If I thought I was the kind of person God would toss a bone to, I'd take it as a sign from up above. Instead I chalked it up to good timing and crossed the street to buy a ticket. Mr. Parker waved at me. I'd practically grown up around his shop, since I played sports as soon as I could walk. He was old but not that old, like thirty or so. I heard he had scored a scholarship for football when he had gone to Foster but blew his knee out after a couple of years and moved back into town. Being forced to come home had made my dad a bitter, twisted guy, but it hadn't seemed to affect Mr. Parker in a negative way at all. He was still in great shape and pretty much the most eligible bachelor in town as far as the older ladies were concerned. I waved back, wondering what he'd do if he knew who I really was. Would he be so quick to wave, or would he have scowled and gone back inside, ignoring me?

"By yourself today?" Ms. Garner asked as she took my money.

"For the foreseeable future," I mumbled, jamming my hands in my pockets as I walked into the theater. As I walked down the aisle, I realized I didn't even know what was playing. I fell into a seat near the front, not really caring about watching the movie.

I should have gone after Kyle, but what was I supposed to say? I didn't have any answers and, to be honest, he was better off without me. No one would give him a hard time if he was by himself. He wasn't worth the time and effort to mock for most people. No one really knew who he was, so at the end of the day there was no profit in tearing him apart. I was the better choice, the one people would get a thrill tearing down. I was the one who had been the most popular jock at Foster, and that meant I had farther to fall than he did. Besides, if he was with me, people would attack him just out of spite. Kyle didn't deserve that. He hadn't done anything to these people like I had.

My karma had come around, and he shouldn't have to pay because I'd been a dick.

The lights went out, and the trailers started. I settled in, wondering if I could catch a nap during the movies, which would be a place to hide until after school let out. I could miss one practice. Everyone would tell the coach I had been absent all day. I'd be golden until Monday. What I'd say Monday, I had no idea. I was barely keeping five minutes ahead of myself, let alone two days.

I needed to stop and think, regroup and figure out what I was going to do. Alone in the darkness of the theater, it was easy to say. I wanted to be with Kyle desperately. I wasn't sure if that was even possible in Foster, but it was what I wanted. Wanted it enough to be mocked at school—but then the thought of what my dad would say made me sick to my stomach all over again.

When I was little, things seemed simple. I'd fuck up, and he'd hit me. My mom was too emotional to handle discipline, and looking back at it I always thought she never wanted to be the bad guy with me since she needed an ally as she waged her emotional Vietnam against my dad. When I screwed up as a kid, and I screwed up a lot, discipline always fell on him.

It started out as spanking, first over his lap with his hand, and later graduating up to a belt. The humiliation made me cry more than the actual blows. I can't imagine what being forced to have sex is like, but being held down while my dad hit me with a belt was as close as I ever wanted to get to it. The helplessness of being held motionless and hit by someone else is about as bad as a situation can get without openly bordering on anything sexual.

Spanking and belting didn't make me a better person.

If anything, the punishments gave me another reason to hate my dad and my life in general. I hated him for hitting me, hated my mom for not stopping him, and hated myself for being such a bad person that Dad was forced to punish me. As I grew older, the spankings became more and more energetic. We moved from belts to hairbrushes to shoes and then finally to fists. The first time my dad punched me was what I imagined getting shot would feel like. No pain at first, way too much shock for anything else to register in my brain. My dad's not a physically weak man, so I assure you he wasn't hitting me as hard as he could. At the time, however, that distinction was lost on me as I gingerly touched my face where he had hit me.

"Don't make me do that again," he'd warned, neatly turning the moment so that, like everything else in my life, him punching me was entirely my fault, and he was the victim. I was smaller, and there was no way I could physically take him on, so I took my revenge in fucking with the illusion of our perfect little family. I'd go out with a couple of guys, get wasted, and then end up puking in the gutter of First Street at three in the morning. A squad car in front of our house with me in the back in cuffs as everyone peeked through their curtains was as bad if not worse than any punch he could throw my way. Having the cops explain that, since my dad was who he was, they'd let my behavior slide was the social equivalent of kicking him in the balls.

When I had started drinking, the punishments evolved from him swinging at me to us throwing down wherever we happened to be at the time. As I got older and bigger, the fights became worse and more destructive. My mom would stand there screaming at us to stop while we went at it like two rabid dogs fighting for dominance. Most nights he was as sauced as I was, so neither one of us felt any pain as we went at it. No pain but loads and loads of anger.

The last time he tried that was a few months ago during summer vacation. I can't even remember what I'd done, but I did know I was done with being a punching bag for him.

He had made the mistake of being drunk while I had been completely sober. By the time I'd reached seventeen, the difference between our physical strengths had dwindled past the point where we were almost even. That night we both discovered I had crossed the line and had become stronger than he was. I wish I could say it was a liberating feeling, that at that moment I felt a rush of power and control in my life. Honestly, though, all I had was disgust and pity for the complete loser I'd let wear me down for so many years. Since then we had stayed away from each other. Whatever I did, right or wrong, was handled by my mother, and my dad stayed out of it. Except, of course, my mother handled nothing.

I felt like I'd been in a tailspin since then.

My life no longer had boundaries, and my behavior had no consequences. What I had always thought would be the coolest way to live my life had turned out to be a fast track to nowhere. When school had started in the fall, I cut more than ever. What did I care about any of this? I couldn't convince the entire group to come with me off campus every time, but every day at least one or two of them would agree, enabling my chaotic and self-destructive tendencies. I was well on my way to completely losing my way when Coach Gunn pulled me aside and informed me I was dangerously close to failing his class, and if I failed, I was off the team.

It was then I realized my life still had a long way to go before it hit rock bottom.

He said I needed to pass the midterm or I was gone. He knew I'd been fucking off for most of the semester, and he was conveying in no uncertain terms that he was done putting up with it. He knew how much I loved baseball, and just the threat of losing it sobered me up instantly. He explained I had a lot of material to cover, and if I didn't pass with a B, I could turn in my jersey and kiss my spot on the team good-bye. As he packed up his materials, he suggested I find a tutor and find one quick.

"Brad? Brad, honey," a voice said from my right.

I realized I had nodded off and sat up so fast my head spun. The credits were scrolling up the screen, and the house lights made me squint. Ms. Garner was looking at me, concerned, probably worried I was drunk and sleeping it off. "The first movie is over," she said pleasantly. "You gonna stay for the second?"

I rubbed my eyes and yawned loudly as I nodded. "Yeah. I'm sorry, didn't get much sleep last night."

"It's okay, dear," she said, smiling. "You want to get a Coke while Barney loads the next movie?"

A Coke sounded good, and I followed her out to the lobby, blinking harshly at the difference between a darkened theater and the afternoon sun. I bought myself a huge Coke and began to sip it as I waited. I wandered around the lobby, wondering if my mom would even say anything if I came home so early in the day, when Jennifer walked by the window. I froze in midsip. She turned to check herself in the window and instead saw me standing openmouthed in shock at the injustice of it all. Thirty seconds either way and I would have been fine. If I had taken longer to wake up, gone to the bathroom instead, decided not to tell the school I was a queer....

She continued to stare at me, no doubt wondering if I was a mirage or not. Finally she turned and headed into the theater, making a beeline across the lobby toward me. Ms. Garner noticed her arrive and began to step out from behind the concession stand to sell her a ticket. Jennifer stopped in front of me. "Hiding?" she asked.

"Thinking," I clarified even though she had nailed it in one.

She looked angry. No, that's not fair to angry people. She looked furious as she began to corral a collection of words in her mind, much like an assassin might arm himself before a kill. "Do you have any idea how horrible today has been?"

I knew how bad it had been for me, but I didn't think that was what she was hinting at.

"I am the laughingstock of the school. People whispering behind my back, everyone looking away as I pass by. What am I supposed to do now?" she demanded.

"I don't have any answers," I answered lamely. It sounded as bad as it had when I told Kyle the same.

"Is it true?" she inquired with her head cocked. I was more than a little shocked, since it was the closest I had ever seen her come to cutting me a break. "Because if you were just sticking up for the lame kid, you can tell people that, and they'd believe you."

And they would, the same idea had been mulling over in my head the entire day even though I hadn't wanted to give it actual thought. I was Brad Greymark, and people wanted to believe I was just a straight guy who had stuck up for some poor, picked-on gay kid rather than accept me being a fairy myself. I suppose people being willing to accept that I'd said what I did to protect someone should have comforted me, but all it did was make me angry.

"One, he isn't lame," I said coldly. She wasn't shocked; this was the language of our little group. Part sarcasm, part vocal evisceration. No one dared share actual feelings or concerns lest they become fair game. Instead, we traded words and phrases that were at best verbal feints and at worst just outright bullshit. "Two, you think today has been any easier on me? You think I can just say something like that and not be—" I mentally pulled myself back from saying scared or terrified since they implied weakness. "—concerned about how it will affect my life? You can't be so conceited that you've made this all about yourself?" Her eyes looked as if smoke might issue from them at any second, she was so mad. "And three, you had to have some clue. After all, wasn't the reason you went out with me in the first place because you didn't want to have some guy trying to get up under your skirt every five seconds? We both know I was the safe choice."

"Maybe I wanted you to get up under it more," she flared.

"Well then maybe you should have dated someone who was into you!"

And for a brief second the mask slipped off her face, and I saw the actual pain that was hiding behind it. That was a mean thing to say to anyone, much less to the girl I had just humiliated in front of the entire school. My expression changed as I tried to apologize. "Jennifer, that wasn't what I—"

I didn't get to finish since she grabbed my Coke and threw it in my face as hard as she could. I felt it burn my eyes as I began to cough from trying inhale at the same time, going down to one knee. The ice had pelted me all over, and it felt like someone had thrown a handful of rocks at my face. "Fuck you, Brad!" she screamed, throwing the empty cup at my head. I was about to try talking again when something that hurt like a son of a bitch hit my head.

"Fuck!" I called as she stormed out.

I tried to wipe my face clean as I breathed through my mouth. By the time I could see again, she was gone, and Ms. Garner was standing next to me, not sure what to do. She had a sympathetic face as she held my class ring out to me. "She... dropped this," she said not wanting to say Jennifer had thrown it at me. I took it and rubbed my head from where it had hit me.

In the silence, Barney walked into the lobby and proudly proclaimed, "Next movie's starting! You better hurry up."

I suddenly needed to be anywhere else but there. I grabbed my ring and fled the scene.

Coke still dripped from my hair when I got out onto the street. I shook my head like a dog who had just ran through a puddle, knowing I could never get in my car this soaked. I took off my jacket and groaned, seeing the white already stained brown after its brown shower. "Oh fuck me!" I cursed, shaking my jacket out the best I could.

"Need a towel?" a voice asked me.

I looked over and saw Mr. Parker leaning in the doorway of his store, finishing a cigarette. He tossed the butt into the street. "You look like you're having a bad day. Come in, and let's get you cleaned up."

He walked back in, and I followed miserably. I think my socks were squishing. How did the Coke get into my sneakers? My entire world sucked.

The store was empty, but the familiar smell of new vinyl and plastic that was ingrained into my brain as meaning "sports" comforted me. "I think I'm dripping on your floor," I said, seeing a puddle form underneath me.

He tossed me quarterback towel. "Use that while I see if I have anything bigger in the back."

I soaked the excess Coke off me. I just knew it was going to be sticky as fuck when it dried. I pulled my T-shirt away from my chest once I realized it was sticking to me. "Get the extra-large Coke," I mumbled to myself. "It's only a quarter more."

Mr. Parker came out with a couple of beach towels in his hand. "Here, stand on that one, and use this one to dry off with."

I spread the first towel under me and stood on top as I dried myself with the other. When I got most of the mess out, I looked up to see that he held a Foster High sweatshirt in his hand. "Your shirt is wasted. Here, you put this on." I pulled my shirt off and tossed it on the floor. I dried off what I could before putting the sweatshirt on. "You've grown since the last time I saw you," he observed casually.

"Thanks," I answered, slipping the sweatshirt on over my head. "Going for Taylor's hitting record this year."

He shooed me off the towel and bundled it up. "I was at Granada same year as Taylor; he was an animal on the field. Good luck with that whole record-breaking thing." He nodded toward the back of the store. "Grab a pair of trunks in your size, and take those jeans off. I'll throw all this in the washing machine."

I grabbed a red pair of basketball shorts. "Since when do you have a washer and dryer here?" I asked as I shimmied out of my jeans.

"Got 'em last year. We do uniform rentals, and not everyone brings them back cleaned," he yelled over the sound of a load going into the dryer. I followed him to the storage/laundry room and handed him my jeans and boxers.

"Thanks for doing this, Mr. Parker. You're a life saver."

He threw some soap in and closed the lid. "Not a problem. Wasn't that your girl who almost tackled me coming out of the Vine?"

I nodded as I sat on a stool. "Yeah, she's a little pissed."

He chuckled. "That's an understatement." He had a small fridge next to his cramped desk. After a second, he opened the door and pulled out two bottles of Coke. "I know you've already had some, but you want another Coke?"

I felt a grin starting in the corner of my mouth and, finally, laughed a little as I nodded.

"Anything you wanna talk about?" he said, handing me one of them.

"You wouldn't understand," I said, taking a long swig.

"Girl trouble?" he asked. I shook my head no. "Boy trouble?"

I started to cough and stared up at him, panicked.

He put down his Coke and began to slap my back. "Whoa there, small breaths. You and Coke aren't a good fit today, are you?"

I looked up at him. "How did you know?"

He arched an eyebrow and then grabbed another stool and sat across from me. "Well, I didn't know anything until just now, but I had a feeling."

I groaned and put my head in my hands. "Oh jeez! Am I that obvious?"

He laughed. "Not in the least, Brad. I just happen to be an expert in spotting things like that."

I began to wonder if everyone in the fucking town knew about me. What if it was just like Jennifer was saying? What if everyone had been talking behind my back, laughing at the queer as he pretended to be straight? I felt even worse than I had before, and I had been pretty sure I had maxed out my misery limit for the day.

At first, Mr. Parker's words hadn't meant anything. Then their significance smacked my brain. Hard.

I looked up. "Wait, what?"

He smiled. I had to admit, for an old guy, he was smoking hot. "I meant I had some experience in seeing things like that in guys like you."

It felt like he was talking in another language for a second. I could hear the words, but they didn't make sense putting them together. "Like me? I don't—how would you—"

Then the other sneaker dropped.

"You mean—you?" I asked, shocked as I had ever been in my life.

He nodded.

"But you're—I mean, you played college ball!" I was flabbergasted. Never really understood that word before now, but suddenly, it was making all the sense in the world. My flabber was more than gasted.

"What? You think there is a straight test you have to pass to get into the NCAA?" He chuckled. "I assure you, just 'cause someone plays a sport doesn't mean he can't like guys."

My mind was going in a million different directions at once as I tried to reset my reality to include the fact that the guy who owned the sporting goods store was gay too. "But you act so—so manly." Man, that sounded lame. "I mean no one would guess you in a million years!"

He shrugged. "No one has, to be honest." Then he thought about it. "Well, my mom, but I don't think that counts. Moms know everything."

"How, I mean, when did you—how did you know about me?" I finally asked.

He finished his Coke. "Saw you and that boy over at Nancy's this morning." He held his hand out to take my empty bottle. "He's in love with you." I handed it over, stupefied by Mr. Parker's words. Someone was watching us? How many other people had noticed us? He saw my concern and shook his head. "Don't worry. You two aren't obvious or anything. Not unless you know what you're looking for."

I wished I hadn't sighed such a huge breath of relief, but I did.

"So what happened? You two break up?"

On one hand it was so insane to be having this conversation with him, but on the other, it was so relieving to talk to someone about it. "He was getting picked on at school yesterday, and he kinda came out."

I began to run my hand through my hair, but it was one sticky mess, and my fingers stalled. "And I kinda… um… came out too."

He looked blown away as we sat there in silence. "Okay! Well I never did that."

"Yeah," I replied miserably. "And now I wish I never had."

He studied me intently for almost a minute before asking. "Why?"

"Why what?" I asked, confused.

"Why do you wish you never said anything? Because you don't like guys or because you don't want the shit storm that comes with it?"

It was an odd question to me, and I had to think on it for a few seconds. I hadn't actually divorced the two thoughts in my head. I was regretting saying anything because of the eventual drama that came with it, not because I didn't like Kyle. "Well, the shit storm I guess."

"And do you like that boy I saw?"

"Kyle," I corrected him.

"And do you like Kyle?"

I nodded slowly. "I do, but—"

"No," he said, cutting me off. "There is no 'but' after that." He seemed angry for a second but then took a deep breath. "Look, Brad, I know I don't know you outside of this store and all, but can I give you some advice?"

"Sure," I said, not sure where Mr. Parker was heading.

"I'm you in twenty years. Consider me…." He took a second and mused on it. "Consider me the ghost of Christmas yet to be."

"It's not Christmas," I pointed out. Mr. Parker wasn't the least bit distracted by my attempt at smoke and mirrors.

"It's doesn't matter," he said, waving my statement off. "Just understand that I am what you will become if you continue down this path. Brad, I was so scared growing up that people would look at me and know I was gay and just freak out that I never told anyone. I dated girls in high school, went off to Florida and dated more girls there, and I was miserable. I never had the guts to be honest with myself. When I blew my knee out and had to come back here—well it felt like being thrown in jail."

I was freaking out because Mr. Parker sounded just like me!

"I've spent most of my life locked in a box of my own making, and it sucks, let me tell you. If I had to do it again—" He laughed darkly. "Well if I had someone like Kyle standing next to me, I'd tell the rest of the world to fuck off and take as much happy as I could grab." And his eyes locked with mine, and I felt a chill down my spine. "Because, Brad, at the end of the day, sports won't make you happy, your friends won't make you happy, and your family will just wonder what is wrong with you. The only way that you'll be happy is if you man up and face who you are."

"A fag?" I asked.

"Different," he said harshly. "Stop using other people's words to hurt yourself. There isn't a thing wrong with what you… what we are. The problem is with other people who can't handle it. You think those people are going to love you? Comfort you? Stand behind you for the rest of your life? I can't make this any clearer, Brad. If you live your life scared of what other people think, then you will always be miserable. And that's the God's honest truth."

"Are you miserable?" I asked him softly.

He stared down, and for a second he didn't look all that much older than me. "More than you can possibly imagine."

The washer stopped spinning, and he got up to throw my clothes into the dryer. His words chased themselves around in my head as I tried to process what he'd said. He was right. I mean, I had figured all that out before, but hearing it from someone else suddenly made it real. I was running scared because a group of people I really didn't like might say something about me? Since when did I care what those idiots thought?

"Look, it's your life." He fished a pack of smokes out of his jeans. "I can't tell you what to do. I'm just saying. You don't want to end up like me. Trust me, living with a life full of regrets is just about the shittiest way I can think of existing." He walked back to the front of the store. "I'm going to smoke. I'll be right back."

"Smoking's bad for you," I said as he walked away.

"So's running from your problems," he shot back as he stepped outside.

He had a point.

I was Bradley Greymark, and that meant something in Foster. Not because of my dad, and not because of my friends. Because of me. I was the guy they followed, not the guy who followed everyone else. I wasn't born a sheep, and no matter how much I might wish I was blissfully ignorant, I wasn't. I might not like being the one in charge, but I was. And I'd be damned if I was going to let that pack of stuck-up idiots dictate who and what I was.

By the time Mr. Parker came in, I knew what I had to do. It wasn't going to be easy, and it wasn't going to be all hugs and puppies, but I had no choice. "So what about now?" I asked him when he sat down.

"What about what?"

"What about now? I've never heard a thing about you, and in this town that's impossible. So what about now? You still hiding?" I would have never spoken to an adult like this before, but for some reason I felt like we were almost equals now. He was twice my age, and he was just as scared of this whole gay thing, which made him more my age and me older than I was when I walked in.

"I wouldn't say hiding—" he began.

"So that's a yes," I cut him off now. "Okay, how about this? If I have the guts to stand up and face the truth, can you too?"

He raised an eyebrow. "Like what? You want me to put a sign up in the front window or something?"

"You think we're the only gay guys in Foster?" I asked and saw his reaction on his face. "Well, maybe, but that doesn't matter. There is this wonderful thing called the Internet. Lets you meet people from all over the world." I grinned and teased him. "I know an old man like you might not know what that is, but trust me, it's out there."

"Hey, I'm not even thirty!" he protested.

"Like I said, old man. But if I am willing to risk it, you need to put yourself out there too," I countered.

"And if I don't?" he asked.

"Well then you're going to be miserable, and I think that's kinda sad," I answered honestly. "You're not a bad-looking guy, and you seem cool. Guys like us shouldn't have to be alone."

"Like us?" he asked, smiling.

"Hot, athletic, gay guys," I replied, giving him a definition.

"So I'm hot?" he asked.

"For an old guy, sure."

We both laughed at that.

"We'll see," he said, shaking his head. "It's not like I have a Kyle wandering around asking me out."

"And you never will unless you take a chance."

He rubbed his chin as he pretended to think about it. "You might be right."

"I know I'm right. This old guy I'm friends with told it to me."

He made a face. "That 'old' shit is beginning to wear thin."

"Then do something about it," I challenged him.

"I'll charge you for the clothes," he threatened.

"Fine," I said as I started pulling the sweatshirt over my head. "You explain why you have a naked teenager in the back of your store."

"Okay, okay, okay!" he cried as he pulled my arms down. "You win! I promise to put myself out there next time I have the chance."

"You mean that? Because if you are just saying it to shut me up, I know where you live, and—" I began to threaten.

"I meant it!" He was laughing now. "I meant every word I said."

"Good," I said, nodding. "And I promise to stop running."

He held out his hand. "Shake on it."

I grabbed and we shook.

My day began to get better.

BY the time my clothes were done, it was about the same time that school was letting out for the day, so I felt safe heading home. I thanked Mr. Parker again before I left and reminded him of our deal. He let me keep the sweatshirt and trunks, which I thought was way cool considering that those things are stupid expensive. I tossed the bag into the back seat and headed out to my house. I wanted to talk to Kyle now, but if he was going through even half of the shit flying around in my mind, he was going to need some space.

And I had to admit I needed to get my head on straight.

I had decided I wasn't going to let what others thought and felt affect the way I lived my life, but that didn't mean I knew what I was going to do about it. I needed a game plan before I brought Kyle in on it. I know if he showed up saying "I want to do this, but I have no idea how," I'd be more upset than I had been before. He had taken the first step, which meant the next one was up to me.

As I turned the corner onto my block, I saw my dad's car in the driveway and cussed under my breath. I had really been hoping to have some time to myself for once without my parents' Mortal Kombat reenactments to distract me. I parked next to his car, which was the identical twin of mine, except black. I had to admit the initial joy of receiving a brand new Mustang had been tempered by the fact that giving the car to me was just another way for my dad to remind me that

I should be grateful to him. I still took the car and thanked him, because I am no fool.

I did hold his tactics against him in my mind, though.

As I walked into the house, I could hear him in the kitchen talking on the phone. I slipped my shoes off, lest I incur the wrath of Momzilla, and tried to race up to my room. Of course that didn't happen. "Brad!" he screamed from the other room. "Get in here!"

"Fuck," I growled under my breath as I turned and marched into the kitchen.

His jacket was off, and his tie was loose, which meant he'd been home for a while. I saw the ever-present tumbler of scotch on the counter next to him and knew he was probably just drunk enough to be dangerous and not drunk enough to eventually pass out. He still had his Blackberry up to his ear as he nodded. "I understand." Pause. "No I'm sure we can fix this." Longer pause. "No, I agree completely, coach."

And that was when the floor seemed to drop out from under me.

"I'll talk to him," he said, giving me a harsh glare. "Thank you." And stabbed the End button. He slammed the phone down and immediately reached for the drink. He and my mom always reminded me of those monkeys that won't let one thing go until they have a grip on something else. It took a lot to get a glass of booze out of their hands, and damn whatever it was that made them put it down. "Why are you home?" he asked, stating each word distinctly, as if he was a lawyer, and I was on trial.

"Blew off school," I said as casually as possible.

"Why aren't you at practice?" he demanded.

There wasn't an answer that was going to be good enough for him, so I didn't even try. "I needed a day off."

"Oh, because you've been studying so hard, right?" He was growing angrier as he went on, and I knew we had just begun. "Coach Gunn told me you were failing history as well as a couple of other classes, and now you're missing practice? What exactly is wrong with you, Brad?"

"I'm working on my grades," I said, trying to end the conversation while we were still just talking.

"And practice?"

"I missed one practice; the world won't end." I could feel my own emotions reacting to his.

"I would have never missed a practice in my day." Which was his normal complaint about anything I did. He would have never done this; he would have never done that. I was so sick of hearing what he would and would not have done. He'd sung that song one too many times.

"Well I'm not planning on being you, Dad, so it doesn't matter what you would have done." I was beginning to lose my cool.

"You'd be lucky to end up as well as I have," he argued. "The way you're going, you'll be a loser the rest of your life."

"Thirty pounds overweight in a loveless marriage at a nowhere car dealership is exactly what people think of when they think of loser." And I'd lost it.

"What the fuck did you just say?" he roared.

"I'm not you! I will never be you!" I shouted back.

"So far, you're doing exactly what I did. Skipping school, getting wasted every weekend with your useless friends. Face it, champ, you're just one broken condom away from this life!" he said, getting in my face.

"That will never happen!" I yelled at him.

"That's what I thought!"

"It's different for me! Trust me!" We were too far gone to back off.

He cocked his head and asked sarcastically. "Oh really, genius? Explain to me how you're so fucking different?"

"I'm gay!"

And there it was.

His face was pale as he stared at me, his mouth open. "What did you say?"

What did I just say?

It was the only weapon I had, so I decided to wield it as well as I could. "You heard me! I'm gay, Dad. So there is no way I'll end up getting some bitch I hate pregnant and being trapped in a life I can't get through without downing half a bottle of scotch a day!" He took a look at the glass in his hand and then back at me as I kept going. "You don't know me, and you never will. I am nothing like you, old man, and if I end up homeless, begging for change on First Street, I'll have a better life than yours."

He swung his hand at me, looked like he was going for a backhand serve, but we weren't going down this road ever again. I caught his hand and held it there, trying to make it look as effortless as possible. "Next time you swing at me, I'm going to swing back," I said, my eyes never leaving his. "And trust me. I hit a lot harder than you do."

He tried to pull his hand back, but I refused to let it go.

"You wanna take my car away? Fine. You wanna throw me out of the house? Great. But you don't get to hit me anymore." I twisted his wrist and made him cry out as he turned, trying to ease the pain. "Got it?"

He nodded silently, and I let him go.

"I'll get my grades up. Don't worry about it," I said, turning around and heading to my room.

I expected him to scream at me as I walked away. I fully expected to hear him cursing and threatening me as I took the stairs two at a time. But he said nothing as I closed the door behind me and locked it for good measure. I sat on the edge of my bed and realized I was shaking. Eight hours? It had only been eight hours since I sat here and wondered what I was going to do with myself. And here I was again, wondering the exact same thing.

I fished my phone out of my jeans and pulled up the picture of Kyle I had taken that morning. I had no idea what to do about him, and it made me feel sick. I liked him so much, but I didn't see any way we could be together and not just be miserable. Every particle of confidence I had felt at Mr. Parker's was gone, and once again I was sure my life was over.

I fell back on my bed and mashed my pillow down over my face before I screamed into it as loudly as possible, cursing just about everything in the world I could think of. If my anger had been a solid object, my scream would have blown through the pillow and smashed a hole through our roof before shooting out into space. I screamed some more, trying to expel as much of my rage as I could, knowing that bottling it up inside would serve no purpose except to make my day worse and worse.

I thought about my last words to my dad and remembered that getting my grades up was what had led me to Kyle in the first place. After Coach Gunn had laid down the law to me about history and what failing it could cost me, I knew I needed to learn history, and learn it fast.

My first thought was to find one of the bottom feeders that hovered around our group. Bottom feeders were people who weren't as popular as the rest of us but lingered around us, waiting for one of us to drop them a crumb of recognition. Most of them were girls who weren't ugly at all but who weren't blessed with the genetic gifts that Jennifer and the rest of her harpies possessed. Jennifer and her clones treated those girls like crap, but I never said anything about it, since the quasi-jocks who vied for my attention weren't any better.

There is something just unappealing about desperation that clings to people no matter how hard they try to conceal it. I never had anything personal against individual wannabes, but anyone who wanted to be around me simply because they wanted to be more popular made me sick. Surviving the endlessly circling pool of social sharks eyeing each other for an opening to take first blood meant that using one of the hoverers was out. There would be questions, and the truth about my grades and the possibility of me being off the team would come out. I'd be a target none of the others could ignore.

I looked around as casually as possible for anyone who knew anything about history, which meant someone who actually paid attention in Coach Gunn's class while trying to listen to what we were going over to see how bad it was. My hunt revealed two things to me. One, that I had no fucking idea what they were talking about. And two, there was a cute-ass blond guy who seemed to know everything. I was shocked I hadn't noticed him before around school. Though I never actually put any real time into wondering what my type of guy might be, I knew right away that my type would look a lot like him.

That day I shadowed him as best I could.

He was like a damn ninja walking through the halls between classes. He moved through crowds of people like he was a ghost rather than flesh and blood. I saw him that afternoon sitting on the steps of the band hall near our table and wondered how long he'd been there and I had never even noticed. I asked everyone if they knew who he was, but like me, they acted as if they were seeing him in school for the first time.

I was intrigued.

The next day I asked about him in the office. The girl who did work study there had a crush on me and would have given me locker combinations if I smiled at her long enough. She explained he was in two honors classes but not in any extracurricular clubs. She knew of him but didn't know him. That seemed to be a reoccurring theme the more I asked around about him.

It was Coach Gunn who knew the most about him.

"You mean Kyle? Smartest kid in any of my classes," he said before class. "Quiet one, but he seems like a good kid." He gave me a grin. "You could do a lot worse if you were looking for a tutor. He's pulling down a 4.2 average."

"It goes higher than 4.0?" I asked, shocked.

"It does for people like him."

After that I knew I had my tutor. I had to find a time I could approach him without an entourage. I didn't want to draw attention to me failing a class, and I couldn't imagine having a group of popular people approaching you just to talk to you would bring out Kyle's confidence. It would have seemed too much like a scene from *Bring It On*, and no one wanted that.

At some point during my memory walk toward Kyle, I fell asleep. Almost two hours had passed before my mom knocked on my door, waking me up. "Bradley," she called, "are you in there?"

She knew I was in my room unless I had crawled out my window and somehow found a way to get down from the second story without breaking my legs. If I had been able to do that, I would have exited stage right already. I sat up, rubbing my eyes, looking over at the clock on my night table. "Yeah, hold on," I said, getting up and unlocking the door.

She had that same perpetually worried look that I associated with small, yippy dogs, the ones that always looked worried, as if someone might step on them. Sure, my mom looked harmless to the unsuspecting eye, but I knew she was a grand master of passive aggressive warfare.

While my dad was overt, aggressive, and loud, my mom was syrupy sweet, always smiling, right up to the lower lids of her eyes. I'm not sure if it was her medication or a defense mechanism, but she never lost her cool. I figured she kept her temper because losing it would mean that whatever my dad had said or done had caused her to react, and that she would not do. "Are you hungry?" she asked, worried. We both knew her being in my room wasn't about dinner, but asking if I was hungry was the excuse she needed to knock on my door.

"No, I'm good," I said, sitting back down on my bed. There was no way in the world my dad hadn't told her what I'd said to him earlier. I mean, in the world of their own private duel to the death, there couldn't be any higher caliber bullet than "You know you made your son gay, don't you?" Mom had come to me seeking not only confirmation that what he had said was true or denial if it wasn't, but also for useful ammunition for a return barrage. Of that I was sure.

She took two steps and stopped just inside my room. I'm not sure that she'd ever been in it. We had a maid who did our laundry and made our beds every day, so I couldn't imagine why Mom would have needed to. "Your dad said you guys got into a fight." Which was like saying that Voldemort and Harry Potter had strong words with each other. "You want to talk about it?"

"No," I answered honestly.

She walked across the room and sat next to me, her hands in her lap. "I don't blame you," she said, nodding.

I wasn't sure if she was waiting for me to say something, but it was very uncomfortable sitting there saying nothing. I wished she would just get to her point and then leave, but we just sat there and continued to say nothing. Waiting.

Finally she asked, "Did I ever tell you what happened when I found out I was pregnant with you?"

I looked over at her, my eyes wide. I wasn't sure what new tactic this was, but there was no way I was going to fall for it. "Mom, did you want something?"

She stared out my window, smiling the whole time as if I hadn't said anything. "Your grandma took me to Dr. Henry." She looked over at me. "He used to be the town doctor when I was your age. He passed away years ago, but he was a nice man." I looked at her, confused, not sure if she had a point or was just rambling. "So your grandma took me to see him after I was—" And she paused as she tried to frame her words properly. "After it was clear something was different with me."

"You were late?" I asked. "Or morning sickness?" That caught her off guard. She looked as if my head had spun a full 360 degrees or as if I had spit green pea soup instead of asking her a normal feminine hygiene question.

"How do you know about that?" she asked as if I had just revealed I knew where that box Indiana Jones was looking for had been buried.

"Mom, I'm seventeen. I do know how babies are made."

The light wasn't great in my room, but I was pretty sure she blushed. After a few seconds, she went on. "Anyway, we went to see him. Back then those home tests were not a sure thing. He took blood that day, and then we waited a few days for the results to come back. So I sat at home for three days. Three days where I wasn't sure what was going to happen to my life. Your father already had his scholarship, so I knew he wasn't going to be any help. I was not even a year older than you are now, and I was a little pissed."

I half smiled as my proper and reserved mom said the word "pissed."

"I mean, I had plans. I wanted to go to college. I planned on traveling. I didn't know what exactly being pregnant would mean. But if I was, I did know everything would have to change."

I frowned a little and interrupted. "If this is supposed to cheer me up...."

"Hush," she said curtly. "So he called back and told me he had my results, and that I needed to be at his office in the morning." She paused for a moment, and I thought she was going to cry. "And I knew what that meant, so I thanked him and hung up the phone and just stood there."

"Because your life was ruined," I said to fill the gaping silence.

She turned to me, and there were tears in her eyes. "No. Because I realized my life was just starting. We all grow up thinking we are going to be one thing or another, and we clutch those dreams to our chests like they are the most important things in the world. But life... life has its own plans for us, and it could care less what our plans are because life is always more important than what people think they want. There are a lot of people in this world who refuse to open their eyes to what life wants of us. They don't understand that life is more important than adolescent dreams. They hold on to those dreams as long as possible, doing everything they can to avoid losing them, no matter what the cost to everyone around them." She put her hand on my cheek, and I felt myself starting to choke up. "I never once regretted having you because I knew in my heart that you would grow up from a fantastic boy to an incredible man. And if I can be even a little part of that, then that is the most important thing I could ever do."

Now I felt myself starting to cry.

"The complications your father and I face haven't been fair to you, but you have to know the way we are has nothing to do with you. The only thing I ever wanted was for you to be happy. And nothing else matters." Tears were falling down her cheeks now, her makeup smearing.

"I want to be happy," I said, the sheer tonnage of today's events finally crashing down over me. I felt myself too tired to keep moving. "I don't know what to do to be happy." I finally cracked. She pulled me into a hug, and I finally just began to sob as she rocked me.

"Stop living our expectations," she said as she comforted me. "And start living your own life." She smoothed my hair absently. "Just be yourself, Bradley; you can never go wrong with that." She pulled back and picked up my phone. Kyle's shocked stare from this morning brought a little smile to her eyes. "This is the boy?"

I nodded.

"He likes you?"

I nodded again.

"You like him too?"

I smiled and looked away as I gave a quiet, "Yeah."

"Then do something about it," she said, handing me my phone. "If you don't, you'll spend the rest of your life wondering how things would have been different if you had."

I couldn't say anything as I took what solace I could from my mother's permission.

After almost a second she added, "Honey, you need to start washing your hair more. It feels like a rat's nest right now."

I laughed for the first time since Kyle left me at Nancy's.

KYLE had been tough to pin down as my history tutor. I remembered trying to get his attention during class with no success. He was either ignoring me or just unaware that anyone might want to talk to him at all. I paused at the classroom door so he'd have to pass me. As he got to me, I raised a hand and opened my mouth to say something, but he just walked past me, never looking up. I don't think that had ever happened to me before.

It was kind of cool.

I couldn't find him the next two periods. He could have disappeared for all I knew. I was just starting to understand why I had never noticed him before. I finally caught a glimpse of him from the back heading down a hallway, and I followed him from a distance. I felt like I was in a spy movie hanging back and tailing him, unnoticed. I saw Josh Walker coming down toward us, and I knew I was screwed. He was on the baseball team, too, and he was, in my opinion, better-looking than I was. He was something like six four with a well-built frame that he poured every day into a pair of Wranglers that should have been illegal. There was nothing nicer than watching Josh walking away from you because his ass was a work of art that required extended appreciation.

As he walked by, I saw Kyle look back and take a quick peek at it.

I froze, wondering if I had just imagined what I'd seen Kyle do. Josh asked me what was up and something about the season that I didn't catch. I watched Kyle walk away, wondering if there was more to this guy than I thought.

Now I stalked with a purpose.

It was easy to follow him since he acted like he was practically invisible walking through the halls. It was as if the thought that someone might be watching him was just not a possibility. The sad part was, from what I saw, he was basically right. I watched him like a hawk, and it seemed no one even gave him the time of day as he navigated the halls. He was a good-looking guy; his hair was naturally a bright blond, and it was shaggy in a way that I thought was cute as hell. Yet if anyone else noticed Kyle, I didn't see it. As the day went on, I became more and more obsessed with him.

The more I watched the more I became convinced he liked guys too. Don't get me wrong, he had mad skills at hiding it, but he was so focused on watching people and staying out of their sight that it seemed that it never occurred someone might be watching him. I caught him checking out a couple of guys, and I liked his taste. The more I watched, the less I cared about my grades, and the more I wondered if he'd like me too.

I realized that I was still chasing after Kyle and wondering, only now I was wondering if I could be the guy he needed me to be. After a shower and some sleep, I got up early the next morning, determined to see him.

I didn't have a clue of what I was going to do, but I needed him to know I was in it for the long haul. My mom had convinced me that if I kept trying to bottle up my feelings, I'd end up as bitter and angry as my dad. Before I headed out of the house, I noticed the door to my dad's den cracked open and a light on inside. Tempting fate, I peeked in for a second to see if he was in there. He was passed out on the couch in the far corner; the den had become pretty much his bedroom recently. Asleep, face smooth, without any lines of anger or disappointment, he looked like himself. I tried to see the person my mom must have glimpsed back before I was born, but I couldn't. All I saw was a guy that had been in the same position in high school that I was. The difference was that my dad had believed being popular really did make him better than everyone else.

Even though I had always known my place in the school's social strata, I never once mistook that as something with any actual worth in the eyes of the world. If anything, the more people looked up to me and idolized me, the worse I felt about myself. I knew I was perpetrating a fraud that had no basis in real life at all. Dad never saw that, believing instead that his position in high school meant something. And no matter how much money he made, how expensive his car was, or even what size house he owned, in the final analysis, my dad was a middle-aged dick still clinging to an illusion and milking it for all it was worth.

I wasn't going to go down that road.

That much I knew for sure.

I closed the den doors and pulled my shoes on as I hopped out toward my car. I had no delusions about the possibility that there was a clock hovering over my car, and the countdown had begun. A couple of hours sober and the realization that his only child was gay would be more than enough to have Dad yank my sweet ride out from under me. I wondered what it'd be like having to get around on foot, and then remembered I had just come out. Being seen walking was the least of my worries.

I laughed at the absurdity of the situation and realized that Mr. Parker had been dead on target: sooner or later everything was going to be all right.

Unlike our neighborhood, the area of town that Kyle lived in didn't seem to have a lot of early risers. In my neighborhood, a virtual army of husbands and fathers came out to spend a good chunk of the weekend on yard duty, keeping the grass short and the weeds in check, while the entire area around Kyle's place was a ghost town. As I pulled in front of his place, I wondered if any kids lived around here. I couldn't imagine not having guys my own age near me as I had grown up. The more I discovered about Kyle, the more I understood how he could have ended up being so reserved. If we had grown up reversed, would he be the popular one and would I end up being the cute guy no one knew about?

Would he have been the jock? Would I have been the—well, no way in hell I was smart enough to be a nerd, so that was out. I still wondered how different we would have ended up instead.

I raised my fist to knock, but the door opened before I could. Kyle stood there, this time looking a lot more awake than he had yesterday. He was angry, but I could see he was trying to keep his cool. "What?" he snapped.

Well, he wasn't trying all that hard.

"We need to talk," I said, hoping he was either going to come outside or invite me in.

"So talk," he said, not budging.

"You really wanna do this out here?" I asked, so not caring if anyone else heard us or not. When he said nothing, I just shrugged and started. "Okay. I'm crazy about you." The joy of seeing his eyes widen in complete astonishment made up for his stubbornness. "I know I was scared, and I handled that like crap, but I'm here now."

"What are you doing?" he asked, almost whispering.

"Making things right," I said with no hesitation. "This isn't going to be easy, and I have no idea what is about to happen, but I know no matter how hard it gets, I'm going to be here for you." I thought about it for a second. "Scratch that, I'm going to be here with you."

He was still speechless, but I could see the emotion creeping up on his face.

"I want to be with you. You, Kyle," I said, pointing at him. "And I may screw up, and I may be stupid, but I am never going to let you be alone." I took a step toward him and grabbed his hands. "I'm here until the day you tell me to go away." I leaned in and whispered in his ear, "And I'm the one who owes you." He looked down and opened his hand. Inside were eighty one cents and my class ring. "You forgot your change."

His face broke into a smile as he hugged me.

"Get in here," he said, pulling me inside.

At that moment I knew I'd follow him anywhere he took me.

BRAD AND KYLE
ORDINANCE
NO. C-3240

Kyle

YOU know what I hate?

Okay, that's a vague and open-ended question, so before you answer, let me clarify it some. You know what I hate about teenage movies? They never show the next day. I mean, sure, maybe the princess *did* indeed date the criminal, but how exactly did they make *that* work? Her friends would never talk to her again once they found out she was actually kissing some lowlife like him. His friends would disgust her with their rude and suggestive talk. Within a week they would be arguing about what to do with their weekend. She would want to go hang out at the mall and maybe see some chick flick, and he'd want to get burned with his friends and maybe play some Xbox. Fighting within two weeks, broken up in a month.

The movie didn't show *that*, did it?

Or what about *Sixteen Candles*? So Jake gets her a birthday cake, and they blow the candles out on their rather flimsy-looking glass table. What's next? Does he think his friends aren't going to be very vocal in their confusion about who the hell this Samantha chick was in the first place? Even though they didn't show many, you know she had to have friends too. Do you think any of them would constantly be asking her what he was like? What were they going to do for fun? She would go to two of his friends' parties before she got fed up with the dirty looks that most of the girls shot her throughout the night. He would insist that she wasn't giving them a fair chance, and she would argue that they were horrible people.

They might even stay together until the topic of colleges came up. Obviously, Jake was headed for an Ivy League college and Samantha wasn't. They'd try a long-distance thing until the freshman mixer during orientation. Jake would be swamped by the first dozen girls who saw him and offered to help him with his homework and anything else he needed help with. When he came home for Christmas, he'd break it to her that they weren't working out, and she'd spend the rest of her life wondering what she had done wrong.

Kind of makes the idea of a sequel pretty dismal, doesn't it?

In the real world, Harry might have met Sally, but the movie doesn't cover exactly how they made it work once the camera was off. Opposites may attract (which I do not believe, by the way), but they don't make for an easy relationship, let me tell you. I may have had the hottest guy in school say he liked me, but I didn't have any faith we were going to be a "we" for any amount of time. We sidestepped the whole *going to school and facing the music* problem that Friday by cutting school.

The fact that we hadn't even decided to date before we had our first actual fight only seemed to drive home the point that our being together was an incredibly bad idea.

I walked out on him in the middle of a diner, for God's sake. I mean, sure, he came back and apologized, and the whole thing with the ring and the 81 cents? Yeah, the boy has game, but now it's Monday morning, and things are different. I don't mean my gown turned back into a sack of flour and the carriage ended up as pumpkin soup, but things between us could not, obviously, be the same, because there were *other* things that remained the same.

Foster High was still in the middle of nowhere, and the students and their teachers and administration were barely a step above the zombies in a Romero movie. I had images of being chased through the quad by a pack of villagers wielding pitchforks and torches while I stumbled forward in horrible lesbian boots with bolts in my neck.

It has been said more than once that I have an overactive imagination.

I paced my small room as I envisioned just about every blood-laden outcome if we were insane enough to show our faces at school again. I was used to being at the bottom of the social ladder. Actually, I was lower than the bottom; I usually hung out in the room next to the place they stored the ladder because people like me weren't allowed to see it. Brad was a different story altogether. He was used to being so far up that I'm sure there were only clouds when he looked down. I had no idea how people were going to react to him coming out.

If what he did counted as coming out.

I mean, he could just say he had been defending me against Kelly, who is a raging asshole. There were ways for him to take back what had happened if he wanted, and that scared me. We had spent the weekend talking about him telling everyone he was gay, about how this wasn't just a phase for him or a knee-jerk reaction to seeing someone get bullied. He had said he was falling for me. I wanted to believe that, but....

But. It always comes down to buts, doesn't it?

I could be okay with being gay, but I lived in Foster, Texas, which meant me being gay constituted a mortal sin. I could be normal if my mom wasn't clinically insane, so that was out of the question. And Brad might be falling in love with me, but I didn't even like myself, so how could he think being in love with me was positive?

I heard two horn blasts and knew I had run out of time to worry.

I grabbed my backpack and ran out the front door, hoping the noise didn't wake up my mother, the sleeping dragon. As I rushed outside, I saw him sitting behind the wheel of his brand-new, yellow Mustang and felt my heart skip a beat in response to the sight. In my world, there are precious few things that can be considered flawless. A weekend where my mother and I missed seeing each other because of our sleeping schedules was perfect. *The Notebook* is a perfect movie, in my opinion. Seasons two and three of *One Tree Hill* were perfect television. And Brad behind the wheel of his car was the perfect boy.

He kept his hair slightly long. Though it was kept in place with product, it always seemed to be one step away from being disheveled. His eyes sparkled with what might be a dangerous energy; he looked like he was half a second from telling someone the punch line to a joke.

And though he had several different smiles at his command, the one he flashed when I walked up to his car looked exactly like the others he'd used when we were together. So far those smiles had been the only actual signs of happiness I'd seen from him since we'd met.

"Well, well, well," he said as I got into the passenger seat. "If it isn't Mr. Stilleno?"

I fastened my seat belt and looked over at him. "Are you feeling okay? 'Cause you sound a little drunk."

His laughter filled the interior of the car and surrounded me like a blanket. "If I was drunk, I'd have hell to pay at practice this afternoon." He leaned over toward me, and I felt his mouth touch mine, and the world stopped spinning for a second. All the air in my lungs escaped me as I leaned in and curled my hand around his head. I ran my fingers through his hair and tried to experience as much happiness as I could in the moment. I was the brave little ant storing food away for the winter. I had no illusions that what came next wasn't going to suck, but right now he was kissing me. And that was awesome.

He leaned his forehead against mine as we sat there, with our eyes closed, which was the closest to prayer I got. "You ready?" he asked after a second.

"I'm scared," I said in a tiny voice that didn't sound like me.

"Me too," he answered. I opened my eyes when I felt him move back. His eyes stared into mine. "But you know what?" I shook my head. "I know things are going to be okay."

I tried not to give him a look of complete shock. "Why do you think that?" He might as well have said that *Deep Impact* was better than *Armageddon* or that Lindsay Lohan was better than Hilary Duff. I mean, things were not going to be okay—he had to know that, right?

Right?

"Because I got you," he said with grin number four, the one he used when he was trying to look all *Ocean's Eleven* about a situation. It looked good on him, but what we were facing wasn't something as simple as breaking into a casino vault. We were in high school in Foster freakin' Texas, and we had just unmasked ourselves as alien invaders.

"Okay" existed nowhere near where we were.

But I knew Brad, and I knew what he was doing.

This was where he tried to assure me that my concerns were valid while actually trying to calm himself down. The voices inside of my head screaming at me that this was a bad idea were echoed in his own. But I was afraid he might not be as adept at dealing with them as I had grown to be. My entire life was a horror movie where I was chased through my head by my doubts and insecurities while that annoying *cha cha cha* sound played in the background. I was willing to play the victim when I was the only one in danger of being made into kibbles and bits, but I could see the real fear behind that grin, and he wasn't *telling* me it was going to be okay as much as he was *asking* me if it was going to be okay.

Behind every strong man is a scared little boy wanting people to tell him it's going to be okay. Remember that, and men will no longer seem as stupid as you think they are.

I gave him a wide grin and grabbed his hand. "Of course you have me. We do this together." It seemed to assure him some. He took a deep breath and turned back toward the steering wheel. "You ready?"

Not even close.

"Always," I lied, sounding completely sure.

He pulled the gearshift, and we headed toward school and our future.

Brad

YOU know what I hate?

Besides the designated hitter and AstroTurf, the thing that most pisses me off is waiting. The only thing worse than being whaled on by your drunken old man is *waiting* for your old man to beat you. Anticipation is one of the most destructive forces I know of in the universe, and that's for good and bad things. It's the feeling when you can't wait to open your presents on Christmas morning—so bad that by the time everyone has woken up, you are so spazzed that you can't help but bug the shit out of everyone. Then you realize how much you're annoying people, and you start to panic because you know it's just a matter of time before you get smacked by your dad, which only makes the panic worse, so now you're trying to overcompensate by being super helpful, which is just as, if not more, annoying than you were acting before, and you just end up freezing up with no idea what the right thing to do is.

Or it's like when you're playing the outfield, thinking the game is mostly over. You're out there counting the seconds before you can get your cup off and take a damn shower. You're hot, tired, sweaty, and to be honest, ready to go home. Your uniform is too tight; it's riding up in places that no guy wants to adjust in front of five hundred clapping fans (including your mom!), and you are just done with it. Sure, you're ahead by one, and there's a guy on base, but all the pitcher needs to do is strike this jackass out and it's over. What could possibly go wrong?

By the way, if you don't know the quickest way to fuck up your day, night, or whatever time it is, think to yourself, *"What could possibly go wrong?"* Fate is a total bitch, and she loves to show off.

And that's when the batter actually gets behind the ball and pops one up into sky.

Now, we've all seen this play. The ball sails up like it's on fire and then starts to fall in a short arc. It's called a rocket because it moves like a jet engine but really goes nowhere but up. So the ball hovers there, looking like it's a mile above your head, defying gravity while it takes in the whole stadium in all its glory. All you can see is a speck of white way up there. Then it begins to grow larger.

And *here* is where anticipation sucks balls.

If you're playing shortstop and the guy smacks one between second and third, everything moves so fast that you have no time to think about it. You catch the crack of the bat against the ball and catch just the hint of something in your vision before your body begins to move. You scoop the ball up and are into your windup toward second before you even know what's happening. More than once, I've been patted on the back for an awesome play before I even knew what I'd done. Whether you make the play or not, a line drive happens so fast you have no time to stress about it.

The fly ball?

All the time in the fucking world.

You've waved the guy next to you off of it—because no one wants to be the asshole who slams into his own guy in the outfield and end up on YouTube. At that moment, time slows to a crawl as that dot becomes bigger and bigger. Now, some guys will tell you this is a routine play and that it there is nothing to it. Let me tell you, there is no such thing as a routine play. Balls like doing strange things when they make contact with a glove, doubly so if the ball senses fear from the catcher. They're like animals waiting for that one chance to race past your legs and out into traffic. Every baseball wants to hit your glove and then jump out so you can be the fucktard who lost the game.

You know your dad is watching you. Your mom. Your friends. Your girlfriend. The girl you wish was your girlfriend. Your buddies. Your buddies' families. Everyone. If they're on your side, they're holding their breath, praying for you to catch it. If they're for the other side, they're cursing you with every bit of energy they have. The guy on first is halfway to second, watching to see if you're going to lose your shit. The hitter has been on first since the late fifties, praying to every god he knows for you to flub. Suddenly your shoes are five sizes too large, and your cover fits you like you're a four-year-old wearing your dad's worn-out Rangers cap. You don't want to glance at the runners, because that is admitting you're going to drop the ball and want to be ready to cut the guy off at third. Also, you never want to take your eyes off the ball, because you know from long experience that the second you do, it will spin violently in any other direction it can, just so when you and the fans look back, everyone wonders, "Why the hell was he so far away from the ball?"

So, basically, this ball has been falling for like an hour and a half.

You feel like you've been out there long enough to go grab a burger and get back before it falls. Yet it's been seconds. You have imagined catching the ball and the team hoisting you on their shoulders in celebration, and you have seen the ball fall through your glove, and people in the stands are throwing food at you. All of this and more runs through your head as that ball swells larger and larger in the sky.

As we drove to school, all I could see was that ball hurtling at me, and I just knew I was going to drop it.

Kyle had no idea how freaked out I was.

At least I hope he didn't. It's hard to read Kyle sometimes. He's smarter than any five guys I know, so knowing what was going on in that head of his is always a tricky proposition. He's always thinking, and that might have been cool if he was a computer or something. For Kyle, thinking can just end up being destructive. It's like he was always playing chess in his mind against himself for stakes that were so high they were damned frightening.

He clung to my hand as we drove, which, I had to admit, helped me relax more than a little. I had already bolted from doing this last Friday, and I wanted to do the same all over again.

Kyle was nervous; I mean, who wouldn't be? But if he knew these people like I did, he'd be pissing himself. I'm sure that, to outsiders, the Popular People might seem like they have it made, but the reality is much different. And a lot darker.

As I park the car, let me break it down for you so you can be prepared:

Only so many people can be popular in a given place at any particular time. I figured out, by the way, that isn't just for high school. The Rule of Popularity Limitation is pretty much universal. As far as I know, it applies all the way to Hollywood and the world in general. There is always a hot girl and then the ones around her. Doesn't matter if you are talking about Marilyn Monroe or Megan Fox, there is always an It girl who captures the boys' attention and the girls' envy. There isn't a rhyme or reason for why this happens, but there is just a something that people see and are attracted to. It isn't about tits or ass or any of that. I mean, sure, the physical stuff *helps*, but in the end, what grabs the attention is attitude more than actual physical looks. And there is only one spot that can be filled by one Girl—or Guy—of the Moment. One.

Like Britney Spears: when she was hot, she was *so* hot. I mean, I remember being seven and thinking I was going to lose it when I saw her videos. She was It and everyone knew that. And then there were the girls around her. Christina Aguilera, Mandy Moore, Jessica Simpson—the list goes on and on. Now, there is nothing wrong with those girls. If you were to break it down attribute by attribute, there were better singers, better bodies, better dancing, better everything. Yet in the minds of everyone else, all those girls were just second to Britney. They were just *girls*. Britney was *It*.

And that is how people are. They fixate on that person. Everyone else is compared to them and always found wanting. I'm sure what I'm saying is nothing earth-shattering to anyone. It's not like I have the launch codes or anything. But here is the rest of that reality: you either know you are It or that you are not It. Knowing that simple fact changes who you are inside for the rest of your life. And not in a sunshine and flowers way, either. Knowing that you're It also means you know you have a shelf life. From the second that someone tags you and you become "It," a timer starts counting down over your head. If you're not "It," you just stare at that clock and wait. There is only a finite amount of attention that people can focus, only a finite amount of attention on one person, and only for so long before their attention shifts. That means if someone becomes more popular, someone else just becomes less popular. It sounds stupid, but it's the way it is for those of us who live on the adoration of others.

Once you enter that race to the top you are forever looking around you to see if there is someone you can pull down on your way. You wonder why pretty girls are so bitchy? Because they know every slur that the other girl takes means one step closer to the top of the food chain. You ever ask yourself why jocks always seem to be fighting? It's because we are just a few IQ points away from pissing on stuff to claim it as our own. We are all sharks swimming in the same small tank, wondering who's going to fall asleep first so the rest of us can have lunch. Not everyone thinks like this—they simply act like this out of survival, and most of it is subconscious behavior.

I always knew that there was something inside of me that, if it came out, would make me the very opposite of everything that makes up a popular person. So I guess I was always aware of how cutthroat popularity was, because it was just a matter of time before it was taken away from me. I could, or at least I hoped I could, handle what I always knew might happen.

Kyle was the one that I was worried about.

He wasn't used to any kind of attention; he'd been careful to avoid any attention at all, for Pete's sake. For someone to go from school unknown to school pariah over a weekend was a lot to ask.

I hadn't realized how long I had been sitting, lost in thought, until Kyle squeezed my hand and asked, "You okay?"

I looked over at him and felt an ache in my chest when I realized how much I liked him. I had never felt like I did with Kyle. Not with Kelly, not Jennifer, not with any of the people I had dated. I had liked them, sure, and they had even turned me on; but when I looked at this boy, my mind lost the ability to comprehend simple concepts like breathing and speech. I couldn't get close enough to him, and knowing how much I needed to be with him scared the bejeezus out of me. But that fear always ran like a bitch every time he smiled at me. The sincerity in everything he felt and said made me feel like a fraud in comparison. Then I saw Julie Benson walk by the car with one of her friends, and they laughed when they saw who I was in the car with.

Just like that, the fear was back.

I slipped my hand out of his and tried to ready myself for this. I could see the uncertainty in his eyes, and I felt horrible, because there was nothing I could do about it. "Look, Kyle, this is going to suck pretty badly, and I can't imagine it's going to get better anytime soon. So let's make a promise. No matter what happens, we don't take it out on each other. It's going to be us against everybody else; the last thing we need is to turn on each other, okay?"

I could tell he didn't understand exactly what I was talking about, but I thought I knew the danger of the next few weeks. We were going to have no one else but each other to rely on, and if we alienated each other, we were truly fucked.

He just nodded and looked as frightened as I had ever seen him.

"Ready or not," I said, trying to show him my most confident grin before we got out of the car.

After I swung the door shut, I forced myself not to
how close the ball was to me.

Kyle

LESS than twenty minutes after I walked into school, I realized I hated
being the center of attention.

The looks I got from everyone—and until that moment, I hadn't
realized how many *everyone* was—as I walked down the hall were
creepy. The whispering from behind me was a little too serial killer for
me. But the suck-cherry on the top of the entire sucky sundae came
when some girl I had never seen before walked up to my locker and
started to talk to me. "So you're, like, the gay guy, right?"

Four years at this high school, two years in junior high, and
another seven years at two different elementary schools, and I was
boiled down to being the gay guy.

I bit back a sigh and closed my locker. "I'm Kyle," I said, trying
not to sound as pissed as I felt.

When I looked, there were, in fact, three girls instead of just the
one. I assumed either they were like a soaking wet Gremlin and
multiplied over time, or I had just missed them walking up. If she
understood the difference between referring to me as "the gay guy" and
using my actual name, the knowledge was lost between her vapid gaze
and her single AAA-battery brain. Clueless, but on a mission, she just
stumbled on with her question. "Um, right. So you're the one who
turned Brad gay, right?"

As stupid as this might sound, I honestly didn't think that there
were people who still believed that.

I mean, sure, I got that I was outed as being gay now and that
people were going to know about Brad and me. But the thought that
some people might be so ignorant as to think someone can be "turned"
gay had just never crossed my mind. Who thinks this crap? Like
homosexuality is a contagious disease. And if it *was* contagious,

wouldn't a group of us have left packages of infected plaid shirts and jock straps lying around to turn the guys we wanted? I was hoping that AAA-Battery girl was asking a sad and completely inappropriate question for the sake of being sarcastic, or maybe making a joke. But I could tell from the unblinking stares from her and her friends, and the way other people slowed in the hallway to hear my answer, that she was asking a serious question.

"Yes," I said, turning to face her directly. "Yes, I did. I took Brad Greymark, one of the most popular guys in school, and used my gay magic on him to turn him into one of us." Her eyes got wide, and she looked at each of her friends' faces in disbelief. I realized too late that she really thought I was answering her honestly. *Foster, Texas, Kyle. Remember. Foster, Texas.*

Before I could say anything else, they began to laugh and wandered off like a flock of peroxide-addled sheep.

A couple of the guys shook their heads at me and walked by, no doubt hoping they could resist my "gay magic." All I knew was that I had probably just made Brad's day worse without even trying. Of course, the thought that my day was just starting to spiral downward hadn't even entered my mind yet.

When I walked into Civics, the buzz of half a dozen whispered conversations stopped. Three guesses who they were talking about. I sat down and pulled out my book while the whispers slowly began to start up again. I caught Brad's name a few times and the word "fag" at least once. I focused my attention on a random page in my book and struggled to find a way to turn off my hearing. If you were wondering, turning off my hearing is not a superpower I happen to possess.

If anything, I had become almost hyperaware of the conversations around me over the years. One of the practical advantages of being socially invisible was that people talked about almost anything in front of you. I had adapted almost secret-agent levels of eavesdropping, and that was messing me up at the moment since I could hear what everyone else was saying.

"I don't get it."

"Him? Why him?"

"I didn't even know he was in our class."

"Brad must be into nobodies."

"He's kinda cute."

That one got my attention, but I forced myself not to look up to see where it came from. I was cute? *Now* I was cute? I mean, how long had I sat here next to these people, but it took this to be considered cute. I swear I didn't understand how the world worked. I had looked up to see how much longer before class started when my phone vibrated in my jeans. I pulled it out and saw a text from Brad.

BRAD: I hate my life.

I knew how he felt.

KYLE: I hate your life too.

BRAD: Hey you started this!! lol

KYLE: You kissed me jackass!!

BRAD: That doesn't count. You threw wood first. <g>

KYLE: I hate you.

BRAD: GTG class starting.

I didn't even notice until I had put my phone away that I had a Stepford robot smile plastered on my face. My face felt weird as I forced it back to normal and had to wonder how screwed up my life was that smiling was considered an experience outside of normal for me. When I did look around, I saw a few dozen people look down quickly, and I realized that I had just added more fuel to the fire.

Thankfully, Mr. Richardson walked in, with the tardy bell right on his heels.

"Okay, settle down," he said, grabbing his own book off the table. "We left off on Rosa Parks last week, and her arrest in Alabama. Anyone want to explain why she was arrested?"

Of course no one raised their hands because if there is anything worse than being the guy who thinks knowing the answer is cool, it's being the person who has to prove they know the answer by raising their hand all Mr. Kotter-style. I wasn't the only person in the room who knew the answer, but I was just as afraid to raise my hand as everyone else. He finally called on someone who mumbled a barely audible, "Um, because she was black?"

There were a few snickers from people, and the person who answered tried to shrink back into their chair. Mr. Richardson gave the room a death glare, which was the teacher equivalent of throwing gasoline on a brushfire of embarrassment before it turned into an inferno of humiliation. There's nothing worse than being laughed at in class while the teacher stomps a foot and claps their hands in an anemic attempt to regain control. It had never happened to me because, until recently, no one could have actually proven I went to Foster High. But I had seen it, and the torture looked horrific.

Mr. Richardson had begun to explain what Rosa Parks was actually arrested for when I heard a fake-ass whisper from behind me. "Maybe she wanted to do it on the bus like Kyle, here, huh?" There is a physical reaction that comes when you realize someone is talking directly to you. It's a bit like a flush, but instead of warmth, it's a chill that transcends any reaction you have had from a drop in temperature. It runs down your spine, and it's what I must imagine being chased in a horror movie must feel like: that moment when the fear turns to panic, and no matter how hard you scream at yourself to move, nothing in your body wants to listen to anything you have to say on the matter.

I knew he saw me stiffen up because his douche bag laughter followed, echoed by the snorting chuckles of two other people. He was performing for an audience.

"That's what you want, right?" he whispered again. "To get it in the back of the bus like a little bitch?"

I should have been scared. I should have been terrified, to be honest. Minus walking into class buck naked, this had been my nightmare for the past decade, hands down. Getting ridiculed for something I had done was bad enough, but being mocked for being gay? I think I would have preferred going to class naked, as long as it wasn't so cold my junk didn't look like it belonged to an infant.

"Least, that's what I heard. Brad bopping his boyfriend on the bus like all good faggots do."

I stress again: I should have been scared. But I wasn't.

I was furious.

I stood up and turned around to glare at the asshole. The look on his face went from cruel leer to absolute shock in two seconds flat. Mr. Richardson stopped talking as the entire class held its breath. "She *didn't* want to sit in the back of the bus, you retard!" I screamed at him. "She didn't want to do it in the back: she refused to move to the back." The people behind him covered their mouths as they reveled in their comrade's embarrassment. "And if you have something to say, why not be a man and stand the fuck up and say it out loud?"

There was an audible gasp as the class reacted to me swearing. There were few taboos in high school that can shock a class of teenagers, but swearing in front of a teacher will always be one of them. "Mr. Stilleno," Richardson called out loudly. I ignored him.

"Does anyone else have anything they want to say?" I asked, looking around the class. "Yes, I'm gay. Yes, I'm dating Brad. I have no idea if he's gay; if you want to know, ask him. And if you want to know what we've done, feel free to describe to me in detail what you've done sexually, and I'll be more than willing to share." I thought people's eyes were going to fall out of their heads from the way everyone looked at me with stark amazement. "It's the twenty-first century; I cannot believe my sex life warrants this much conversation. Are we done?"

My heart was pounding in my chest like it was a gerbil trying to escape Richard Gere's house.

I'm sorry, that was uncool of me. Richard Gere has done nothing to me but make me love him in *Pretty Woman*, and for me to lash out like that was just tacky.

My heart was pounding in my chest like it was a kid trying to escape Michael Jackson's house.

See? Again uncool. I am a huge MJ fan, and he's dead, so again, my bad.

I was close to pissing my pants as I realized I had stood up in front of the entire class and essentially dared them to ask me about my sex life.

I turned around and saw Mr. Richardson gaping at me with no earthly idea of what to do next. "What to do when the gay kid loses his shit during class" was not covered in the teacher handbook. I grabbed my book and backpack and tossed my stuff inside. "Don't bother," I said, saving him the trouble. "I'm on the way to the principal."

The room was dead silent as I slammed the door open. Insane or not, I knew I just did something that most people would have thought impossible for me less than an hour ago.

I just gave them something else to talk about.

This was the second time in a week I'd been in the principal's office. Two times was exactly two more times than I had been in the last ten years combined. Mr. Raymond walked into his office, no doubt holding my file, which I'm pretty sure was heavier than it had been last week. He sat down behind his desk but said nothing as he kept reading whatever it was that was contained within my mythical permanent record. I am sure Mr. Richardson had called over before me and informed them of my Rosa Parks meltdown and that Mr. Raymond was once again stymied by what the hell was wrong with me this time.

"Kyle," he said, closing the folder. "Another bad day?"

I don't know if it was nerves or just a lifetime of pent-up frustration bubbling up despite my best efforts, but a sharp bark of laughter escaped my mouth before I could stop it. When I saw the blatant lack of amusement on his face, I tried to sober up, but it was too late, I had caught the giggles. I'm not sure if The Giggles is an ailment that is unique to the socially undeveloped, but I know that I had a bad case of it. Helpless to do anything else, I covered my mouth and looked away from the ever-deepening scowl spreading across his features.

"Did I say something funny?" he asked, no doubt hoping his tone might act like a glass of cold water in my face.

No luck.

"Bad day?" I asked, wiping the tears from my eyes. "Bad day? Mr. Raymond, I have been having a bad life so far."

He cleared his throat as he waited for me to regain my composure.

"I'm sorry, sir, but no, I'm not having a good day." I tried again without the laughing. "I suppose that's because I came out last Thursday, and it isn't going well." His only reaction was arching one eyebrow in surprise, so I went on. "Kelly kind of cornered me, and I just admitted it. So I suppose it's out there now, and it's been a hard morning so far. A guy in Civics class began going on about it, and I lost it."

He had his fingers steepled in front of his face, which looked confused, as if my words were in some foreign language and he had to translate them. After a few seconds of silence, he finally asked. "So, then, you admitted to others you were gay?" I nodded, not sure what part he hadn't heard the first time, but hey, better late than never, right? "To other students? You actually said it out loud?" Another nod. "Well, then, I'm afraid there isn't much we can do about it."

I tried not to drop my jaw in shock.

"You had to be aware that this news was going to be taken with some trepidation by most," he went on, getting up from behind his desk and starting to pace the room. "This is North Texas, Kyle, and people around here just aren't going to accept it." He looked back to me, and I saw not one iota of compassion in his face; if I didn't know any better, I would have said he was angry. "Now, if anyone threatens you with physical harm or actually hits you, of course, we will intervene, but you had to be ready for this when you 'came out'." He added air quotes to the last two words, the distaste in his voice evident.

"I didn't come out; I was being bullied by Kelly," I retorted, trying to get my metaphorical feet under me.

"Either way," he said, opening my file quickly and scribbling something down on the first page. "I would suggest just staying away from those people for the time being."

"How long would that be?" I asked, not so much shocked as I was pissed.

He looked up again. Closing my folder, he offered, "We are only six months away from graduation."

I could say nothing to that. I was floored: he pretty much told me to just tough it out until school was over. When it became obvious I wasn't going to say anything back, he added, "Second period is ready to start. You might want to make sure you aren't late."

Part of my brain realized he was dismissing me, because I got up and grabbed my backpack automatically. The rest of my brain could not believe this was happening. "So you aren't going to do anything?"

His gaze got stern as he realized I wasn't just going away. "There are over a thousand students in this school, Mr. Stilleno, and I can assure you a majority of them will not agree with your 'lifestyle choice'." Again with the air quotes. "If you were expecting special treatment, you were wrong."

"Special?" I sputtered, wondering if I had hit my head and woken up in the fifties.

"As long as there is no physical threat, there is nothing we can do," he informed me with all the emotion of a fish. "We can't make people like what you are."

I knew this would be bad, but I never imagined it would be *this* bad.

The bell rang, and he looked up at the clock. "You're going to be late," he said in a casual tone, as if we had just been talking about what was for lunch.

I turned around and walked out, knowing if I opened my mouth again I was going to scream.

And probably not stop.

The next period was about the same: whispers that stopped when I walked in, giggles as I went by, a couple of rude suggestions from behind my chair, and a long line of nothing from the teacher. I thought maybe Mrs. Jackson didn't know what was going on, but that thought was dashed when Mr. Raymond walked in halfway through class. He pulled her aside and whispered something while they both glanced over at me. That's the moment I realized: everything that had occurred so far was just a prelude to the fuckery that was about to follow.

Or, in other words, my bad day had just begun.

Brad

THIS day could not get any worse.

Bad enough that I was getting the Elephant Man treatment as I walked down the halls, but as I walked by I could hear the Creeping Whisper follow me all the way to class. The Creeping Whisper is a virus that moves from person to person as Patient Zero walks down the hall. I steadily ignored the buzz the best I could, but I could hear what they were saying when they thought I was out of earshot, and none of it was surprising.

"There he is; I heard he turned gay."

"Kelly Aimes is saying that he tried to make a pass at him during football camp."

"I heard Jennifer say he kept trying to get her to sleep with him and his boyfriend; that was why she broke up with him."

It's nice to know that, no matter how long and well you may think you know someone, the human instinct to cover the crack of the ass supersedes everything, and when the chips are down, it's every man for himself. I expected Kelly to lie like a dog, but Jennifer was surprising, even if I couldn't blame her. She had been broadsided by this, and if I had possessed even a tenth of the feelings I previously had stated out loud for her, I would have given her a heads-up before my declaration. I wish I could say that I wanted to hurt her, even a little, but the truth of the matter was, she didn't even cross my mind when I kissed Kyle.

So I couldn't fault her for bashing me.

My first class was English, a class I always found slightly confusing, since most of what the teacher bitched about had frighteningly little to do with actual English. We learned some kind of weird, formal version of English that I've never heard one person in my entire life use. Worse, every year we were forced to rehash what we'd learned before and then soak up some more odd rules about things like subjunctives.

As with all my classes, I sat with whatever members of the team were there with me. We usually commandeered a corner in the back and spent most of the class busting each other up while waiting for the bell to ring. So I headed to the back, where Sam and Oscar were already sitting, and tossed my backpack on my desk.

They both got up at the same time and moved to a couple of seats on the other side of the room.

I spent the rest of the class sitting in the back with no one sitting by me. I was so depressed I couldn't even be pissed. I'm not sure what I had thought people's reactions would be, but that one move alone kind of floored me into stunned silence. I spent the whole hour just wondering if this was how the rest of my senior year was going to be. When the bell rang, I ignored everything and just focused on what was in front of me and nothing more. It took me a couple of minutes to realize that what I was doing was how Kyle had spent the past four years of high school, and who knew how many years before that.

I eased up on my pity party a little and realized it was tough all over.

I had gym second period, and I'd been looking forward to letting off some of the pent-up aggression that had been building since last Thursday. I tossed my backpack into my locker and had begun to strip my shirt off when I heard a voice ask from behind me, "What the fuck do you think you're doing?"

I yanked my shirt off and tossed it aside as I turned around and found Cory, Tony, and Josh standing there with their arms folded, looking very pissed. "What the hell?" I asked, already fed up with this day, and it was only second period.

Tony repeated himself slowly, "I asked, what do you think you're doing?" He was obviously the ringleader, because I could see Cory and Josh just hanging back, letting him do all the talking.

Obviously they weren't going to go away until they had their fun, so I just played along. "I'm dressing out for gym, the same as I've done for the last four years; can I help you?" Tony was in shape, but we both knew he wasn't in my league. I was curious how far he was going to push this shit.

"This is the boys' locker room," he said with a sneer. "Not a fag hangout."

I am going to be honest with you, I assume he was trying to say "hangout," but I'm not sure because he never finished the word. My fist made contact with his jaw half a second after "fag."

He went down hard. Maybe he thought I was going to have a little more patience than that, and I'd caught him off guard. Blood gushed from his nose, and I'm sure he had discovered he'd read that one wrong. I moved to follow up, hoping to end things once and for all. I thought if I rearranged Tony's face now it might quiet the rest of these assholes before things got out of hand. But as I descended on him, I suddenly realized why exactly Josh and Cory had tagged along.

They each grabbed one of my arms and pulled me off Tony, holding me in place while he scrambled to his feet. Now, I might have been in better shape than Josh, Cory, and Tony individually, but all three of them together were more than strong enough to keep me down. I caught a glimpse out of the corner of my eye: other guys were watching silently, but not one of them made a move to help me. Who could blame them? This wasn't some four-eyed geek getting bullied by a couple of jocks, or a freshman getting hazed by seniors who had a hair up their ass, this was one of the most popular guys in school being beat down by three other guys who one week earlier might have taken a bullet for him.

This was Darwinism at its finest, a pretty good representation of how the dinosaurs fell into extinction.

Tony's first punch into my gut didn't hurt that much. The second not so much, either. By the fifth I found my abs were burning from the impact, and it was getting harder to breathe, a fact that was evidenced by the dots starting to form in front of my eyes. My head fell forward, and I could taste blood in my mouth by the eighth punch.

Someone shouted "He's coming!" across the locker room, and they let me go instantly. I fell to the cement floor like a sack of potatoes, my limbs refusing to answer as I screamed for them to get me upright again. Coach Nuess ran up to us. I'm sure he was speaking English of some kind, but the sound of blood rushing in my ears made him sound more like a *Peanuts* teacher than an actual human being. The three musketeers had, of course, fled already; they were by their lockers changing out while I spit up blood onto the floor as air entered my lungs again.

"Greymark, what the hell is going on?" he asked, no doubt shocked to find me lying on the ground doing a pretty fair impression of a cartoon damsel. "What happened?" he asked, seeing the blood pooling up under me.

I scanned the locker room, and no one would meet my eyes.

Everybody was intently studying either the ceiling or the floor as I struggled to find something to say to him. My instinct was of course to name as many names as I could. It's human nature to point fingers, to bring down retribution on those who have wronged you, but human nature and common sense were two creatures that rarely met in a teenage boy's mind. So instead of sounding like a little bitch and pointing a finger at them I simply said, "I slipped, Coach. My bad."

Of course he didn't believe me. I was shirtless, and my stomach was bright red in a way that only physical contact with another human being could produce. There was more blood under me than was contained in my whole body (at least the way I saw it). The only way that happened was a fight, and we both knew it. Also, we both knew that there wasn't much he could do about it unless I said something.

Which I wouldn't.

"Brad, come on," he said in a low voice. "What's going on?"

Rationally I knew he was trying to help, that the concern in his voice came from that place, but that wasn't how I took it. Every single syllable just dripped with pity to me, and I couldn't stop myself from reacting to it. "I said I slipped," I said a little too loudly. "Can I change out now?"

He looked at my stomach and then at the blood. "No," he answered bluntly. "Go to the nurse. You're not in any shape to work out." He was pissed, and I guess in his shoes I would have been too; I mean, it was his ass if something did happen to me, and I wasn't even trying to help him.

I put my shirt back on and grabbed my backpack before turning to leave. I saw Tony and Cody standing by their lockers, both of them with shit-eating grins on their faces. They didn't look human to me: they looked like hyenas leering at wounded prey, biding their time.

Before I got out the door, someone shouted. "And stay out, fag!"

I had never been so pissed in my life.

Since I had turned seven, locker rooms had been my safe haven. They were a place to prepare for battle, to goof around with friends, and to literally strip down to nothing before building myself up again. I know to most guys a locker room is just a smelly place where you're forced to change clothes every day, but to me it was so much more. And now it was gone.

I stormed off across campus. My stomach was killing me, but it was nothing compared to the feeling of betrayal that swamped and fogged every breath. Why did being gay matter? How was I different? Nothing had changed, and yet everything had changed. I hated the contradictory logic of it with every fiber of my being. I wanted to hit someone, I wanted to cry, and I wanted things to go back to the way they were.

By the time I made it to the nurse's office, I was a mess.

The bleeding in my mouth had stopped, but it was obvious I wasn't going to be doing crunches anytime soon. I must have looked worse than I felt because when I walked into the room, the nurse got up and ran toward me. "Brad? What happened?" she asked in a worried voice.

"Tripped," I answered as the emotions came rushing up inside of me. I felt one racking sob escape from my mouth, and it was like a dam somewhere broke, and everything came rushing out. I just began to cry helplessly, my ability to actually articulate words finally deserting me.

I don't know if she understood me or, because she'd been a high school nurse for a long time, she understood my tone more than the words, but she led me over to one of the three narrow cots and sat me down. "Just relax here for a minute." Her voice was soft, her kindness triggering all kinds of emotional explosions in me. "Do you want me to call your parents?"

I stared up at her, wide-eyed. Talking was still beyond my ability, but I shook my head with what I assumed was a pleading look on my face. It must have been enough, because she tried to calm me by saying slowly, "Okay, okay. You just want to rest here for a second?" I nodded, hating this feeling of weakness that had descended on me. This wasn't me, this wasn't who I was.

At least it wasn't who I used to be.

I lay down on the bed, resting my head on the pillow for a moment, hoping if I closed my eyes for a while maybe I'd wake up to find all this was merely a nightmare. That my life hadn't come crashing off its tracks and wasn't headed toward a head-on collision with everyone—except one person—in school. *Two* periods. Less than two hours into my day, and I was already nursing my wounds in the nurse's office like a little bitch. How could I handle this for the rest of the year? Screw that—how could I handle the rest of the day?

I just didn't have any answers.

Kyle

WHEN I walked into History, I instantly knew something was wrong.

There was a pack of jocks sitting over where Brad usually sat, laughing their asses off. There wasn't anything new about that; it seemed like all they did was sit off to the side and laugh at their own jokes. What made my spider sense tingle was the way they stopped when I walked in, watching me for a second before bursting out into a new round of guffaws. I looked around to see if Brad was with them, but when there was no sign of him, I began to worry.

I sat down at my desk, still not sure what was so funny.

Tony pantomimed punching someone. A couple of his other friends were almost crying from laughing so hard. I wasn't sure where Brad was, but it was getting pretty late; we had made an agreement not to push things by walking into class together like we were a couple. After all, Foster, Texas, could only handle so much before it broke, so we had decided on trying to keep it as normal as possible. Still, I would have assumed he would have been in class by now since he was dangerously close to being tardy, and he didn't need any more points against him in addition to his academic performance, or lack thereof.

Mr. Gunn walked in, and everyone settled pretty quickly. There were few teachers on campus who attracted the kind of respect Coach Gunn did. It wasn't just the fact that he looked like he could bench-press a dump truck, though it helped. He was just a very no-nonsense kind of man, and no one ever dared to see if they could push him even a little bit. The jocks quieted down because they knew he could end their little jock lives in seconds. Everyone else went quiet because Mr. Gunn always looked like there was an even chance he would slug you if you pissed him off.

The tardy bell rang, and still no Brad. Worry stood up and began to wave a hand for attention.

Coach Gunn had begun to go over the homework we were supposed to have done over the weekend when Nurse Wilder walked in with a note. Everyone stopped, wondering who she had come for since she rarely left her office unless she was pulling someone out of class. Coach Gunn paused as she whispered something to him and handed him the folded paper. He glanced at it, and both of them looked over to where Brad usually sat. Tony and his pack of idiots burst out laughing but tried to cover it when Coach Gunn shot them a look.

That was when I knew something had happened.

It was like sitting on a hot plate knowing something was wrong with Brad and not being able to do anything about it. Nurse Wilder walked out, and Tony and his idiots went through another round of chuckles, which just pissed me off even more. Coach Gunn cleared his throat, which was the equivalent of DEFCON 2 for him. The room quieted down some, but being quiet didn't mean squat to me. They obviously knew something, and the fact that I didn't was torture.

Time ceased to have meaning; my mind kept narrowing in on what had happened to Brad. I knew Coach Gunn was talking about something, but my entire focus was on Tony and the way he whispered to his friends when he thought the coach wasn't paying attention. I wished I had some kind of super hearing or could read lips like a spy so I could decode what Tony was saying. I must have been staring like a freak because one of his friends noticed and pointed it out to him.

He turned and looked at me angrily.

Obviously homophobia outweighed common sense, because he interrupted Coach Gunn out of nowhere and screamed at me. "See something you like, fruitcake?"

Last week I would have looked away quickly. The Kyle I was last week would have been intimidated by his attack and would want nothing more than for people to forget I existed. Seven days ago, Tony would have been able to do that with impunity.

Unfortunately for both of us, it wasn't last week.

"No," I answered him from across the room. "I'm into guys."

Obviously most of the class had been just waiting for some sort of action: we had everyone's attention almost instantly.

"What the fuck did you just say, faggot?" Tony jumped out of his seat.

I stood up as well. "I said I'm not into ugly girls!"

As with most high school conflicts, the atmosphere automatically turned toward the gladiatorial. The "fight, fight" chant began somewhere in the back of the class, and the effect of the word on Tony and me was almost chemical. I have no idea what I thought I was going to do to him, but I did know I wasn't backing down. He knew exactly what he was going to do, and we both knew he wasn't backing down, either. His fists were clenched, and it was painfully obvious that he intended to take a swing at me. I'm sure this was an intimidating concept to most guys my age since nine out of ten "fights" in high school ended up like Kelly and me: some shouting followed up by chest bumping and snarling with an occasional shove or two. Throwing an actual punch was as rare as it was surprising, so I am sure Tony thought the threat of a punch would be all he needed to do.

What Tony didn't know was that I had been punched before.

In fact, I had been punched by guys much older and much bigger than he was, so the thought of having him swinging at me was not that scary. It was simply an annoyance. There had been times when my mom hadn't wanted to discipline me, for whatever reason. At those times, she sent her boyfriend du jour into my room to take care of the problem.

Tony started to swing, and I ducked under his reach easily. Coach Gunn grabbed me from behind, but instead of my shirt, all he had was a handful of my backpack. I jumped at Tony's stomach as I shucked the pack off my shoulders. I connected with him, and we both went flying backward. His desk was knocked to the side as we fell; he grabbed the front of my shirt before we hit the floor.

Which was when my knee connected with his groin.

I wish I could say that when I jumped at him I had a whole plan to take away the advantage of his superior reach and follow it up by a shot to his balls, but I didn't. All I knew was that there was something wrong with Brad, and this asshole wouldn't stop laughing about it. The blow was more about my legs being too long and his crotch getting in my way. He let out a satisfying scream as every single part of his body froze, waiting for the inevitable explosion of agony that every man loathes.

He let go of my shirt as he went from the offensive to the defensive instantly. His hands moved up to block his face, which might have been the end of it, if something in me hadn't snapped. He stopped being a human being to me, ceased being Tony and became something else entirely.

He was something weaker than me. And he had hurt Brad.

Seeing him flat on his back, unable to defend himself, I kneed him again, this time not for Brad but for me. I didn't know anything until Coach Gunn yanked me off Tony in one solid motion. I struggled in his grasp, but I was like Mario trying to get free from Donkey Kong. It just wasn't happening. There were sounds coming out of my mouth, but honestly they weren't in any language civilized people spoke. I had a flash of Tony's eyes, wide in shock, as he lay on the floor, wondering where his day had gone horribly wrong while the rest of the class looked on in voyeuristic glee.

And once again, I was the bad guy.

"Kyle!" Gunn said, shaking me back to my senses. I stood tiptoe so he wasn't holding me up off the ground, and I felt like a little kid being scolded by a father I never knew. I tried to shake him off me, but the man was no fool; he held the back of my shirt like you hold a puppy by the scruff of its neck. "Tony, get your ass off the floor now," he barked, ignoring me completely. As the other boy got to his feet, he said in a voice barely above a whisper, "If I let you go and you go at him again, you're going to have to deal with me. Do you understand?"

I did indeed understand.

Tony stood a few steps back from me, the other two jocks flanking him on either side like secret service agents in football jerseys. He was trying to regain his game face, but I could see the very real shock in his eyes as he looked at me. There was being surprised by something and then witnessing something impossible, like water bursting into flame or something falling skyward. What had just happened was honestly beyond his level of comprehension, and it was going to be a while until he was okay with the idea that not every nerd would take being bullied without doing something back.

"What was that about?" the coach asked once it was clear that I wasn't going to pull a Wolverine and try for two in a row. Of course he said nothing, since I had broken the cardinal rule of high school existence. I had landed the first punch. Like some ancient chivalrous code of conduct or the whackjob coeds on reality TV, the person who hit the other first was always at fault.

"He just came at me." Tony was obviously trying to walk that fine line between being the victim who had just been attacked and the jock—the cool guy who was, of course, at no time threatened by the situation. "Maybe it's his time of the month," he added with a smirk.

I took a step toward him, and he flinched closer to his two clones.

Gunn wedged himself between us, but I had made my point so stood my ground. "Kyle, explain yourself."

Before I could answer, Tony interjected, "He's a fag, Coach. He's mad because I don't swing that way."

The coach spun on him and screamed, "Wright! Stow that shit!" A couple of people chuckled, and Tony realized he wasn't on a football field surrounded by like-minded muscle heads. Jocks on football fields responded to swearing, but in a classroom words like that caused far more trouble than they were worth. In a more subdued tone, he said, "We don't call people things like that here."

"But I'm not calling him anything he isn't, Coach!" Tony pointed at me. "Ask him!"

Gunn turned to look at me. "Is this true?"

Remember the good old days when I was just invisible and miserable? Good times.

"Am I gay?" I said as confidently as I could. "Yes. Am I attracted to him?" I said, locking eyes with Tony. "No, since I only like men and not little bitches who can't take a hit."

Tony took a step at me, his fist raised, but obviously Gunn was ready. His hand engulfed the enraged jock's fist before it even got close to me, stopping him in his tracks. "Next time anyone takes a swing at anyone, I am going to be the one hitting back." He glanced at both of us. "We clear?"

Tony took a step back, rubbing his hand. "Yes, sir," he answered, half pouting.

I just shrugged.

"Stilleno, to the office. Wright, sit down now," Gunn ordered after a second.

I was going to argue the punishment until I remembered that the office was where I had been wanting to head to before this asshole had opened his mouth. Instead, I just turned and walked out of class; the only thing on my mind was finding Brad.

Brad

I MUST have passed out, because when I opened my eyes again, Kyle was there.

"Am I dreaming?" I asked as I tried to sit up. There was an ache that felt like I had just done a thousand crunches, and I instantly fell back onto the cot. "Okay, so not dreaming."

"Don't get up," he said a little bit too late. "Are you okay?"

I nodded, keeping my eyes closed as I tried to focus past the pain. "Peachy." I was unable to keep myself from wincing.

I heard him sigh and mumble, "So I guess we're broadening the definition of okay to include massive abdominal pain." I cracked one eye open and saw the worry on his face. "Did Tony do this?"

That brought me up short. I didn't care how much it hurt, I moved myself into a sitting position. "Where did you hear that?"

Something moved across his features so fast I thought I might have imagined it. His eyes got cold, and his lips pursed in what anyone else would have called fury. I had never seen anger from him before. Even back at the diner he hadn't shown this much emotion. Just as quickly, though, it passed, and my Kyle was back. "I didn't hear it, I just figured it out." I gave him a look that made it obvious I did not in any way believe that. He was smart but not even Sherlock Holmes could have come to that conclusion. When Kyle saw I wasn't buying it, he added, "I heard him bragging about it in History." My pulse began to race, and I clenched my fists in frustration. He put his hand over mine and said with a smile, "It's okay, I'm pretty sure his stomach isn't feeling any better right now."

I looked at him in shock. "Did you hit Tony Wright?"

He looked down shyly and shrugged. "I didn't actually hit him," he answered quietly. "I may have tackled him to the ground and then kneed him." I know my mouth fell open in amazement when he amended it with a proud, "Twice, to be honest."

I have had friends before.

I mean, I had a lot of people who called themselves my friends over the years. When someone is the golden boy of the school, there is no shortage of people trying to gain favor in one way or another. I don't say this to brag; I am just making you aware. I have never felt as if I had been lacking in the companion department. But as I looked up and realized that this guy, this wonderful boy who never wanted more than to be invisible, had just gone toe to toe with the school's running back to defend my honor, I knew for a fact that everyone who had come before meant nothing compared to him. I had possessed acquaintances and lackeys, sycophants and hangers-on, in every shape and variety. In all my eighteen years I had never seen what I saw sitting on a crappy nurse's bed as he knelt next to me.

It was at that very moment I realized I was in love with Kyle Stilleno.

If you'd asked me last week, I would have told you I never wanted to be saved by someone else. The very thought that I might be so weak as to need another person to come charging in to rescue me would have been insultingly ridiculous. I stand over six feet tall, weigh 179, and can bench press 275 pounds on a good day. Until that moment, lying beat to hell on a cot in the health office, the thought that I needed to be saved from anything had never entered my mind.

The cold hard fact was that I hadn't needed to be saved now, but it just felt so fucking awesome that someone had tried that I couldn't help myself.

I leaned forward and threw my arms around him. He stiffened in surprise as I squeezed him tight while I forced myself not to cry. He relaxed and hugged me back. I could feel him rest his head in the crook of my neck as we both surrendered to each other for a moment. "You're crazy," I whispered to him.

I felt him chuckle. "That's one word for it," he replied tiredly.

I pulled back and looked into his eyes. "What's another?"

His eyes were watering too, as we stared directly into each other's souls for a brief second. "Love?"

I felt my mouth explode into a smile before the emotion actually registered with my brain. There was literally nothing I could do to stop myself from kissing him.

So I did.

It was a perfect moment, and for a few seconds, the pain and anguish of the day seemed to fade away as I was engulfed in the emotion he generated effortlessly in me. I had never felt like this about anyone before, and I didn't know about him, but I didn't want it to ever end.

Which of course it did, seconds later.

"That's enough of that," a voice warned from the doorway. Kyle practically shoved me away as we both looked over to find the assistant principal, Mr. Adler, standing in the doorway, scowling. "If you're feeling better, Mr. Greymark, perhaps you and Mr. Stilleno will join me in my office?"

He didn't wait for an answer; instead he just turned around and walked away.

Kyle looked over at me nervously, and I had to laugh. He could fearlessly face off against football players but the possibility of getting dressed down by an assistant principal caused him to shake in his boots. It was just too cute.

"Well, if it gets too bad, you beat the hell out of him while I'm on lookout," I said to him wryly. He lightly punched my shoulder, but I had made him smile, and that was enough. I tried to stand, but my stomach rebelled on me again, and I paused, unable to suppress a groan. It was the wrong thing to do, of course, because now he knew how hurt I was.

"Don't get up!" he said, almost pushing me back onto the cot.

"How long you think he's gonna wait for us?" I asked, trying to keep my balance. "Just help me get upright. I'll be fine." Of course I had no idea if that would be true or not, but I couldn't worry him about it. It was pretty evident by the look on his face that he knew I was conning him, but there was no denying that Adler was waiting for us to show up, and if he had to walk back here again to get us, it was only going to make it worse.

"I'm fine," I assured him when he didn't move to help me. "I promise."

He tried to stifle the sigh of frustration as he helped me up, but I could still hear it.

It hurt like hell, but by leaning on his shoulder I was able to get upright. Once I was standing, the pain wasn't so bad. As long as I didn't clench my abs by bending over or laughing I should be fine. I looked over at him and nodded. Kyle had a look on his face that made me feel like I was going to collapse at any point. He stayed close as we walked out of the nurse's room and toward Adler's office.

Everyone tried not to stare, but they were about as subtle as a car wreck as they looked at us and then away quickly. The whispering didn't help any, either, but what was I supposed to do? Shout at them? Demand to know what they were saying? I knew what they were saying. *So those are the gay kids, and I heard the red-haired one used to be straight, with a girlfriend and everything.* It wasn't the curiosity that pissed me off, it was the look of pity in their eyes. They watched us like we were condemned men walking toward the electric chair.

No, that's not right. Let me rephrase that.

We were rightfully condemned men walking toward the electric chair; sad, but it was what we deserved for what we had done. That was what really pissed me off.

"Take a fucking picture!" I snapped at them when their curiosity became too much to deal with.

Kyle put a hand on my shoulder and whispered, "Just ignore them."

I felt like turning around and kissing him right there to make a point. Throwing him down on the ground and making them watch us was a nice pipe dream but probably had more to do with my attraction to him than anything else.

Adler wasn't alone when we walked into his office.

He had another assistant principal with him along with Mr. Davis, the head principal of Foster High. The only time I had seen Davis out of his office was when he accepted all the credit for one of our teams going to state. Like it was his fat ass that had been sweating blood, sweat, and tears on the field. Having him in the room stopped me cold, though; he did not spend his hard-earned calories for anything this side of an apocalypse.

"Ah, good; you're both here," Davis said, gesturing to the two chairs in front of the desk. "Brad, Kyle, thank you for coming." The insinuation that he said it as if we had a choice made me sick. "We've had some problems today, have we?"

I was about to say something rude myself when Kyle popped off with, "No offense, Yoda, but can we get down to it?" I looked over at him in shock, and he just shrugged back at me. "What? We both know this isn't going to end happy."

The two assistant principals shifted uncomfortably, but Davis glared at Kyle for a moment before going on as if he hadn't been interrupted. "As you know, here at Foster High, we don't tolerate any kind of fighting at all."

He was about to go on, but Kyle interrupted him again. "So the guys who beat him up will be facing some form of punishment?" he asked, pointing at me.

"You were the one who was sent to the office for fighting, Mr. Stilleno," Davis said with a chill in his voice.

"So I should have let the guys that were belittling me in front of the class just continue?" Kyle asked back.

What the hell had gotten into him? I'd never seen him this pissed off before, and that was including the time I almost broke up with him before we even started going out.

Davis seemed to take a second to gather his thoughts before starting again. "Okay, bottom line, boys. We have a strict rule against PDAs on campus."

I was confused, since I owned an iPhone, and Kyle's cell barely counted as a phone. I guess my confusion was evident, because Kyle explained, "Public display of affection." And then it started to sink in.

Mr. Adler asked Kyle, "You weren't giving him mouth-to-mouth, were you?"

"You've got to be kidding me" was all Kyle responded with. He looked like he was ready to swing at somebody the way he stood, his arms at his side with hands clenched in anger.

"You'll find we aren't, Kyle," Davis said in what I am sure would be a sympathetic tone to anyone within earshot. "What you two do on your own time is fine and good, but as long as you are on campus you will *not* engage in it again. Is that understood?"

I felt like I was three inches high, but if anything, Kyle just seemed to get angrier.

"So this is going to be enforced for everyone, right?" he asked. All three men stared at him like he was some kind of lower life-form that had had the nerve to address them. "Every cheerleader I see sucking face in the quad, and the people in the halls grabbing a quick feel between periods, they won't be tolerated either, right?"

Davis didn't even blink. "I haven't seen that." I bit my lip rather than ask him when he'd ever left his office to see anything.

"But if you do," Kyle pressed. "That will not be tolerated either, correct?"

Adler's face grew redder and redder as Kyle kept arguing. Finally, he exploded. "We will not allow your kind of filth on campus!" Davis tried to quiet him, but Adler ignored him. "What you two freaks do to each other is your own business, but you will not go around exposing other kids to your perversion."

"Robert!" Mr. Davis barked at him, effectively cutting him off. "Go get a drink," he suggested, though it was no suggestion.

Adler stormed out as Davis tried to calm the room down some. "We are not discussing the rest of the school, we are talking about the two of you. Period." Kyle seemed ready to jump out of his seat and scream, but he bit his tongue. "You'll find that though this is a free country, there are some places that certain types of behavior are just not tolerated." He leaned forward on the desk toward us. "You'll find Foster High is one of those places."

Kyle stood up so fast that I saw Davis flinch back reflexively "Are we done here?" he asked.

"Consider this a verbal warning," Davis said. "Next is suspension, and after that, expulsion."

I felt my stomach do a backflip. Expelled? How could I ever get a scholarship if I was kicked out of school? I stood up quickly and cut Kyle off before he could speak again. "We got it, sir." Kyle gave me a look, but I ignored it. "It won't happen again."

"See it doesn't," Davis suggested. His tone of voice would have been enough to set *me* off, but the threat of expulsion shut me up.

I turned and maneuvered Kyle out before he could make it worse. I shushed him until we were outside; he looked like he was about to spit fire. When we were a good distance away from the office, I let out a sigh of relief. "Are you trying to get us killed?" I asked.

His eyes widened as his mouth opened. "Are you kidding me?"

I tried to keep my voice down. "I can't get expelled, Kyle. I can't!" I grabbed his arms and tried to will my worry into him. "As it is, I'm on academic probation for baseball. You think they are going to let me play if we keep playing chicken with the principal?"

I could see the hurt in his eyes that I wasn't on his side, but this wasn't about love and fluffy feelings. This was real life, and as much as I hated it, they were right. This was north Texas, not California. No one was going to be okay with two guys going at it right in front of their eyes. He had to see that, he just had to.

"Brad," he said after a few seconds. His expression was so full of sadness, of grief, that my aching abs clenched again instinctively. "What makes you think they are going to let you play baseball, period?" My grip on him collapsed as what he'd said crashed through my anger and fear. He stood close but didn't touch me, knowing, I think, that I needed to hear what he'd said. Blindsided, I reached for him, and only then did he reach back. Grabbing his hand was like grabbing an ironwood rod: for those seconds, I didn't need anyone other than him to be there.

When he spoke, I heard the same rage that had filled him when he'd seen me in the nurse's office.

"What they are doing is wrong," he snarled. "And if we don't do something, who will?" I had no answers, and he knew it. He shook his head, not angry at me, but sad; then he gently pulled his hand from my grip and walked away.

Leaving me feeling more lost than ever.

Kyle

THE rest of the day was as bad as you'd expect.

Everyone knew something had gone down, and apparently they also knew we had come down on the wrong side of said something. Every adult who saw us watched us like we were wearing black trench coats and just casing the joint, and every student smirked like they had caught us doing something wrong. Brad was quiet, and I couldn't blame him since I think he was just coming to terms with how fucked we were. I had imagined how horrible it would be if I ever had to come out, but those images were nothing compared to the reality. We sat on the steps of the music room in silence as people walked by, staring at us like we were rare animals on display.

"And if you look to your right you will see a mated pair of North American homosexuals. Please don't get too close, they spit."

I picked at my sandwich as I watched Brad. He seemed worse than depressed or upset—he looked beaten. He didn't look up when someone walked by, no matter what they said, and they were saying plenty.

"Hey, look, it's the queer couple."

"I didn't know we had a gay bar out here."

"Are they filming *Queer as Folk?*"

He didn't even acknowledge their existence until Kelly walked by.

"Hey, Brad," he called out, all casual, like he'd just run into him at the mall. "Lemme ask you something."

Brad looked up at him with eyes devoid of all life, and I felt myself shiver a little.

When Brad didn't say anything back, Kelly just kept talking as if he had. "You don't mind if I go out with Jennifer, right? 'Cause I'm sure she is dying to know what it feels like with a real man."

Brad choked back a groan as his muscles protested and stood up in a second; if I hadn't been ready there would have been no way for me to stop him. His chest pressed against mine angrily as I blocked his way. He roared at Kelly, which was bad, since his mouth was right next to my ear. "Come say that to my face!" I was leaning into him with all my strength, and he was still moving down the steps toward Kelly. "Walk up here and fucking say that to my face!"

Kelly took a step back, playing it off like he was pretending, but I had seen his eyes grow wide for a second before he realized I was holding Brad back. "Hey, look!" Kelly called out to the guys around him. "He wants me to go up there and get in his face." Turning to Brad, he spoke slowly as if speaking to a child. *"I'm not like that."* He pointed at his chest. *"Me straight, you fag!"*

Both Brad and I went down another step, and I knew I couldn't keep him back for much longer. I screamed over my shoulder at Kelly, "Get out of here, you asshole!" It just made him and his friends laugh even louder. I looked at Brad and pleaded in a voice only he could hear, "Please, please don't do this." No response. "If you hit him, you're gone, you know that?" Still nothing. "You won't be able to play baseball."

That got his attention.

His eyes locked with mine, and I could see the green in them was brighter than I'd ever seen before. It took me a second to realize it was from tears. In a pretty accurate imitation of what I had said before, he sarcastically asked me. "What makes you think they're going to let me play baseball?"

It felt like he had slapped me across the face.

My hands dropped, and he pushed past me instantly. I heard him and Kelly start to go at it, but I honestly couldn't focus on anything but the fact that Brad blamed me for everything. I wasn't the one who kissed him. Well, I kissed back, but he started it! And I wasn't the one who asked him to come out in front of everyone! I was the one who was telling him at the time not to do it. But this was my fault?

I turned around and found Kelly and Brad chest to chest, each one daring the other to make the first move. I imagined I could smell the testosterone as I approached them. Ignoring Kelly, I stepped between them and glared at Brad. "Are you kidding me?" He took a half step back in shock, but I wasn't letting him. "You're pissed at me? Do you think it is my fault they aren't going to let you play?"

"I didn't say that!" he answered quickly, making it pretty obvious that was exactly what he had meant.

"Sure sounded like it," I answered just as quickly, making it even more obvious I was calling him on his bullshit.

"Well, I didn't mean that," he said in a much lower voice.

"Then what did you mean?" I held my breath for his answer.

It was obvious he didn't know what to say. He opened his mouth and then closed it once he saw how angry I was. I might have let what had happened go, seeing how flustered he was, but that wasn't going to happen, because Kelly had to open his big mouth.

"Awww, look," he said from behind me. "Lovers' quarrel!"

I spun on Kelly and slammed the flat of both my palms into his chest. His arms pinwheeled as he fell back into his friends; they caught him before he hit the ground and then pushed him toward me. I raised my fist, and part of my mind realized I was about to throw my first punch at another human being in anger.

And then Brad pulled me out of the way.

Kelly stumbled past where I was, his fist passing through where I had just been standing. Now it was Brad holding me back as I fought to follow up on Kelly. "Knock it off," Brad said in my ear. "Five-0!"

I had no idea what he was saying until I saw Mr. Adler moving through the crowd in the quad like a shark through a school of minnows. I stopped fighting with Brad as he got closer. Kelly got his bearings and looked over at me with a look that resembled an angry bull. "You're fucking dead, queer!" he screamed as he hurled himself at me.

"*Aimes!*" Alder screamed, stopping the jock in midstride. His head whipped around, and he stared at the man like he was a mirage for a moment. "What is going on here?"

Kelly looked to Brad and me and then back to Adler. "He… I mean…."

Mr. Adler leveled a stare at me. "I thought we'd talked about this?

I pointed at Kelly. "He just took a swing at me and called me a queer, and you're looking at me?"

He took a step closer to me and said, "You're not making this easy on me, Mr. Stilleno."

I fought back the urge to laugh. "Am I supposed to be?"

"He pushed me first!" Kelly fired back, sounding like a five-year-old.

"Is this true?" Adler asked me.

I threw my hands up in exasperation. "I give up." I shrugged Brad's hands off me and grabbed my backpack.

"Going somewhere?" Adler asked.

I looked at Brad, who wouldn't meet my gaze. I sighed and said to Mr. Adler, "According to you, I'm going to hell if I don't change my ways."

I expected him to brush it off, to just ignore the verbal jab and to push on. Instead he said loud enough for everyone to hear, "Not according to me, according to the Bible."

I felt my mouth sag open in disbelief.

"Perhaps you should go home for today," he said after the laughter from the quad had died down. "We obviously have things to sort out."

I pushed past him and ignored the leering faces of the people I passed on my way off campus. I knew Brad wasn't following me, and at this point, I didn't care.

I was alone again.

I know, I know! That line is so emo I should have black eyeliner on while I listen to Paramore on my iPod, but it was how I felt. It wasn't fair; I had spent my entire life preparing for a life lived in solitary confinement, and though I hated it, I was at least ready. I had stockpiled more than enough emotional supplies to prepare myself for the winter of my discontent.

Oh God, I think I *am* emo.

Anyway, I had a bomb shelter's worth of self-pity and platitudes stashed in the depths of my consciousness like a paranoid shut-in waiting for the inevitable zombie outbreak to occur. Sad songs and digital copies of *The Notebook* stockpiled in my own Waco-style.... Okay, I'll stop with the weird metaphors.

To sum up, I had been ready for a life lived with Healthy Choice meals and cats until Brad crashed into me like Paris Hilton after a long night of appletinis and cosmos. Dammit, okay, last metaphor, promise. I walked into my house and froze because there was something deadly wrong with the living room.

It was clean.

Well, maybe not clean to you, but for our place, this was clean. The drapes were open, which meant the room was exposed to actual sunlight, a rarity unto itself. The beer and weed table, what normal people called the coffee table, was clear of all debris, and it looked like it had been wiped down recently. All those signs could mean only one thing.

She was sober.

"Kyle?" she asked, coming around the corner, a bottle of glass cleaner in her hand. When she saw me standing at the door, she said, "What are you doing home?"

Great, just great.

"I don't want to talk about it," I said, making a beeline to my room, not even close to being ready to deal with a cognizant mom.

"What about school?" she asked to my back as I slammed the door. "Kyle!"

I threw my backpack down and tried not to notice the comparison between my behavior and a kid that needs a nap. My mom went through phases like this every few months, and it drove me crazy. She'd get this new zest for life, swear off drinking and getting high, become obsessive-compulsive about getting her life back on track, fail at it badly, go out at the first sign of failure to commiserate with her old friends, get wasted, go on a binge.

Lather, rinse, repeat, puke.

During those times, though brief, she became aware of how distant we were, and she'd try to compensate by being a cross between Donna Reed and a serial killer. She'd want to know how I was feeling and how school was and even if I had homework or not. It was nauseating to me on many levels, the main one being that over the years I had grown used to rationalizing her behavior as if she was clinically insane. As long as she continued to act insane, I was okay with it. But when she came at me all normal-like and sounding like a mom, it just reminded me that she wasn't crazy, she just didn't care whose life she ruined with her antics.

That was normally when I got really pissed.

Before I could get a good head of steam under me, she threw open my door and walked in. "I can let a lot of crap slide because normally you are more than capable of taking care of yourself, but when you walk in the door in the middle of a school day and don't even bother with an excuse, that's when I know something is wrong." She crossed her arms across her chest. "So what's happened?"

"What do you care?" I shouted, unable to handle the frustration that was quickly fermenting into rage inside of me. "Since when do you care about anything around here but yourself?"

I don't know if I was surprised or disappointed that she didn't look hurt or even slightly uncomfortable. She just kept staring at me. "Since now. What is wrong?"

"Go away," I said, sitting on my bed. "Just leave me alone."

I could feel her just standing there, not moving, not talking, just staring at me. I didn't want to cry in front of her. I didn't want to cry in front of anyone, if we are bringing the topic up, but life always seemed to have other plans. Finally she began to turn and then stopped. "You know, Kyle, you say I'm never there, and all I care about is myself, and I understand why you'd say that. But later, when you are busy hating me in your mind and you tell yourself I never tried, I want you to think about this, right now. I am here, trying, and you are the one telling me to leave." Her voice sounded tired and sad. "And we both know this isn't the first time."

She was right. She had tried before, and I always pushed her away. I didn't want to get used to her being there or start to depend on her. I never wanted to get used to being able to count on someone besides myself because I knew sooner or later they would just screw it up, and I'd be where I started in the first place. Alone. At least this way, I was ready to be alone and was never disappointed.

She began to close the door, and my mouth moved before my brain could stop it. "I'm gay!"

She paused before turning slowly to come back into the room. My heart was pounding so loud it felt like it was going to burst out of my chest all Indiana Jones-style. There was a buzzing in my ears that made everything muffled as I waited for her next words. I thought she might take some more time to consider it, but instead she just responded with a simple "Okay."

I blinked a few times, not sure now if I'd heard her.

"Okay?" I asked back.

She shrugged. "Okay."

I stood up. "Just okay? Seriously? I tell you I'm gay and all you can say is 'okay'?"

She cocked her head. "Are you upset because I'm not reacting?" She laughed shakily to herself. "Did you want me to be upset at you?"

I didn't know what I wanted. Did I want her to be mad? Did I want her to freak out and throw me out of the house? I was so fucking confused.

"Kyle, what happened at school?" she asked with real concern in her voice. I felt the walls in my head starting to break as all the emotions I had been holding back began to spill out. One sob slipped out of my mouth, and I began to crumble. "Kyle, why are you home?" she asked, taking a step closer.

I felt my resolve give out from underneath me as I began to cry and cry and cry.

And I didn't know if I would ever stop.

Brad

I WATCHED Kyle walk away and felt my heart shrivel up and die.

So much for not turning on each other.

Half of me wanted to run up to him and just hug him until graduation. The other half wanted things to back to the way they were and for all of this to have been a bad dream. Life without Kyle? Life without baseball? Stuck in this town for the rest of my life? Dead-end job, being considered a freak by the people who used to be my friends?

"Screw it," I said as I started to run after him.

I felt a hand grab my arm and spin me around. Kelly looked me right in the face, no malice, no sneer, just an intense look of concern. "Dude, what is wrong with you?"

I pulled my arm away angrily. "Get out of my way, Kelly," I snarled.

"Are we going to have another problem?" Mr. Adler said once it was clear Kyle was not coming back.

"No problem, sir," Kelly answered quickly. "Just trying to talk some sense into him."

I opened my mouth to protest, but then I saw the old man nod in agreement and say, "Well someone needs to. Carry on."

Kelly pulled me aside as the crowd dispersed, obviously disappointed that there had been no bloodshed. I let him pull me around the corner to the alley between the music building and the gym. I watched as he made sure we were alone before he hissed in a fake whisper at me, "Have you lost your fricking mind?" This wasn't normal Kelly, and it would have been obvious to anyone who had grown up with him. He wasn't being mean or sarcastic; in fact, it looked like he was actually worried about me. "Do you have any idea how bad you've screwed up?"

My knee-jerk reaction was to argue, but I stopped myself. "How?" I asked, wondering where he was going with this.

He checked again for anyone listening. "Look, dude, you had everything, and you're blowing it over"—he looked like he was about to spit, the way his face scrunched up—"over fag shit?"

"Don't call it that," I warned him.

He held up his hands in apology. "Fine, gay shit, whatever. You really want to throw your life away over something that stupid?" I didn't have an answer for that. "Your popularity, your chance for a scholarship? Bro, what are you thinking?"

I hated that he was making sense. It was as if my inner fears and anxieties had been given voice through Kelly, of all people. I just shook my head. "I don't know."

He took a third look around and took a step toward me. "Look, man, if it's about getting off, we can deal with that." He put his hand over my crotch and leaned in to kiss me. I was so shocked his lips actually touched mine that I couldn't even process it. I felt his tongue press against my closed mouth, and that was it.

I grabbed his hand and took it away from my dick. I squeezed it hard, causing him to jerk back from me as he screamed in pain. I twisted his wrist slightly, and he went down to one knee almost instantly, trying to move so the pain was less crippling. "Let me see if I get this straight," I said, putting the slightest amount of force into the hold. "I can like guys as long as it's you?" He shook his head, but I ignored it. "I get to keep my friends and my life as long as it's you who sucks my cock? Really, Kelly? Was that how you saw us ending up?" It was right then that I realized Kelly might have taken more away from us fooling around at football camp than I thought. As with most things in my life, I had been so busy worrying about myself, I completely forgot there were two of us in that bed. Some random kid turned the corner and saw us and ran off instantly. I was running out of time.

I let go of his hand, and he sat there rubbing it for a moment. I knelt down to make eye contact with him. "Was that the plan, Kelly? You and me, we get wives, have kids, but then go off up to the lake to fish every weekend? Some random hotel now and then?" I could see him fighting back tears as he dropped his gaze, and it wasn't because of the pain. "Is it worth it? Is all this worth never having what you really want?" I wasn't angry at him anymore. All of that rage and fury had turned to pity as I began to feel like I was just kicking a three-legged dog. I grabbed his chin and made him look me in the eyes.

"There is nothing in that life that is worth not being who you really are," I told him in quiet words, no longer sure if I was talking about him or me. "Play their game, and you will end up a miserable imitation of the man you could really be." I moved my hand down his cheek in the only actual display of affection I had ever given him. "I'm sorry, Kelly, I shouldn't have treated you like that." He pressed his face against his shoulder, trapping my hand for a moment. He looked so miserable it was heartbreaking. I could see his future unfold in front of me instantly.

He was going to graduate, then wander from one meaningless job to the next. Maybe get some girl pregnant, have to marry her and settle down. He'd probably get a job on one of the ranches out here just to pay the bills. He'd be in rest stops and dirty bathrooms on the weekends, blowing strangers in a vain attempt to quell the hunger that was just beneath the surface of his skin. Never able to face who and what he really was, he'd grow up to be a miserably angry man who wondered why life was always against him.

He sounded just like my dad.

I pulled my hand free as a couple of people raced around the corner, eager to see what they were sure was round two. Instead they saw us kneeling there, as if in prayer. I held my hand out to help him up, and I saw his face change in a flash. The change was so fast and final that I swore I could hear the door slam on the prison cell of Kelly's life. He'd made the decision that quickly, as soon as someone might actually have seen him and me.

He pulled back from me, slapping my hand away. "I said no, you faggot!" he yelled, making sure everyone heard it. "Stop asking me!" He stumbled away from me, making a great show of how disgusted he was by me and my gay advances. Some people nodded, as if that went along with their preconceptions of who I and all gay people were. But I saw more than a few look at him with narrowed eyes, obviously not buying it.

He ran away from me, no doubt ready to spread the news in his own Paul Revere way. I could just hear him: *The gays are coming! The gays are coming!*

I just sighed and stood up, feeling like I was already an old man.

No one said a word to me as I walked past. I couldn't blame them. If I had been standing where they were, I'd have no clue what to say, either. The bell rang, and everyone began to scatter toward their classes. I looked at the path Kyle took and thought about trying to catch up with him, but I honestly had no idea what I was going to say.

I opted for going to class instead.

To save time and sanity, let me recap what my last three classes were like:

Walk in. People whisper. Sit alone. Ignore people staring at me. Rush out the door as quickly as I can. Try to figure out what to do between periods since I am basically avoiding everyone. I had never been the first in a classroom before, and let me tell you, I hadn't been missing a thing.

The only advantage of having no one to talk to was that it gave me time to think. Everything I'd said to Kelly was true, but the words meant nothing when I tried to apply them to me. I'd always had a plan to get out of this town. I was going to play my ass off, get a scholarship to a college on either coast, and never look back. Fuck my friends and their two-faced ways. Fuck my parents and their series of civil war reenactments. And fuck this one-horse town and everyone who thought it was the center of the world. I had dreamt of seeing that "Welcome to Foster, Texas" sign that sat on the outskirts of town in my rearview mirror since I could remember.

Kyle was not part of the plan.

That wasn't fair. Liking guys wasn't part of the plan, and it should have been. I'd spent so much time running away from what I truly was that I shouldn't be the least bit shocked at how it turned out. Like any other bimbo in a horror movie, I had actually run toward the horror I had been trying to flee, and it was going to cost me. Blaming Kyle was just me doing what I always did, deflecting responsibility to anywhere but me.

I wandered into the locker room and began to change out for practice, my thoughts a million miles away.

"Greymark!" Coach Gunn's voice echoed through the locker room. I froze in place, my fingers stopped at the third button of my jeans. I looked over and saw him walking toward me with three other guys from the team in tow. "What are you doing?"

I wasn't sure what exactly he was asking, but I had sinking feeling I wasn't going to like it. "Changing out for practice?" I offered.

He shook his head as he stepped closer. He started to speak. "You can't—" And then stopped as he noticed we had an audience. "Don't you idiots have somewhere else to be? Like running laps?" They scattered pretty quickly. In a lower voice, he started again. "You can't be in here." I shook my head in confusion since I had spent most of my high school life in this locker room. He obviously didn't want to elaborate, but when he saw I wasn't getting it, he sighed and put a hand on my shoulder. "Brad, you can't be in here any more than I can let one of those guys change in the girl's locker room. It isn't allowed."

I felt my face grow red with embarrassment. I pulled my shoulder away from him angrily as I heard someone laugh a few lockers back. "What do you think I'm going to do?" I asked him as I pulled on my shirt. "I've changed out here since I was a freshman, and now I can't?"

The coach didn't look like he was enjoying this any more than I was. "Things have changed, Brad, and you know it. People are going to be uncomfortable undressing next to you, and you should have thought of that before you...." I could tell he was trying to find another way of saying "coming out" but nothing was coming to mind. He finally just said, "You should have thought of that before telling everyone your business. I'm sorry, Brad, but you can't be in here."

I pulled my sneakers back on. "Then where am I supposed to dress out?"

Now he looked like he'd swallowed a bug. "Brad, you can't be in here."

"I got that, so where do I dress out for practice then?"

And then the other shoe dropped.

"You're kicking me off the team?" I practically screamed at him. When he didn't say anything back, I lost it. "I gave you four years!

Four fucking years of blood, sweat, and tears, and you're kicking me off the team? I got you to state last year!"

"You weren't gay last year," he responded without expression.

"Yes, I was," I blurted out. "The only difference was that you didn't know."

"No, the only difference was you didn't feel the need to stand in front of the school and announce it." He didn't sound nasty saying it, but it hurt nonetheless. "This is out of my hands, Brad. You can't be here."

I looked past him and saw the rest of the team staring at me. Some were flashing me shit-eating grins, others looked shocked. One or two actually looked upset. No one said anything in my defense.

Fine.

With what little pride I had left, I grabbed my stuff and walked out of the gym for the second time today. This time, though, it felt like it was for the last time.

I threw my duffel bag into the backseat and burned rubber out of the parking lot. I was so pissed I couldn't even see straight. As the Mustang screamed past the school, I saw the banners hanging on the back fence proclaiming it the proud home of the Foster Cowboys. I resisted the urge to stop and pull the damn banners down and light them on fire. I just kept driving. I turned on my stereo and blasted it as loud as I could, driving toward nowhere in particular.

Which, if I thought about it, was a pretty good metaphor for my life.

I had been heading toward this point for so long I couldn't remember a time when I wasn't sacrificing everything along the way just to get me once inch closer to the goal of getting out of this town forever. It didn't matter if I dated Jennifer and never told her I liked guys, because the longer people thought I was straight the better my chances were of getting away. Who cared if I pretty much treated people around me like crap? Once I left for college, I'd never see them again, so what did it matter? And so what if my parents were one bad night away from reenacting some of the better parts of *Fight Club*?

They had gotten as much mileage out of using me as a bargaining chip as they could; I didn't owe them a damn thing. And who cared if I wasn't happy?

Certainly not me.

Though I didn't mean to, I ended up at the lake, at the same spot I had taken Kyle when we skipped school. Before, it had been my old stomping grounds, a place where I had practically grown up. Now it felt like an alien planet. All of its previous luster and appeal were gone, and for the life of me, I couldn't remember what I had ever seen in it. I tried to remember the nights and the parties and all the fun I was supposed to have had here, but nothing came to mind. Instead, it looked like a crappy lake in a crappy town that I was never going to be free of.

It looked like a goddamned prison, a prison of my own making.

Kyle

I CAN'T think of many things that people would consider universal.

As human beings we spend so much energy arguing over every little thing it's easy to forget sometimes that deep down we are all the same creature. White, black, straight, gay, liberal, conservative, all those labels do is point out how different we seem, when the truth is almost everybody feels the same way about the important stuff.

For example, when you see someone in pain, you want to help, and when you are in pain, you want help.

If you had asked me a week, a day, hell, even an hour ago if I would think these words, I'd have thought you were completely freaking insane, but as I knelt there and sobbed, I only had one desire running through my bones:

I wanted my mom.

It sounded so stupid and trite that I was embarrassed for even feeling it, but when she knelt down with me and put her arms around me, all the walls I had erected over the years to keep the sorrow and the pain away from my life shattered. I was overwhelmed. The more she comforted me the more I ached, as a lifetime of emotional venom began to seep out of my heart. I told her the story the best I could between huge, earth-shattering heaves. I have no idea how she understood me, but I had just to assume moms speak Crying Children. She didn't interrupt me or ask any questions, she just sat there and absorbed the tale without any indication of judgment.

When I was done, I felt exhausted and drained and more than a little bit embarrassed. I dried my eyes and got up slowly. "So, yeah," I said, sniffling. "So basically my life sucks." She didn't smile; she didn't so much as chuckle. "So, say something," I said after agonizing seconds of silence.

"They can't do this," she said, a clarity in her eyes that I couldn't ever recall seeing before.

I scoffed. "I beg to differ since they are doing it."

"No," she said, standing up. "You don't understand. They can't do this."

That was when my spider sense started to tingle.

"They can't discriminate against you because of that," she said with more force. "It's against the federal law."

"Don't," I said, trying to cut her off at the pass.

"Kyle, you can't let them do this to you," she implored me. "You have to stand up for yourself."

"No, no, I do not," I countered with emphasis on the "no." "I just need to get through the rest of this year and graduate. Nothing is gained by making them even more pissed at me."

She gave me a stern look. "That's the old Kyle talking."

"No, that's the me Kyle talking. See? This is me talking, and I am saying no."

She shook her head and held her tongue, but I knew this was far from over. "It's not fair," she said as she was walking out of my room.

She paused at the doorway. "And I know life is not fair, that doesn't mean you just accept it."

She closed my door and was gone.

If I had run a marathon fully clothed in the desert I wouldn't have felt this drained. It felt good to unload, but it didn't change that I was still in the same situation I was before I lost it. I slipped my shoes off and lay back on my bed, feeling like I was a thousand years old. She was right, what they were doing wasn't fair, but what the hell could I do about it? They held all the cards, and even if the school was somehow on my side, the other students would still treat me like trash no matter what.

And then there was Brad.

It felt like the bed was pulling me into it as I began to nod off. Every impulse I had was to try to help him, but I didn't know how. Even if I distanced myself from him now, he'd still be outed and just as shunned as I was. We were both screwed, but the difference was he had so much more to lose than I did. I was just a loser that turned out to be gay, the only difference now was that people openly shunned me instead of doing it unconsciously. If Brad lost baseball, I didn't know what he'd do....

That was the last thought I remember having.

A jumbled series of images made up my dreams. I saw Brad shirtless, tied to a pole like a scarecrow, bloodied and beaten, held up only by the ropes. He was surrounded by the school, students and staff, all of them screaming at him like an angry mob of villagers attacking a monster. Kelly was holding a baseball bat and brandishing it at Brad's head like he was about to try for a stand-up triple. I would have been more concerned if part of my brain hadn't realized that most of this imagery was pulled from the pilot of *Smallville* so I kinda knew it was a dream.

When I woke up it was dark out, and I was drenched in sweat.

I sat up, trying to remember what I could from the dream before it faded away into wisps of nothing, but all I could focus on was that Brad had been in danger. I got up and checked the living room for signs of life and possibly food. I wasn't too surprised to find my mom gone. It wasn't 2:00 a.m. yet, which was the time most alcoholics turned into pumpkins. I should have known that her moment of clarity was another mirage created by years of wandering this desert by myself. I grabbed a banana and headed back to my room, wondering how many times I was going to run at that football of hope, knowing she was going to pull it away eventually.

I thought about taking a shower but decided I was just going to stink myself up all over again, so I just pulled off my clothes and went back to sleep.

Brad

A TAPPING sound on my car window woke me up instantly.

I jerked away in a blur and ended up slamming my knee into the steering wheel. "God damn!" I called out as a light blinded me from my left. I held up my hand as images of alien abductions flashed though my head.

"Brad? Bradley Greymark?" a voice asked on the other side of my window.

The aliens knew my name?

More rapping on the window. "Son, are you Bradley Greymark?"

My eyes began to adjust, and what I had been so sure just seconds before was a nasty green alien with a taste for brains began to look more and more like a policeman.

"Son, I need you to roll down this window."

The words started to make sense as I fully woke up. I rolled down the window and was greeted by a gust of freezing air. "Jesus," I muttered, my teeth starting to chatter.

"Are you Bradley Greymark?" the policeman asked me again. I nodded as I turned on the heater. "Bradley Greymark the baseball player?"

Not so much.

"Yeah," I snapped, willing at this point to say anything to roll that damn window up. "That's me, why?"

He frowned slightly at the attitude, and I realized that snark might not be the best tack to take with the cop. "Because your parents are going nuts and half the force is out looking for you."

I stopped myself from commenting that half the force was three guys and probably a mule and instead dug my phone out of my pocket. I tried to turn it on, but the screen just stayed black. I hit the button again, and sure enough, nothing. The cop pointed at it and said, "It helps if you charge them, I've heard."

Obviously snark was okay when *he* thought of it.

"What time is it?" I asked, realizing it was pitch black beyond my windshield.

"Going on 4:00 a.m.," he answered without checking. "You been drinking?"

I shook my head. "Just cut school and fell asleep."

He considered my answer for a moment and then took a step away from the door. "Why don't you get out of the car." I looked at him and bit back the "Are you kidding me?" that was right on my lips. Instead I sighed and climbed out into the cold night. He shone his flashlight into my car, no doubt looking for empties littering the backseat or something as incriminating. When it was obvious I didn't have Jimmy Hoffa on ice in my backseat, he turned his attention to me.

"So, bad day, huh?" he asked casually. I nodded, wrapping my arms around myself, trying to keep warm. "Yeah, I can't imagine letting your freak flag fly is the least stressful way to spend a day." I looked over at him in a daze, but before I could say anything, he grabbed my shoulder and spun me toward the car. "Hands on the roof, legs apart." I was too shocked to protest as he began to pat me down. "Yeah, the whole town knows about you. That kind of news spreads quick," he said as he began to move his hands over my chest and then lower, toward my waist.

"I'm—" I said, trying to form actual words in my head. "I'm sorry…" was all I could manage. The whole town? Oh God, how was I going to live this down?

"Why?" he said, almost whispering in my ear. "I mean, you wanted everyone to know, right?" he said as his hands moved from my waist to the front of my pants. I began to move, but he was pressed up against me. "Do not move," he growled. "I know how you queers like this," he leered, his hands unbuttoning my jeans.

"Stop," I protested, afraid to fight back but wanting him to stop.

"You sure you want me to?" His voice sounded like it was inside my head. "After all, isn't this what you deserve?"

There was a tapping sound on my window, which woke me up instantly.

I jerked away in a blur and ended up slamming my knee into the steering wheel. "God damn!" I called out as a light blinded me from my left. I held up my hand as images of being raped by a cop flashed though my head.

"Brad?" a voice asked from the other side of the light. "Brad, it's Officer Miller. You okay?" I fought away the images of the nightmare when I realized the strange cop had been a figment of my imagination. "Brad?" he asked, this time concern lacing his voice.

I nodded and rolled down my window. "Sorry, bad dream."

I saw the sun had just gone down over the lake, and the sky was still a strong cobalt, making it maybe between six or seven.

"I saw your car parked out here and just wanted to make sure you were okay." Which was probably a half-truth, since Miller had personally taken me home in the back of his squad car more than once.

I nodded and rubbed my eyes. "I cut school and fell asleep."

He chuckled to himself. "Son, it's Monday. Kind of early in the week to start skipping, isn't it?"

I nodded as I checked my phone to see if I had any missed calls. "I have a feeling it's going to be a bad week."

"Oh, come on, son. It can't be all that bad. How bad can it be at your age?"

Instead of answering, I just turned the engine over. "Thanks, Officer Miller, I better get home."

"Stay out of trouble, Brad," he said, putting his flashlight away. "And get home safe, okay?"

I nodded as I rolled up my window and waved to him as I drove away.

The town was packing it in for the night as I drove home. I was surprised that we didn't roll the sidewalks up after a certain point. It was dark when I pulled into the driveway. My dad's car wasn't there, meaning he was working late or just decided to drink at the dealership. As I walked in the door I could smell something cooking, and my stomach growled, reminding me that I hadn't eaten since lunch, and even then, I hadn't finished it. I slipped my shoes off and hung up my jacket.

"Bradley?" I heard my mom call out from the kitchen.

I slid into the kitchen on my socks. "Food?" I asked eagerly.

She laughed as she shook her head. "How was school?"

My mind froze as I debated what to tell her. My first instinct was, of course, to lie, that being what I always did. The word "fine" was halfway to my lips before I stopped myself. She knew about Kyle, and if anyone was going to not lose their mind over baseball, it would be her. What did I have to lose?

I did not like the answer of *nothing* that came to mind.

"Not good," I said sitting down at the table.

She paused serving for a moment. "Define 'not good'."

"Well," I said, running a hand through my hair. "The coach found out about Kyle and um… kinda kicked me off the team."

She put the plate down and turned toward me. "What?"

allowed hard as I tried struggled not to just break down. "He I couldn't change out in the locker room because of—well, you know. So I can't be on the team."

Now, I have seen my mom mad before, in fact most of the time she was around my dad she was pissed, so I assumed that I had seen it all. I had seen her scream, cuss, and throw dishes across the room. I had seen her grab my father's clothes and throw them over the stairs into a pile in the foyer. I honestly believed that I had witnessed every conceivable shade of anger that might come from her. But as she stared at me from the stove with cold fury in her eyes, I realized up to this point I had never really seen her truly angry.

"He said that?" she asked, her voice sharp and clipped. "He actually said you couldn't play anymore?"

I nodded.

"What time is it?" she asked more to herself as she grabbed the address book from the phone. She began to slap through it angrily as she pulled the phone from the charger. I watched her stab in a number and wait for an answer. "Carol? Hi, it's Susan. Are you still on the school board?"

I waited a few seconds, but it was obvious if I wanted dinner, I needed to get it myself.

Today had seriously sucked.

Kyle

I WOKE up to my mom knocking on my door.

I sat up, confused, since seeing her awake this early was akin to having Bigfoot do a soft shoe shuffle across your campsite. "What's wrong?" I asked instantly, before I was fully awake.

"Nothing," she answered, smiling. "Brad is here."

I started to say, "Tell him I'll be right out," but she stepped away from the door, and he walked in. "Nice hair," he said with that damn grin.

I fell back onto my bed. "Does anyone understand the concept that I might not want to see people right after I wake up?"

He closed my door and shrugged his jacket off. "Well, if you weren't so cute in those boxers...," he said, lifting my covers.

"*Hey!*" I exclaimed, slapping his hand away.

I saw him pause for half a second. "Or lack of boxers...."

My face burned with embarrassment. "Can you please hand me something out of the top drawer?" I asked, trying to force time to go backward so the last thirty seconds were just beginning to happen.

He opened the drawer and began shuffling around. "White. White. Gray. Oh, look, striped!" he said, holding up a pair with thin blue lines.

I wrapped my blanket and bedspread around me and jumped out of bed. "Seriously?" I grabbed for them, but he pulled them away playfully.

"Why are you so bent out of shape?" he asked sincerely. "You do know I've seen you before, right?"

"Please just give them to me," I pleaded, trying to grab them again.

In one movement, he stepped forward and wrapped his arms around me. I was trapped in the cocoon of my bedding. "I really want to know... what's so horrible?"

I sighed and leaned my head against his chest. "I hate the way my body looks," I replied in a miserable tone. "Please let me get dressed."

When he didn't say anything for a few seconds, I looked up. He was just staring at me, those green eyes almost glowing in the morning light. "You mean that? About hating your body?" I nodded, wondering if this was a world-record way for a day to become shitty. He dropped his hands and grabbed the front of the blankets. He began to pull them open as I freaked out. I clutched them shut as hard as I could. "Don't," he said softly. I shook my head as he slipped his hands underneath the blanket and moved them around the small of my back. "Let them go," he said. "Please."

This must be how rats felt when faced with a cobra, those eyes boring into you, freezing you in place. I could feel myself begin to shiver as my hands relaxed. The blanket and bedspread fell to the ground, leaving me standing there naked as the day I was born. He took a step back and looked at me from head to toe. His face showed nothing of what was going on that head of his, and I felt myself begin to shake harder.

"You are so beautiful," he said, moving back toward me. His hands moved over my chest and then slowly down to my abs. "You have no idea how perfect you are." His fingers traced over me from my stomach to my hips and then to my ass. Everywhere he touched goose bumps followed, making me shiver involuntarily. His lips touched my shoulder and began to move down as he talked. "You shouldn't"—kiss—"hate anything"—kiss—"anything so perfect." When he reached my belly button, I felt the warmth of his tongue, and I heard a moan slip past my lips against my will. "Never hate anything about yourself," he said, pushing me down onto my bed. I fell backward, and he followed me, his head hovering over my growing member.

"My mom…," I said, the words choking in my throat.

"I locked the door," he said, smirking evilly.

His mouth moved down, and all I knew was ecstasy.

Brad

I LOVED turning him on.

I had never done this before; in the past I had always made sure that Kelly was the one on his knees. But as Kyle spread his legs, I didn't care about what was gay or whether who did what made the other one in charge. His fingers skittered through my hair. I think he was trying to stop me, but when I moved my tongue I felt them clench into fists; he pushed me down onto him. Every gasp he made sent a chill through my own body, every time his hips left the bed, I could feel my own body respond.

It wasn't anywhere as bad as I thought it would be; if anything, it was awesome.

My hands fumbled with my jeans as I pulled myself free of my boxer briefs. I heard him whisper my name, and I heard myself groan in response. Why hadn't I done this before? Why had I always been so afraid that doing this would break me? As I felt him get closer, my own hand sped up. My entire life at the moment was composed of making him explode. I didn't care about my ego, my reputation, or my masculinity. I loved him, I really did, and if I could make him happy in any way, then I was doing the right thing.

"I'm… I'm…," he panted as I felt him begin to pulse in my mouth.

The second he went, I felt myself follow.

His whole body shook as his hands dug into my head. His hips were off the bed as he thrust again and again. I felt like I was floating as my own orgasm consumed me. I don't know how much time passed before he fell back to the bed, his softening tool slipping out of my mouth. My hand was a mess, and I tried to catch my breath as he lay there, his body covered in a fine sheen of sweat.

I found a bath towel on the floor and wiped my hand clean before climbing up onto the bed. I moved next to him, pulling him against me. "Good morning," I whispered to him. His eyes were still closed as a wide, contented grin spread across his face. "You like that?"

He looked over at me. "Do you have to ask?" He lunged toward me, his mouth pressing into mine as he kissed me hard. "You… that was…," he said between breaths.

"I love you," I said, summing it up for both of us.

He paused and looked me straight in the eye. I had never seen a blue as perfect as his eyes. "You really do, don't you?"

I raised an eyebrow. "What else can I do to convince you?" I could see him beginning to tear up. "What's wrong?" I asked, concerned.

He shook his head. "Nothing," he lied. "I just... I just feel like I've ruined your life."

He tried to bury his head against my chest, but I stopped him, holding his chin up so he would look at me. "Listen," I said with as much honesty I could put into my words. "I didn't have a life before you. All of that was... was just a waste of time." I put my hand over his heart. "This, this is the first real thing I have ever felt. You didn't ruin my life, dummy." I smiled at him as my own eyes began to mist up. "You saved my life." When he kissed me, I could feel all the words he couldn't say move through us, and I knew for the first time since we met....

Things were going to be okay.

Kyle

WE barely made it to school on time, but I have to admit, I didn't care.

As I sat in first period, I found if I thought about what had just happened for too long my mind would begin to fuzz up, and I'd just sit there with a goofy grin on my face. I think I might have looked like I was in the middle of a stroke since Mr. Richardson stopped his lecture and actually asked me if I was okay.

No, that wasn't embarrassing at all.

It was weird, because things seemed completely different than they had yesterday. I mean people still stared, and sure, they were whispering, but I couldn't waste the energy needed to care. I just walked by them and thought about this morning, and suddenly, they didn't matter anymore. I saw Brad in the hall between third and fourth period, and we just looked at each other as we walked toward each other. My cheeks hurt I was smiling so hard, and the twinkle in his eye from his grin made me want to jump him right then and there.

"Hey," he said, his whole face lit up.

"Hey," I said back, my chest swelling with emotion.

"Good day?" he asked. I saw just the hint of mischief in his eyes, and I felt my body react.

"Better than average," I answered, which made him laugh. "Hey, I know a place we can eat lunch in peace today."

A couple of girls walked by, their heads turning to gawk at us as they passed.

"What are you supposed to be? Paparazzi?" Brad snapped at them. They turned and shuffled off quickly. When he turned back to me, I was barely holding back laughter. "What?" he asked. "Like they were looking at a traffic accident or something."

"Yeah, so… lunch," I said, trying to steer the conversation away from the negative.

"Okay, wherever you want to go," he said, distracted.

"Ignore them," I said quietly. He looked back to me, and I gave him a smile. "They aren't worth getting upset over."

I saw him sigh and nod. "See you at lunch?"

The tardy bell rang, and people began to scatter. I took a look to make sure no one was looking before I leaned in and kissed him on the cheek quickly. "Love ya," I said as he stood there in shock, a hand covering the skin where my lips had touched.

Brad

AND just like that, my mood changed.

I wandered through the rest of my classes, my mind lost in everything Kyle. I had no idea where he got the strength to put up with all this, but every time I felt like I was done, there he was. Anyone looking from the outside might think I was the strong one, but I felt like a little bitch next to him.

When the lunch bell rang, I saw the usual suspects assembling at the Round Table. Kelly had taken over my old seat. I had a feeling that should bug me more than it did but the only thing I could think was that I hoped he had more fun there than I'd had.

"You ready?" Kyle asked, coming up from behind me.

I nodded over at the table. "Did I look that arrogant sitting over there?"

He looked at Kelly and shook his head. "He looks like a punk sitting there," he said with a warm smile. "You looked like a king."

I hadn't felt like a king, but it was nice that he saw me that way.

Instead of heading into the quad, we turned the other way, toward the auditorium building. I had to admit I never really found myself on this side of school, since at Foster, baseball practice counted as a Fine Arts credit. Kyle seemed to know his way; he maneuvered down the halls without hesitation. We ended up in what used to be a balcony overlooking the stage. Now, however, it looked like it a storage room. "Ta-da!" he said, gesturing to the space.

I looked around as I walked in. "How did you know about this place?" I asked.

He shrugged as he took a seat. "Spent a lot of lunches by myself. I like exploring."

I felt bad for a moment, but I saw that he wasn't upset or even dipping a big toe in pity. He was just stating a fact, and that, for some reason, made it even worse. I sat down next to him as he dug through the paper bag he'd packed his lunch in. "Cookie?" he offered, a chocolate chip cookie in his hand.

"I love you," I declared out of nowhere.

"It's store-bought; trust me, it's not all that," he stated somberly.

I laughed and had leaned over to kiss him when the door opened.

"Oh," someone said from behind us.

Three guys and a girl stood at the doorway looking in on us. They were all dressed in dark clothes, and the guy who had spoken wore dark eye makeup and had black lipstick on. The other three weren't dressed as severely, but they were all clearly part of the alternative crowd. Foster didn't have a huge goth population, but the few there were pretty militant. "What are you guys doing up here?" he asked, recovering from the shock of seeing intruders.

"Eating lunch," Kyle said, holding up his bag. "More than enough room," he said, gesturing to the other seats.

The girl put her hand on his shoulder and whispered something, but he shook his head at whatever she'd asked. "No, we don't have to leave," he said, walking in all the way. "They're the ones who are lost."

I clenched my fists and began to stand up, but Kyle's hand on my arm stopped me. He told me to calm down with his eyes before looking back at the other kids. "We're not lost, we're just looking for a place to eat lunch."

Another guy had joined the original four; he called from the door, "Jeremy, let it go."

Jeremy wasn't going to let it go, though. "What's wrong with the Round Table?" he asked, his disdain practically dripping from his lips. "Couldn't get a reservation?"

This was ridiculous. I was not being browbeaten by a damn goth; that was where I drew the line. "Look, Jeremy," I said, standing up. "We don't want any trouble; we just want to eat lunch. Why don't we just all calm down and think a second." He froze, and I realized he had thought I was going to hit him. Instead, I put my hand out and said, "My name is Brad, and this is—"

"I know who you are," he said, cutting me off. "You don't even know who I am, do you?" I had to admit I didn't. "You and your friends threw beer bottles at me last year outside the bowling alley. You guys screamed 'drama fag' and took off." I felt my stomach plummet. "Ring a bell?"

I shook my head, feeling like a complete asshole.

He laughed, and I felt something in me cringe. "You don't remember me? Or you don't recall because you jerks have done it more than once?"

"Both," I admitted, not able to look at him.

"Come on, guys," Kyle said, standing up, moving between us.

"You can stay here, Kyle," Jeremy said, not taking his eyes off me. "You, I have no problem with, but he is going to have to go."

"You know me?" Kyle asked, the shock obvious in his voice.

Jeremy scoffed. "I've had a crush on you since the fourth grade; pity you never noticed." I could see the blood drain from Kyle's face as he realized he might not have been as invisible as he thought. "Just because douche bag here is experimenting with his sexuality, it doesn't mean he's an outcast." He practically spit at me. "It just means karma works, and that bad things do happen to bad people sometimes."

I could see Kyle beginning to get that look on his face which meant he wasn't about to back down. I decided to make things easier for all of us. "It's cool," I said. "I'll see you after school." I began to walk out, and though it cost me, I refused to look away, just nodded at each person as I passed. The look of hatred and disgust on the other kids' faces made me want to puke. I turned back to Jeremy. "For what's it worth, I'm sorry."

Sad thing is, I really was sorry, but I knew it meant nothing.

Kyle

I WAITED until Brad was out of earshot before I turned to Jeremy. "What the fuck was that?"

It was obvious he wasn't expecting that kind of reaction from me. "You can't tell me you are attracted to that asshole?"

I ignored his question because I knew that wasn't what he really wanted to know. "I get that he and his friends were dicks to you, and that sucks. But you know what it's like to walk around this town and have people hate you for no other reason than you're different, right?" He nodded. "Then why the hell would you treat anyone else like that?"

He looked like he had eaten a bug from the expression on his face.

"You may not like him, but he stood right next to me when no one else would. He came out to the entire school for no other reason than he liked me. He didn't have to do that; it would have been so much easier to deny everything and stay who he had been, but he didn't. So whatever problems you may have had with him, he is ten times the man of anyone else I have ever met. So back the fuck off." I was out of breath, and I hadn't even realized my fists were clenched. I didn't know what to do with my protective instincts when it came to Brad, but evidently my body did. I forced my fingers out of the fists and tried to look calm.

"Would you have even gone out with me?" he asked after a few seconds of silence.

I sighed. When had I started feeling so tired all the time? "You said you've known me since fourth grade?" He nodded. "And in those eight years, did you ever talk to me? Just walk up and let me know how you felt?" A quick shake of his head. "He did," I said, pointing to where Brad had been. "He came after me and told me that he liked me." I saw the way Jeremy seemed to deflate as what I was saying hit home. "You don't get to say that I wouldn't go out with you. You never even asked."

"Jeremy," the girl said, trying to distract us. "We have to get those chairs set up, and we're losing time."

"The school board can bite me," Jeremy answered, turning away from me.

"School board?" I asked, looking at the girl.

She nodded. "They are having some emergency meeting tonight, and we have to get the auditorium set up for it."

"Dammit," I said, rushing past her and out of the room.

I caught up with Brad halfway across the quad, out of breath. "School—school...."

He looked at me like I was a retarded stroke victim. "Yes, we're at school."

I shook my head as I tried to catch my breath. "School board...."

"You're bored with school?"

I stopped and looked up at him. "What is wrong with you? The school board is meeting tonight."

He shrugged. "And?"

"And they only meet at the first of the month. This is an emergency meeting," I explained.

Another shrug. "Still not getting it."

Thank God he was cute.

"What do you think they are going to be talking about?"

"Um, school stuff?" he offered hopefully.

Cute, I reminded myself. *And sexy.*

"Us. They are going to be talking about us," I explained slowly. "They are going to have to come up with a policy." He still wasn't getting it. "There isn't a policy yet! They can't kick you off the team because there isn't a rule that says players can't be gay." His eyes opened wide. "We still have a chance to change things."

"How?" he asked, excited.

"I don't know yet," I admitted. "But I need to find a copy of the school rules," I added as my mind raced a million miles a second. "I'm going to check the library."

"What should I do?" he asked.

"Um... no idea," I had to admit.

He nodded. "Okay, then, good plan."

"I'm sorry, but honestly, I am going to be sitting in the library reading. Do you want to do that?" I asked, knowing the answer.

"Not really," he admitted sheepishly.

"Then go to class, and don't worry about it."

He gave me a grin. "So you're going to save me again?"

I smiled back. "I'm going to try my hardest."

"If we weren't in the middle of the quad, I would kiss the shit out of you," he whispered.

I felt my face get warm. "I'll hold you to that."

He gave me a little push. "Go on, then, be a superhero."

I turned around and headed toward the library, I had a purpose now, and that changed everything. I couldn't fight people like Kelly or intimidate guys like Jeremy. In fact, when it came down to it, there wasn't much I could do to help us out. But sitting in a library and studying the school charter to find out what the board could and could not do? That I could handle.

I refused to stand by and be a victim of this.

Brad

SO it's possible I might be dating Batman.

If you had asked me last week what the school board was, I might have told you that it was what they used to spank kids back in the Stone Age, but Kyle knew better. I wasn't sure how the coach could kick me off the team if there wasn't a rule against me being on it, but he had. Only there was no rule that said Coach had the right to do that. And Kyle knew what to do with that piece of information, even if I didn't. So I spent the rest of the day watching the clock in anticipation that he would find something we could use. When the last bell rang, I flew out of the class and made my way across the quad.

It hit me that this was the first time I had ever willingly dashed *toward* a library.

When I pulled open the quiet solid-glass door, I was struck by two things: one, there were two entire stories of books; and two, if I was forced to be anywhere this quiet for more than five minutes, I might lose my mind. I looked around for Kyle, but I only saw some nerds grouped together in the back of the foyer. They looked like they were playing dice or something. The goth guy at the theater had known Kyle: maybe these guys might too. They *were* sitting in one of Kyle's favorite places at school: book land.

"Hey," I said, walking up to them. "Do you guys know a guy named…."

They had all froze in place like deer in the headlights.

Oh God, did I beat you guys up too? I thought to myself, realizing there was so much more room for my day to get shittier.

"We aren't bugging anyone," gulped the one that was sitting behind some kind of folder that was standing up, hiding the papers he had behind it.

"I'm not saying you are. I'm just looking for—" I began to explain.

"I just bought these pants, please don't trash me," another of them begged.

"I'm not going to trash you," I assured him, referring to the practice of grabbing random freshmen and stuffing them into trash cans. I had never done it myself, but I had indeed stood and laughed while the other guys did it. Last year it had been sort of funny. Now, seeing the abject terror in their eyes at the sight and sound of me, I couldn't recall one amusing thing about it.

"Go get Mrs. Linson," the main guy told his friend. Mrs. Linson was the school librarian and the current frontrunner to be discovered as a child-eating witch before she died. The library was her domain in the same sense that hell was the domain of Satan. Since I didn't have a bucket of water handy, I knew if she did come over I was pretty much a dead man.

"I'm not here to beat you up," I said angrily. All three of them moved away from me, and I felt sick to my stomach about how these guys were gaping at me. In a calmer voice, I said, "I am looking for someone. Kyle? Blond hair, skinny?" They continued to stare at me for a second, no doubt waiting for me to spring my trap on them. "I'm serious, have you seen him?"

"He didn't do anything, either," the main one answered.

I put my head down and rubbed the bridge of my nose as I began to name the lineup of the '96 Rangers in my head. I got to Palmer and decided to try again. "Okay, look, guys, I'm Brad, and I am looking for my boyfriend, Kyle Stilleno. He is about so tall, shaggy blond hair, skinny, and was in here after lunch. I am not here to beat you up, or beat him up. In fact, I am out of the beating business. I just want to find him."

There was an oppressive silence as they stared at me for almost a minute, their mouths open in shock. Finally, the main one said, "Kyle Stilleno is gay? Wow, I had no idea."

That took me aback. "You know him?"

All three looked at me like I had just stated as truth that the world was flat and that if you went too far there would be dragons waiting for you when you got there. "Of course we know him. He has the highest GPA in Foster High history, hands down. He aces every honors class he's in. Shoot, he already has college credit!"

One of the other guys nodded. "I saw him recite the periodic table from memory one time in Mr. Ethan's science class."

Holy crap. Kyle was, like, a nerd celebrity.

"Have you guys seen him?" I asked, hoping I had calmed them down enough to get an actual answer.

Two of them shook their head but the third nodded. "He was in here earlier, on the computer, but he ran out about an hour ago."

"Shit," I said, looking around in vain. "And he didn't say where he was going?" I asked hopefully.

"Not to me, but he might come back," he offered. "He's in here a lot."

That took me aback. "Really? Why?" The three of them glared at me harshly as I mentally rewound what I had said, trying to find where I had offended. "Nope," I admitted. "No idea what I said wrong."

The main guy shook his head disappointingly at me. "You know, if more jocks actually dared to walk in here more often, so many of them wouldn't be failing." That was way too close for comfort. He gestured to one of the empty chairs at the table. "You can wait with us if you want."

"Sure." I shrugged, taking a seat. "Why not." I looked at the papers and dice in front of them and asked, "What are you guys doing?"

"Role-playing," one of the other guys explained. When he saw the confused look on my face, he added, "D&D," which did nothing to help me. "Dungeons and Dragons?"

"Oh," I said, recognizing that name. "This is Dungeons and Dragons?" I gestured to the papers and dice. "Where are… you know… the dungeons and dragons?"

The main guy rolled his eyes. "In your head. It's role-playing."

"That doesn't mean anything to me," I admitted flatly.

"Give him a character sheet," he ordered one of the other guys. "Roll him up something easy, like a warrior."

One of the other guys moved over toward me, sliding a piece of paper in front of me. "Okay, this is your character sheet," he began to explain. "First things first: you need to pick a name."

I looked from the piece of paper to him. "I have a name. It's Brad."

The three of them covered their mouths as they chuckled at me. "No, a name for your character," he said after a few seconds of laughing. "I'm Jeff, by the way," he said, offering his hand. "That's Mike, and the DM over there is Andy."

I shook his hand. "DM?"

"Dungeon master," Andy explained. "I run the game."

I nodded again, still no closer to figuring out what the hell we were doing. Jeff handed me a pencil. "You're going to be a warrior, so pick a name first."

"Warrior? You mean like Conan?" I asked, looking the character sheet over.

"Yes, exactly," he exclaimed, but Mike interrupted him.

"No, Conan was a barbarian; don't tell him he's a warrior." I looked over at him, confused, because he seemed really worked up over the fact. He went on, "Lancelot was a warrior."

This time Andy spoke up. "No, Lancelot was a cavalier," he explained to Mike and then looked at me. "Have you read any of the *Dragonlance* books?" I shook my head. "*Lord of the Rings?*"

"I've seen the movies," I offered.

He scoffed, making it clear that the movies did not count. "Fine. You know Gimli." I blinked blankly at him. He sighed. "The dwarf. With the beard."

"Right, the one who fought with the pretty guy from *Pirates of the Caribbean!*"

From the way they all looked at me, I was pretty sure that wasn't the right answer. "His name was Legolas, and he was an elf," Andy explained with a cold tone.

"Okay, so I'm an elf?"

"You're a dwarf," Mike corrected me.

"No, we haven't decided that yet. All we know is, he's a warrior," Jeff countered.

"But why would he be an elven warrior?" Andy asked from behind his screen. "The bonuses are just wasted on that class."

"That's not true," Jeff began to argue. "There are elven warriors, and they have natural—"

"Guys?" I tried to interrupt to no avail. "Guys." Still nothing. "*Guys!*" I barked. They all looked at me like I had grown a second head. "You do you know I have no idea what the three of you are going on about, right?"

They looked at each other and then back to me. "Okay, just do what we say," Andy said as Jeff took the piece of paper from me and began to roll the dice.

For the next hour or so, they began to walk me through the story that I was this guy who learned how to fight and owned a sword or some shit; I didn't catch it all. We ended up going to these abandoned mines where we were jumped by goblins, which, from what I gathered, looked like Gremlins when they went bad. I didn't catch all of it, but what I did understand seemed very cool.

We were about to charge into the lowest level, where a black dragon had made a lair, when Mrs. Linson walked over to the table. "Okay, boys we're closing soon, so wrap—" She stopped in midsentence when she turned from scanning the little study cubicles to look at the D&D players and saw me sitting there. "Mr. Greymark? Are you bothering these young men?"

And I had almost forgotten how much of an asshole I had been for a second there.

I was about to defend myself when Andy said to her, "He's okay, ma'am. He's just playing D&D with us."

She looked at me skeptically, one eyebrow raised, as she asked, "*You're* playing Dungeons and Dragons?"

I nodded, showing her my character sheet. "I'm not bothering them; we're about to kill a dragon."

I don't think she completely bought it, but there wasn't much she could do about it. "Well, be that as it may, I need to close up before the school board meeting."

Fuck.

"Is that now?" I asked, jumping up.

"It starts in about thirty minutes," she answered slowly, not sure why I would care about the school board.

"I need to go," I said to the trio. "Do you keep this or do I?"

Andy looked at me. "You're going to play with us again?"

I nodded, handing him the piece of paper. "I wanna see if the dragon has any phat loot!" He took it in disbelief as I ran out of the library. "See ya!" I called out as I exited.

Dark had already fallen. I didn't like the feeling as I raced across campus.

I had no idea how I lost so much time pretending to be some guy with a sword, but I had, and it had been fun. Why had the jocks always picked on guys like that? What exactly was so wrong with them that we used to seek them out just to be dicks? Were we just a pack of wild dogs, sensing weakness in others and lunging at it? Was that what we were beneath the games and the jostling for position and awards? I felt sick to my stomach as I ran into the auditorium, hoping I wasn't too late.

What I found was Mr. Adler and Mr. Raymond with five other old people sitting up on the stage behind a desk, looking at me, puzzled. There was a podium in the aisle where people could address them, I assumed. Mr. Adler called out to me. "Mr. Greymark, this is closed to students." The "so get the hell out of here" remained unsaid but understood. A few people had taken seats in the first row. As I began to turn, I saw one of them was my mom!

"Mom?" I said, stopping in shock.

She waved but didn't get up. Adler shouted now. "Out, Mr. Greymark!"

What the…?

I stomped up the center aisle, looking behind me about five times, making sure that was indeed my mom, and I wasn't just having some kind of hallucination. The door closed behind me, and I knew there was no way I could not know what was going on in there. I smiled and took off toward the balcony where Kyle and I had started to eat lunch. If I stayed near the back and behind what remained of the stored chairs and tables, no one from below would be able to see me. Luckily, the stairway door was unlocked. Jeremy and his crew would have to come back to put everything away, so they'd left it open. Once I reached the balcony, I stayed low in case one of those old geezers had crazy eagle eyes or something.

I poked my head around the end of a table and began to eavesdrop.

"…over the previous minutes. We can move on to new business," I heard Adler say in a pissy tone. He did not sound like a happy camper. "Coach Gunn, I believe you have something to bring up?"

I looked down and saw Gunn was sitting on the other side of the auditorium, almost as far away from my mom as possible. Any farther and he'd have been sitting in the side hall. He stepped up to the podium and began to talk to Adler and the board. "Mr. Raymond, members of the board, I have coached football and baseball here at Foster for over fifteen years. And in that entire time, I have to admit, I've never come up against a problem such as this. As you know, school sports are incredibly important to any school, and to Foster, perhaps more than most. A lot of our kids come from families that cannot afford to send their kids to a four-year college, and a sports scholarship is the only chance they have of attending a four-year university. Because of that, each and every spot of any team has to be considered not just for the student, but for the entire team. If we don't win, they don't go to college. It's that simple. So when there is an element, no matter what its source, that disrupts team morale to the point of perhaps losing critically important players, we are forced to act for the betterment of the entire team."

Well, if I'd had any doubts this was about me, they were gone now.

"Now, I have no personal thoughts one way or another. But when members of my team come to me and say they have found out something about a student that makes it impossible for them to play on the same team as that student, I have to investigate."

Mr. Raymond interrupted him to ask, "And what student were they talking about?"

"Bradley Greymark," Coach Gunn answered.

"And what did they find out that made it impossible for them to stay on the team with Mr. Greymark?"

Gunn paused, taking a breath as if steadying himself to say it out loud. "They said he had recently admitted he was a homosexual."

I heard a few people on the stage as well as in the audience murmur to themselves for a few seconds before Mr. Raymond got their attention. "And, Coach Gunn, did you confront Mr. Greymark about these rumors?"

"I did."

"And what did he have to say?"

Gunn leaned into the microphone. "He admitted they were true."

More murmuring, this time much louder.

This time Mr. Adler asked the question. "Coach Gunn, what did the students that came to you say was their problem with having Mr. Greymark on the team?"

"They said that they would feel uncomfortable about changing clothes with someone who would gain sexual pleasure from seeing them in a state of undress."

Well, that was bullshit, because I knew the idiots that had talked to him, and they wouldn't understand half of those words. This was starting to sound real rehearsed.

"Coach Gunn, do we have coed locker rooms?" Adler asked.

"No, sir."

"And why is that?"

Like he needed to explain that?

"Because it would be highly inappropriate for boys and girls to be in a state of undress together. Especially at their age."

A few people chuckled, but so far, nothing was funny to me.

"Well, it seems to me that we do indeed have a problem," Raymond said, taking back control of the meeting. "What would you suggest we do, Coach Gunn? In the best interests of the team, of course."

"I don't think it is fair to make students who are clearly uncomfortable with his lifestyle be forced into a situation where they have to do something like expose themselves." He made it sound so rational, so damn logical, that if he had been talking about anyone else but me I might have agreed with him.

"Sounds reasonable," Raymond said, pretending to mull it over as if this was the first time he had heard the proposal. "Thank you, Coach Gunn, you may sit down."

Gunn shuffled back to his seat, and I saw my mom glaring at him.

"Now, we have a proposal in front—" Mr. Raymond had begun to say when the doors burst open with a crash. Kyle walked down the aisle with a stack of papers in his hand.

The cavalry had arrived!

Kyle

I WAS late, and I knew it.

The parts of the city charter I needed weren't online, and that had meant running all the way to City Hall to get copies printed. I had them; there was no way they could do this legally, and I had the proof. I ran down the hall, throwing the doors open in an explosion of noise that was as regrettable as it was unavoidable.

Every pair of eyes was on me.

I couldn't see anyone in the seats because of the low light, but the school board was illuminated perfectly. If looks could kill, Mr. Raymond would have cut my head off by my first step down the center aisle. A small part of me screamed orders, telling me to turn around and run away, that this was not how I behaved. I was supposed to be invisible, unnoticed by everyone. I wasn't Perry Mason, interrupting the trial in the middle of testimony to submit new evidence. Even though it was small, running was a powerful impulse, one I might have succumbed to last week.

Before Brad.

"I need to address the board," I said, holding the papers up. "You can't do this."

Mr. Adler stood up. "No, Mr. Stilleno. You can't do this. School board council meetings are closed to students, as we explained to your... friend, Mr. Greymark. You need to leave."

I stopped halfway down the aisle. "Seriously?" That I did not know.

Mr. Raymond leaned forward. "Very seriously, young man."

"Crap," I said to myself as I started to think I might have done all my research for nothing.

"So you can rule on Brad's future, and I don't mean just at this school, but he can't be in the same room to face his accusers?"

I froze as I heard my mom's voice. She was sitting in the front row with two other guys I didn't recognize.

"The rules are very clear in this matter, Ms. Stilleno. Your son will have to leave," Raymond began to explain.

She looked back at me and just smiled. "Go on, we got this."

I looked at my papers in despair. All that work for nothing?

"Mr. Stilleno, do you need to be escorted out?" Mr. Raymond asked.

I looked up at him and considered flipping him off but thought better of it. I turned around and walked out of the auditorium, pretty sure we were dead. I tossed the papers into a trash can as I passed it and began to lumber outside, dejected.

"Hey!" I heard someone whisper. I looked over and saw Brad standing at the stairs to the balcony. "Come on!" He gestured to me. "They can't see us up here."

I grabbed his hand, and we sneaked upstairs where we could see the entire meeting. "Where have you been?" he asked.

"Wasting my time, obviously," I replied, feeling like crying, I was so upset. This was not how the story was supposed to end. I was supposed to charge in and knock down the walls of bigotry with my well-researched information. Not get shot down halfway into the room like an idiot. He squeezed my hand, and I looked over to him. He was just staring at me so intensely I wondered if I had something on my face. "What?"

"You're a superhero," he said, leaning in and kissing me. I could swear the whole room tilted as I closed my eyes and kissed him back.

I might have stayed in that coma if I hadn't heard Mr. Raymond call the meeting back to order. "If we can continue, we have a proposal in front of us. Does anyone have anything they want to add to the discussion?"

"I do," a woman's voice called out.

"That's my mom!" Brad whispered.

I could hear Mr. Raymond sigh from up here. "Mrs. Greymark." He gestured toward the podium.

Brad's mom walked right up there looking three kinds of pissed. I had only seen her that one time at Brad's and wondered how someone that small could hold her own against the behemoth that was Brad's father. Seeing that look on her face, I understood now; he was the one I should be worried about.

"Mr. Raymond, members of the board. If you think I am going to sit back and let you discriminate against my son like this you have another think coming."

"Mrs. Greymark—" he began to explain, but she just kept talking over him.

"My husband and I pay taxes in this town. We have donated a sizable amount of money and time to this school and the baseball team. In fact, I have personally baked cookies to raise money to go to state last year. Where we won a championship, if I remember, based on my son's performance. While the years of effort, training, and sacrifice that my son has dedicated to this school obviously mean absolutely nothing to you, they do mean a great deal to me and to my husband. With all that in mind, please justify to me your decision to remove Brad from the team. Now."

Mr. Adler waited to see if she was done this time before talking. "Mrs. Greymark, we are in new territory here. We have never had to deal with an openly gay student, much less an athlete."

"But you have had gay students before," my mom said, standing up.

"Mrs. Stilleno, you do not have the floor," Mr. Raymond protested.

"If you thought you were going to treat our sons like second-class citizens and then have an orderly meeting where we pass the conch around to talk, you're dumber than I thought." There was laughter from the audience, and I saw Brad look at me in amusement.

"Dude, your mom is epic!" he said, smiling.

"Yeah, when she's sober," I said, more to myself, but he was right. She did sound kind of badass down there.

"You have had gay students and athletes before," she said when the noise quieted down.

"If we did I didn't know of it," Mr. Adler admitted. "In fact, I don't know a gay person in all of Foster."

"Yes, you do," a male voice said as someone stood up next to my mom.

"Holy shit!" Brad said, his eyes wide with shock.

"Who is that?" I asked, squinting my eyes.

"Mr. Parker," he said, obviously amazed.

"Mr. Parker from the sporting goods store?" I asked, stunned. "Mr. Parker is gay?"

Brad nodded. "Yeah, and he's way cool."

I was going to ask how he knew that, but they started talking again.

"Mr. Parker," Raymond said, obviously upset. "You're gay?"

"Yeah, so you know at least one," he answered proudly.

Raymond and Adler talked among themselves for a second as they tried to regroup. After a few minutes, Adler looked over to him. "Be that as it may, you were never a student here, Mr. Parker, so your point is moot."

"I also know for a fact that Matt Wallace is gay, and he played football here for three years." More talking and argument, but Mr. Parker just kept talking. "Now, two of those years Foster went all the way, so you're telling me there were morale problems then too?"

"No one knew he was gay!" Adler protested.

"Yeah, we did," another voice called out. I saw Scott Ritchie, one of the best quarterbacks Foster had ever had, stand up. "We all knew, but we didn't care." He added in a gruff voice, "He played as hard as his brothers did, and that was all that mattered."

"What exactly do you think we would do in a locker room that is so different than what we've been doing for years?" Parker asked. "Do you think we're going to start touching guys? Molesting them? Are you saying gay guys, unlike straight guys, who are models of chastity, are just unable to control their urges? We've been getting naked in front of you guys for years, and no one ever died from it. So what is different now?"

Mr. Raymond's face was getting red now. "Mr. Parker, it's like the military. Though we can't condone it, if nothing is said—"

"No, it's not," another voice said, standing up. This one was in Navy whites and looked like a big guy.

"No fucking way!" Brad exclaimed.

"Who's that?"

"Aaron White. He played ball for Granada last year." Brad was obviously blown away.

It was obvious Raymond was losing it. "And who are you, young man?"

"Petty Officer White, and I can tell you that this hellhole is nothing like the military. I spent four years here hiding who and what I was, hating Foster the entire time because of it. I couldn't wait to get out. What you're doing is going to crush not only Brad but any gay player that comes after him. And you can try to justify it as morale or for the team, but it's really just about you not liking gay people."

Now they weren't murmuring. There was outright talking as people began to argue with each other. Mr. Raymond was trying to get control back, but there was too much chaos. Finally he slammed his hand down on the table a few times and screamed, "*Order!*"

Everyone jumped at that and began to take their seats, well-behaved, former high school students to the end. "Be that as it may, we have lost sight of the reason for this meeting. The proposal is to prohibit openly gay students from playing on any school-related sports team. We have heard your concerns: now let's vote."

Both of our moms screamed bloody murder, and I saw Mr. Parker stand up too, but it was obvious that the board was going to vote no matter what anyone with a brain might say.

"All in favor of the ban?" Raymond asked.

Every single one of them raised their hands.

"The motion is—" he began to say when the doors flew open again.

"Now who?" Brad asked, unable to see the door since it was under us.

Everyone stopped and looked in silence.

Slowly, as if there was nothing on the line at all, Brad's dad walked down the aisle toward the podium. I saw his wife smile and move aside, letting him take her spot.

"Nathan," Mr. Raymond said, obviously nervous. "Please don't tell me you've come to admit you're gay as well."

No one laughed at that.

"No, Frank, I'm here to speak the only language you understand," he said, turning to his wife. "I assume the passionate plea for equal rights and an end to bigotry didn't help?" She shook her head, and I could feel the "I told you so" emanating off him. "Did you have a chance to discuss the federal laws?" he continued blandly. She arched her eyebrows and glanced at the members of the board, silently condemning them to the lowest class of Permian slime creatures she could imagine.

"And what language is that?" Raymond asked.

"Money," he answered with a shark's grin. "You do this to my son, and I will sue this district for every dime it has. When I'm done, I won't only have your job, but I'll own the whole damn school. Under the city charter, what you are doing is illegal."

"No, it's not," Mr. Raymond argued.

"Yes, it is!" I screamed, standing up.

Whoops.

Everyone on stage shot me looks as sharp as shark's teeth when the audience looked up at me. I might as well talk; I was fucked anyways. "According to the city charter, municipal funds cannot be used in any function that can be considered segregated or restrictive towards any member or group of the student body."

Brad stood up next to me. "Yeah! What he said."

I saw his dad nod.

"The boy is right," Nathan said, getting Mr. Raymond and the school board's attention. "Ordinance number C-3240." They looked at him confused so he began to explain. "It was originally put in there for racial segregation during the sixties, but it is worded so it includes any ban based on bias. You can't stop a student from playing if they are black, a girl, or even gay. I am begging you, pass the ban." His eyes flashed as Mr. Raymond began to sweat. "It doesn't matter to me if he goes to college on a scholarship or on the settlement the state of Texas will give me after hearing what a mess you made of this. But either way, my son is going to college. And if you don't think I'll call the feds in to back me up, you're dreaming."

One of the ladies up on stage next to Raymond pulled him aside and began to whisper to him. Brad's dad gestured angrily for us to get down there. "Busted," Brad said with a huge grin on his face.

By the time we got to the floor, everyone on stage was gabbling, and it was obvious that the board in its little nest didn't agree anymore. Brad went and sat next to his mom, and I headed over to mine, where she sat with Mr. Parker. "Surprised?" she asked, knowing full well I was.

"Did you bring him?" I asked, pointing to Mr. Parker.

"Tyler and I went to school together. I've known he was gay since he was your age," she said smugly.

"You did not," he argued.

"Oh please," she replied sarcastically. "The only thing you were missing was a purse."

Mr. Parker made a face as he sat back in his chair.

After a few minutes, the board stopped arguing, and Mr. Raymond began to speak into the microphone. "In light of the information the board has just obtained, we move to strike down the ban and reinstate Bradley Greymark on the baseball team." He looked over at Brad. "But there will be arrangements made for you to change out somewhere away from the others, same as if there was a female on the team."

There was a cheer from most everyone in the seats, but I didn't notice because all I was looking at was Brad. And he wasn't happy. I knew what he was going to do half a second before he did it, but by then it was too late.

"So is there any other new business or can we adjourn for the—"

Brad stood up. "I have something."

The entire auditorium went silent as he took his father's place at the podium.

Brad

I WALKED up to the podium knowing my dad wasn't going to just move aside.

"What are you doing?" he practically growled at me.

"Making things right," I said, trying to sound braver than I actually felt.

He stared a hole through me as his hand squeezed the life out of my upper arm. In a voice barely above a whisper he said, "You fuck this up and you will spend the rest of your life working at the dealership because there is no way I am going to pay for your dumb ass to waste four years getting drunk at a college."

I looked back at him, the calmest I had ever felt. "Who are you kidding? We both know you couldn't afford to send me anywhere for a year much less four." His face began to grow red. "I know exactly what I am risking Dad." I pulled my arm away. "Some things are just too important to ignore."

He wanted me to say more, but I refused to look at him, instead just staring at the school board, who had obviously had enough of me for one day. "Don't screw this up," he said as he let me pass. I saw him take a seat next to Mom, and they both had that look on their faces that said they thought I was about to screw the pooch on this.

"Mr. Greymark, you got what you wanted today," Mr. Raymond said, sounding about as patronizing as anyone I'd ever heard. "What more could you possibly—?"

I looked over at Kyle, and I could see he was nervous. As our eyes met, he gave me a smile and a nod that told me, even though he had no idea what I was about to say, he was with me. "I want to address the bullying problem on campus." Both Raymond and Adler rolled their eyes as I began to talk. "There is a problem at this school, a problem that has existed for a long time with nothing done to stop it. Hateful, spiteful acts that go unchecked and ignored by the teachers and the staff."

Mr. Raymond sighed as he leaned into his mic. "Mr. Greymark, are you saying you want special protection against people being mean to you because you're gay?"

"No," I answered as firmly as I could. "I am saying I want everyone to have protection from people preying on them and making their high school life hell." Raymond sat back, obviously confused about where I was going. "Kids in this school are beat up, put down, and generally made miserable by other kids, and the faculty turns a blind eye. I know this because before today I was one of the ones making them miserable. We stuff them into trash cans, slam them into lockers, call them names between classes, and a lot worse. And yet every time this happens, it's justified by saying high school is tough, and kids will be kids." I took a deep breath and leveled a look at them.

"You're wrong. High school doesn't need to be that. You're failing us, and worse, you're failing yourselves. You think you've done something here because you were blackmailed into putting me on the team? You're going to use this as proof that Foster is progressive and not a closed-minded, hostile community, and you're wrong. There isn't anything wrong with being different, and that needs to be understood by everyone. Wrong is wrong, different is good. If we were all the same, life would suck, and it would be a pretty boring place all around. But you don't let different grow in Foster High; hell, you don't even let it exist. There's a much bigger world past the outskirts of town, and if you want all of us to be ready for it, you need to start teaching us now. No matter who you are or what you are, there is a place for you somewhere. I already know half a dozen kids that are counting down the seconds until they can blow this town and never come back. I know because I am one of them. Is that what you want? A whole generation of children hating where they grew up because you were too afraid to accept them for what they are?"

This had to be the most I had ever talked in front of people in my life. My heart was pounding, and I was sweating, but I couldn't stop, not now.

"I'm not asking for special protection, I am asking for universal protection. I am asking you as adults, as our teachers, to do something about it and to do it quick. Because I don't care what you have decided or what my dad threatened you with. I am not going to play ball for a school that can't accept me for who and what I am. I don't even want to go here. So you have a choice, Mr. Raymond: fix your school and its policies or deal with the consequences."

"And what would that be, young man?" Raymond asked, daring me to finish the threat.

"He won't go here anymore," my mom said, standing up. "I'll put him in Granada."

I saw Kyle's mom stand up too. "So will I," she said. "So will a lot of parents."

"Exactly how long do you think you can run a school with no students, Mr. Raymond?" I asked him with a smile. I looked at the rest of the school board. "Thank you for your time."

And I walked away.

I could hear people clapping as Mr. Raymond tried to get order back, but I didn't care. I meant what I said. I wasn't going to go to a school where people could be treated like shit, and no one did anything about it. Period.

Kyle ran up to me and threw his arms around me. "Who's the superhero now?" he asked.

I gave him a grin. "You know, I was just sitting there asking myself, what would Kyle do?"

I saw him smile back and knew there wasn't a chance in hell I would ever let him go.

"You know the school has a strict policy against public displays of affection?" he asked in mock outrage.

I looked over to the stage and back to him. "They can get over it." And I kissed him.

I can't tell you the day I started to lose who I was but I can tell you the very moment I found out who I really was.

It was the moment the blue eyed boy kissed me back.

Author's Note

Everything that happened in this novel to Brad and Kyle has happened to an actual gay or lesbian student in the United States. If you are not aware of how bad it can be in high school for teenagers coming out, please be aware it is worse than you think. There is nothing harder than trying to find your own identity in this world, and that is only made worse by intolerance from the people we trust to protect us. Though this is a work of fiction, similar experiences are happening right now to students all over the world, and their stories do not always have a happy ending.

If you are a gay or lesbian student being bullied in high school, you can contact the It Gets Better Project at http://www.itgetsbetter.org. If you are just someone being bullied in high school regardless of your sexuality, you can find help at http://stopbullying.gov.

If you are a parent of a gay or lesbian teen and want information or resources on talking to them about it, please go to http://www.pflag.org.

You are not alone and it *does* get better. There is always another choice out there, and if you think you are alone, you are not. If you are feeling suicidal, please visit http:// www.suicide.org/gay-and-lesbian-suicide.html for help. Your story is just as important as this one— please don't end it early.

With love and sincerity,

John Goode

JOHN GOODE is a member of the class of '88 from Hogwarts School of Witchcraft and Wizardry, specializing in incantations and spoken spells. At the age of fourteen, he proudly represented District 13 in the 65th Panem games, where he was disqualified for crying uncontrollably before the competition began. After that he moved to Forks, Washington, where against all odds he dated the hot, incredibly approachable werewolf instead of the stuck-up jerk of a vampire, but was crushed when he found out the werewolf was actually gayer than he was. After that he turned down the mandatory operation everyone must receive at sixteen to become pretty, citing that everyone pretty was just too stupid to live, before moving away for greener pastures. After falling down an oddly large rabbit hole, he became huge when his love for cakes combined with his inability to resist the commands of sparsely worded notes, and was finally kicked out when he began playing solitaire with the Red Queen's 4th armored division. By eighteen he had found the land in the back of his wardrobe, but decided that thinly veiled religious allegories were not the neighbors he desired. When last seen, he had become obsessed with growing a pair of wings after discovering Fang's blog and hasn't been seen since.

Or he is this guy who lives in this place and writes stuff he hopes you read.

Also from John Goode...

HarmonyInkPress.com

1 900L

CPSIA information can be obtained at www.ICGtesting.com
Printed in the USA
LVOW11s1937080415

433776LV00018B/1132/P